W9-BMD-181

The
Delightful
Life of a
Suicide Pilot

ALSO BY COLIN COTTERILL

The Coroner's Lunch
Thirty-Three Teeth
Disco for the Departed
Anarchy and Old Dogs
Curse of the Pogo Stick
The Merry Misogynist
Love Songs from a Shallow Grave
Slash and Burn
The Woman Who Wouldn't Die
Six and a Half Deadly Sins
I Shot the Buddha
The Rat Catchers' Olympics
Don't Eat Me
The Second Biggest Nothing

The Delightful Life of a Suicide Pilot

COLIN COTTERILL

SOHO
CRIME

Published by
Soho Press, Inc.
227 W 17th Street
New York, NY 10011

Library of Congress Cataloging-in-Publication Data

Names: Cotterill, Colin, author.
Title: The delightful life of a suicide pilot / Colin Cotterill.

ISBN 978-1-64129-177-4
eISBN 978-1-64129-178-1

Subjects: 1. Paiboun, Siri, Doctor (Fictitious
character)—Fiction. 2. World War, 1939-1945–Southeast
Asia–Fiction. 3. Laos—Fiction. 4. Thailand–Fiction.
Classification: LCC PR6053.O778 D45 2020
823'.914—dc23 2019051328

Printed in the United States of America

10 9 8 7 6 5 4 3 2 1

For her invaluable contribution to the research behind this last book in the Dr. Siri series, I should like to thank my wife and best friend, Kyoko, who also cooks a jolly good quiche. For their last-minute reading of the rough manuscript, my thanks to Kirk, Robert, Lizzie, David, Rachel, Kate, Bob, Leila, and Steve. Thanks, too, to Margaret and Charlie whose contributions have made this a better book. If you want to delve more deeply into the world of yokai, please visit the amazing yokai.com website. And for their belief in Dr. Siri over the years and their boundless enthusiasm, I should like to dedicate this book to the lovely people at Soho Press to thank them for making me feel special. Sayonara.

TABLE OF CONTENTS

CHAPTER ONE
Every Body Has a Story to Tell

There was a myth. Not a ghostly urban legend that might cause little children to wet their beds, but a disturbing notion nevertheless. It was likely begat from the mischievous storytelling of a doctor not unlike Siri Paiboun, the ex-national coroner of the People's Democratic Republic of Laos, who was known to smudge the lines between fact and fiction. The myth went something like this: after you're dead, your hair and nails will mysteriously continue to grow. Any qualified physician would snigger at such a thought. But no matter how unlikely the possibility, there were those who swore to have witnessed such a phenomenon. And all those doubting so-called "experts" needed to do was to take the key from beneath the welcome mat at the Mahosot Hospital morgue in Vientiane, let themselves into the cutting room, and slide out the only occupied freezer tray. And once they pulled back the sheet they would see for themselves. Comrade Thinh still sported a fine head of hair that was just a little too long to be called respectable. His nostril hair, on the other hand, had sprouted remarkably since his arrival on the slab. It was currently a good six centimeters long. Mr. Geung, the lab assistant, had already combed it into a neat mustache and was certain that before too long, there would be enough for a goatee.

Comrade Thinh's corpse had been in the morgue for almost a week with nothing to do but nurture this nasal display while his wife and his mistress argued their respective cases for taking the corpse home. It was fortunate for Thinh that he was dead because the two women were loathsome creatures. He'd probably inflicted a broken neck upon himself to be rid of them. The decision was currently in the hands of an ad hoc council composed of members of the Vietnamese Central Committee, naturally, all men. That it should be under consideration by such a lofty team was a testament to the importance of the deceased and the potential ramifications of sending him off to the wrong pyre.

Dr. Siri was no longer connected with the morgue in any official capacity. His lot now lay behind the portal of his wife's noodle shop, where he sat between shifts at a rear table with a cup of coffee and a book, any book. His illegal library had been destroyed some years earlier, and 1981 Laos was not a world hub of literature. The one bookshop had five Lao translations of Soviet Communist rhetoric, a shelf of official reports, and a three-year archive of the weekly edition of the *Passasson Lao* newsletter. The rest of the space was occupied by dusty sports equipment and stuffed endangered creatures with marbles for eyes and the terror of that final chase frozen on their faces. But once you have a reading habit it's a bugger to shake off. No love nor money could produce a Proust or Victor Hugo in Vientiane, so Siri read the minutes of the last Central Committee conference and the proposal for the next three-year development plan. And, of course, he read and reread the script of his motion picture that would never make it as far as the silver screen. He yearned for something creative and stimulating to enliven his dull days. As is often the case, a strong-enough yearning was just enough to tweak fate into action.

He had promised never to set foot in the morgue again but there was something about postmortem nostril hair growth that was far too tempting to pass up. As soon as Mr. Geung arrived for his evening noodle shift and passed on the news of the body in the freezer, Siri was on his bicycle and peddling in the direction of Mahosot with Ugly, the thrice-almost-dead mongrel, trotting along behind. There were no cars on the road. A recent survey had suggested there was a total of fourteen thousand motor vehicles in Laos. Eleven thousand had no access to gasoline because the scant offerings were monopolized by the government. Children were growing up bemused by these four-wheeled, moss-covered monuments in front yards.

It was a balmy evening that followed a balmy day at the end of a balmy month. The hot season lurked beyond the mountains of Vietnam, awaiting its cue to bake the Lao capital, but until it made its entrance the calm evenings brought out a procession of girls and boys doubling up on bicycles like amusement park duck targets hoping to be hit with a smile or a nod. They pedaled so slowly it was inconceivable the momentum was enough to hold them upright. Siri had invented the word "crtia," which was a microscopic step up from "inertia" and perfectly described flirtatious cycling. He shamelessly teased the girls he passed and they pretended not to hear him. But there was no disguising the small curl of lip, the flutter of eyelashes. No woman is deaf to a compliment.

The morgue door was ajar. Siri left the bicycle and Ugly in the shade of a nipplewort tree and kicked off his old leather sandals in the foyer. He passed the office where he'd sat many hours trying to make sense of ancient French forensic pathology texts and entered what was called the cutting room. There, leaning over the freezer tray, were Chief Inspector Phosy and his wife, Nurse Dtui. They looked up mid-chuckle.

"Ah, Siri," said Phosy. "I didn't think you'd be able to stay away."

"I've spent too many happy hours staring into offal to give it all up completely," said Siri.

"Have you seen this, Doc?" asked Dtui. She was pretty and slightly more rounded than usual. He refrained from asking her if she was pregnant just in case she wasn't.

"I hope you aren't making fun of the dead," said Siri.

He joined them and couldn't hold back a guffaw of his own when he saw the corpse. Mr. Geung had fashioned a splendid mustache; it was true it had outgrown a Poirot and was approaching the realm of a Fu Manchu. Siri tugged on it to be sure it wasn't a practical joke. It held firm.

"Well, I've seen some things," said Siri, "but this takes the prawn cracker."

"Do you think there's any connection between the nose hair and the death?" Phosy asked playfully.

"Not for me to say anymore," said Siri. "Whose case is it?"

"Dr. Mot announced the cause of death," said Dtui.

"Ah, then we'll never know for certain," said Siri, no fan of the current coroner, a recent returnee from the Eastern bloc. As Siri often said, it was a miracle he'd graduated after studying in a language he couldn't speak. He did have a certificate suggesting he was qualified to perform autopsies.

It was framed and hanging on his office wall beside a similar certificate claiming he was proficient in porcelain glazing.

"And what brings you both here, apart from the obvious sideshow?" Siri asked.

"I was asked to investigate the case personally," said Phosy.

"I thought they'd strapped you behind a desk."

"They let me out every now and then for delicate matters," said the policeman.

"What's delicate about this?" Siri asked. "I heard from my inside source that your man here had too much to drink and fell off a cliff. What Mr. Geung couldn't tell me was why all this warrants so much attention."

"And that all comes down to who he is," said Phosy.

"Who is he?"

"Does the name Bui Sok Thinh ring a bell?"

"Not a tinkle."

"He was the son of Bui Kieu."

"Still nothing ringing in my ears."

"Perhaps he was after your time," said Phosy. "He's one of the richest men in Vietnam."

"I thought we'd obliterated wealth," said Siri. "Did something happen to communist dogma while I was napping?"

"The inevitable happened, Doc," said Dtui. "It's the same here. Lots of good intentions but no money. A few years of failed cooperatives and natural disasters and there's no budget for infrastructure. So we fall back on good old cronyism. We call the rich guys back from life-long banishment overseas, borrow a few billion here, make a few deals there."

"Ooh," said Siri. "Your wife's grown horns."

"She's bored with being poor, I think," said Phosy. "She's waiting for me to accept my first graft so she can buy a refrigerator."

"I feel that refrigerator will be a long time coming," said Siri.

"That's what I try to tell her."

"Never mind, Dtui," said Siri. "You're still comparatively young. It's not too late to find yourself a sugar daddy."

"No hope there," said Dtui. "Sugar daddies like them wafer thin with silicon breasts."

"Sounds awful," said Siri. "Give me a good old-fashioned naturally buxom girl any day. But back to hairy nose here. Did he get a share of his daddy's wealth?"

"They sent Thinh to Italy to study during the war. His family had a lot of mandarin money to invest in Europe. Thinh made a fortune in war profiteering. When Uncle Ho took over Vietnam the Viet Minh found themselves short of funds so they started courting the Bui clan. Thinh brokered a deal for the Italians to drill for oil in the gulf of Tonkin. Thinh ran the company. The income from that amounted to a large chunk of the country's GNP."

"And how do you go from that to a cold slab in a foreign country?" Siri asked.

"He was very high-profile in Hanoi and he liked to get away and relax when he had a chance. He had a soft spot for our very own Vang Vieng; peaceful, beautiful scenery and nobody knew him there. He'd fly the family helicopter down. He had a hidden chalet in the hills. He liked nothing more than to hike up to the karsts with a few bottles of very expensive wine in his pack, sit on a ledge, and watch the river. Simple pleasures. In the early days he'd take his wife. I'm told she is a sow of a woman as well as the daughter of a Vietnamese politburo man. She soon tired of those hikes and he soon tired of asking her. He took himself a younger girl to be his minor wife and she was in better shape. Didn't mind the trekking. They'd sit on the ledge and drink to Mother Nature . . ."

". . . and probably play a few rounds of paper, scissors, stone," said Dtui.

"I tell you, Madam Daeng and I never tire of that," said Siri.

"Thinh could have had his choice of beautiful, loose women to be his mistress," said Phosy. "But he was apparently a glutton for punishment, and he selected a plain, opinionated girl who was the daughter of a Viet Minh war hero. I hear she has the temper of a rabid Chihuahua. She's claiming that the major wife was with him on his last trip to Vang Vieng and that she pushed him off a ledge when he was drunk. The wife laughed off that allegation and countered that it must have been the mistress who accompanied Thinh to the mountain and killed him."

"Why do we think either of them had to be there?"

"A goat herder saw this Vietnamese man hiking there last weekend. He was with a woman. Too far away to identify her."

"And what's to be gained by killing him?"

"The first wife stands to inherit a hell of a lot," said Phosy. "If she's convicted of murder, the money will go to the minor wife. And the concubine's father happens to be on the board of directors of the drilling company. He'll no doubt be pushing for an inquiry."

"Any children?"

"No."

"Other siblings?"

"Apparently not."

Siri looked around at the morgue he'd worked in for five years. In that time, it had been refurbished first by the Chinese, then by the Soviets, but it still looked neglected. The air conditioner wheezed. The corpse carts limped like old supermarket trolleys. Not even Mr. Geung's "Twelve Puppies to Make You Laugh" wall calendar could inject any passion into that old building. Siri walked to the freezer that had not contained Comrade Thinh and fought with the handle for a few seconds as always. Inside were the jar of water and four tumblers. Mr. Geung always left them there just in case the morgue had visitors. They didn't see a lot of use. Naturally, there was no ice. The freezers got their name from a short-circuiting accident following which Nurse Dtui and Daeng had spent several hours attempting to thaw out a body with the aid of kettle steam and a two-bar heater. The equipment had frozen nothing since. Siri poured his guests a glass of cool water each and returned to the matter at hand.

"All right," he said, "even if one of the women in his life was there, how do we know he just couldn't stand them anymore and stepped off the ledge to be rid of them?"

"Everyone who knew him swears he's the last person on earth who'd commit suicide; fun-loving, over the moon with the Italian project. He even seemed fond of the women in his own way. No business pressure. No political bullying. He loved his life."

"Yet here he is," said Siri. "Dtui, why didn't you do the autopsy?"

"I'm just a nurse," she said.

"A nurse with a deep knowledge of forensic pathology," Siri countered.

"But no certificate on my wall," said Dtui. "Not even in porcelain varnishing."

"I'll print you one," said Siri. "It seems all you need these days is a bit of paper with one illegible signature at the bottom."

He pulled back the sheet that covered the corpse.

"Look," he said. "Dr. Mot didn't even bother to cut our friend here open."

"Said it wasn't necessary," said Phosy. "Said it was obvious the victim had died from multiple injuries sustained whilst bouncing off rocks on his way down the cliff. Said the empty bottles proved that he was so drunk he probably didn't feel it."

"May I?" Siri asked.

"Go ahead," said Phosy.

Siri turned the corpse on its side and studied the back.

"No handprints, no bruises, no indication he was hit with anything," he said. "It is possible he stepped up to relieve himself, took one pace too many, and peed himself to death."

"Then why would the wives deny they were there?" Dtui asked. "They could have explained what happened and there'd be no evidence to say otherwise."

"Unless it wasn't one of them," said Phosy.

"Good thinking," said Siri.

"I'm wondering whether he went to Vang Vieng alone last weekend, met a local girl, and took her up into the mountains," Phosy continued. "She might have panicked when he made advances and pushed him away."

"Even if it was an accident, she'd still have given birth to a buffalo from the shock of it," said Siri.

"No way she'd admit to being there," said Dtui.

"And Vang Vieng's a small community," said Phosy. "They'd set up a force field around one of their girls."

"You wouldn't even get to talk to her," said Dtui.

"Unless we could convince her we know it was an accident," said Siri, lowering the corpse onto its back.

"How would we go about that?" Phosy asked.

"I have no idea just yet, but every body has a story to tell if you just show a little patience. Do you suppose our intrepid Dr. Varnish has exhausted all his autopsy skills?"

"He said there's nothing more to be learned," said Dtui.

"Then he wouldn't mind me tinkering a little."

"I doubt he'd notice."

"Splendid. Then I shall return tomorrow at dawn with my tool kit and my faithful lab assistant."

CHAPTER TWO
My Friends Call Me Toshi

Dr. Siri arrived at the noodle shop a little too early to beat the evening rush. Diners had already filled the small open-fronted restaurant but they weren't there for the Mekong views. They'd come to enjoy the best noodles in the capital. Government workers in khaki or white shirts had eaten away the frustrations of another day of paperwork and inefficiency. Lady teachers in stiff cotton *phasin* skirts had kicked off their uncomfortable shoes beneath the tables and sighed off another day of explaining how Marxist-Leninism had affected the shifting of the tectonic plates. Karl and Vladimir had been a busy pair since '75.

Standing on the uneven pavement was a scrawny man dressed as a farmer but wearing a splendid post office helmet from the old regime. He never entered the restaurant unless invited by Siri himself.

"Comrade Ging," said Siri. "I've told you, you really don't have to get permission to go inside."

"Oh, I'm not here for food," said Ging as always. "Just doing my duty delivering mail. Officials of the Lao Postal Service do not request or expect remuneration for doing something of which we are proud."

There was no mail delivery service in Laos. Letters were either sent to post office boxes or to a large *poste restante* sack, much of the contents of which would never be claimed. There were as many postal workers slitting open and censoring mail as there were selling stamps, and customers could never be sure of what subversive material their mail contained. Comrade Ging sold stamps. But on his breaks and after work he would don his helmet, wrap a homemade post office armband around his boney bicep, and deliver unopened mail to residents he knew would show their gratitude. Madam Daeng's noodle shop was one such place.

"Do you have something for us?" Siri asked.

"I do." Ging smiled, reached into his back sack, and pulled out a parcel the size and shape of an Omo washing powder packet. He nodded and handed it to Siri. "And with that, I'll be on my way."

Siri was tempted to let him go but he knew his wife would berate him for doing so. And it was nice to have mail delivered.

"Perhaps you'd be kind enough to join us for a meal," said Siri.

"I . . . I don't think I'll have time."

"Madam Daeng would be pleased if you could spare a few minutes."

"Well, I . . . All right, then. To keep Madam Daeng happy," said the man, walking triumphantly into the restaurant. He removed his helmet and found an empty stool. Mr. Geung welcomed him by name and Geung's wife, Tukta, served him without asking what he wanted. In fact, after forty years in the postal service, all he really wanted was respect.

"What's that?" Daeng asked her husband. She was bent over the noodle trough. The steam wafted around her like a dream sequence but she never seemed to work up a sweat.

"Parcel," said Siri, heading for the stairs.

Daeng could have repeated her question but a simple eyebrow raise stopped him in his tracks.

"Feels like a book," said Siri. "Heavy. Ging just dropped it off."

"That's very nice for you," said Daeng, ladling out four bowls with the deftness of a conjurer. "But don't you think our customers could use a bit of *maître-d'*ing?"

"Darling, your noodles sell themselves. They don't need promoting."

"After a day of dealing with bureaucracy our customers appreciate a little sympathy and a few laughs. We aren't just a noodle shop. We're a wellness agency and you are the doctor of compassion."

"But I . . ."

"The book can wait."

The book waited until 8 P.M., when the customers had all returned to their overcrowded homes, the tables were cleared and clean, and Mr. Geung and Tukta were back in their room talking to the baby that wouldn't be born for another six months. Everyone was aware that the odds were stacked against a woman with Down syndrome producing a healthy child. And when the father also had Down syndrome those odds tumbled into infinity. But, like Dr. Siri, Geung had friends in other dimensions and he'd been shown their daughter in a dream. Geung said she looked a little like Sarinthip Siriwan. Siri pointed out that it would be a most difficult birth considering the size of the Thai actress. The couple laughed at that for a week.

"So, are you going to open it?" Daeng asked.

"I was wondering what the chances are that it's a bomb," said Siri.

They were sitting on the riverbank sipping their after-noodle rice whisky cocktails. The lights of Sri Chiang Mai on the Thai side were all out; probably another power cut. The Thais were renowned for creative wiring. So, with the moon yet to make an appearance, the darkness was thick: like staring out over a landscape of tar. Daeng got to her feet.

"Where are you going?" Siri asked.

"You don't expect me to sit beside you if it's a bomb, do you?"

"I don't know. It could be romantic, splattered across the Mekong together, our parts floating side by side to Cambodia."

"There's nothing romantic about dismemberment, Siri. I'm off to the ladies' room. You can open it while I'm gone. I'll listen for the bang."

Guided by the single lamp in the shop behind her, she scampered up the bank. Not bad for a seventy-year-old. Siri took his penlight out of his top pocket and held it between his teeth—teeth that he could still proudly call his own, all thirty-three of them. From the same pocket he removed a Soviet army knife and flicked open a blade. He sliced through layers of thick masking tape and removed an inner skin of brown paper. Inside that was a plastic bag followed by several layers of Thai newspaper and another plastic bag, all taped securely.

When Daeng returned, Siri was sitting in a pile of assorted wrappings, holding a somewhat smaller parcel in his hands.

"We used to play that when we were children," she said.

"Play what?"

"You give someone a gift and by the time they've unwrapped it there's nothing inside."

"How cruel you were," said Siri. "No, I feel I'm almost down to the meat. Just one more layer of tissue paper and . . . there."

At last he found what was most certainly a book of some kind. The cover was made of a sort of skin; leather perhaps. It was dotted with a dark mold and smelled rancid. He opened it carefully but all he found were blank pages.

"Hmm," he said. "That's odd."

He turned the book to what should have been the back and there on the rear cover were two small Chinese-looking initials branded onto the skin. He opened it to the back pages, where he was met by line after line of neat handwritten text.

"Chinese?" said Daeng.

"Japanese."

"Can you read it?"

"I'm afraid not. I picked up the numbers when we were in the underground and the Japanese were threatening to invade. Thought it might be useful for recognizing times and dates in captured documents. But I didn't get around to the letters. They don't use the same date system as us. It starts with the reign of the current emperor and that began in . . . 1926. So the number here is probably Showa Eleven. I'm assuming this is a diary and it starts in 1937."

"And there I was thinking I only married you for your body."

"It's a two-for-the-price-of-one package, Daeng. No extra cost for the genius."

"So, 1937? Japan's at war with China," said Daeng.

"This starts July seventh."

"Stop showing off."

Siri flipped through the pages, right to left.

"It's beautifully penned," he said. "Someone's obviously put their heart into it. Every page neat and precise. Not a crossing-out or a smudge; not so much as a wine stain. There's a week or two between each entry. And it looks like the writing gets more confident. Much stronger. It's as if the writer's gouging the ink into the paper. And I . . ."

"What?"

"Daeng. Look at this."

She leaned over the page.

"Well, I'll be," she said.

The Japanese text ended halfway down the page and was replaced with the date 12/30/1940, in Western numerals, and the Lao sentence *My name is Kangen Toshimado* (咸元利圓). The Lao lettering was childish but it was legible, and to Siri's eyes, it seemed to introduce a sudden burst of fun: a hibiscus sprouting suddenly in a cabbage patch.

"Our Comrade Toshimado's learning Lao," said Daeng.

Siri turned the page and there was Toshimado agreeing with her.

I am studying Lao, he wrote.

A week or two had passed in diary time but he'd obviously been practicing his lettering. Daeng turned the page and read the entry for 1/6/1941.

I am Japanese. I am a major in the Imperial Army of Japan. I am thirty-four years old. My friends call me Toshi.

With every page they turned, the Lao language seemed to spread like a virus over the paper. On 1/24/1941 he attempted his first full page. There were mistakes here and there but they all suggested that Toshi was enjoying his journey through this new language. He wrote about traveling across the Lao countryside with his friend and eating and drinking local delicacies. He threw it all down on the page, hang the consequences. Suddenly, after three years of beautiful but disciplined Japanese text, his words had flamboyance.

The penlight was made in China so neither of them was surprised when the feeble beam gave up the ghost. It was a sign of the times. Soviet donations were ugly and almost indestructible. Chinese donations looked like the originals but didn't work, yet the donors still believed the third world should be grateful.

"Let's go inside and read some more," said Daeng.

"A riddle first," said Siri. "Why do you think someone would send me the diary of a Japanese soldier?"

"Because they knew you were desperate for reading material?"

"I admit it will be fun to read but they've gone to a lot of trouble to get this to me in one piece. My guess is that there has to be a point."

"You sure there isn't a letter in there?"

"I didn't look."

He held up the diary by the spine and, recklessly, fanned through the pages. At first nothing happened. Then a single page came loose. It was caught briefly in the lamplight from the shop as it surfed a breeze. It was almost impossible to follow its course but it was clear to both of them that it was headed in the direction of the river. Before it could hit the water it was out of sight.

◙ ◙ ◙

Dr. Siri and Mr. Geung arrived at the morgue just before the sun rose. They'd both held on to their keys for old times' sake. The place didn't get a great deal of use. It wasn't that people were no longer dying, rather that decisions were made at higher levels as to whether anyone really needed to know how or why. As in all good socialist states, the mechanism of secrecy was the most oiled. Mr. Geung pulled out the sliding tray and was delighted to see that Comrade Thinh's nose mustache had grown a good two centimeters since his last visit. But, to their unrelenting surprise, the hair on Thinh's head was also considerably longer and the finger- and toenails had begun to curl into claws. It defied all logic but this was a mystery that would have to wait. Their purpose for visiting the morgue was to find answers to more earthly questions. They lifted the body onto the cutting table and removed the sheet. It served no purpose other than modesty and Comrade Thinh really had nothing to be modest about.

"You see, boy," said Siri. "If you have enough money, women can forgive the smallest of transgressions."

Geung snorted.

"Perhaps it w-w-was too cold in the freezer," he said.

"A chicken doesn't become a sparrow after a night in the icebox," said Siri.

"You're speaking ill of-of the dead."

"I know. And I'm sure he'll make me regret it when he gets to the otherworld. But first, to work. What do you see here?"

"Broken bones," said Geung.

"Many?"

"Left arm three places, shhhhoulder, both legs, ankles, ribs, and probably more."

"Good. All consistent with falling onto rocks from a cliff. See anything inconsistent?"

Geung looked at the doctor querulously.

"I . . ."

"Yes?"

"I have D-d-down syndrome."

"So?" said Siri. "That doesn't make you an idiot."

"I don't have . . . I-I-I'm not qualified."

"Nonsense. How many times have you sat in on our autopsies?"

"Forty-seven."

"Right. And there I was thinking it was a rhetorical question. Just take a look at our friend here and tell me what your gut says."

"It says 'Grrrr' sometimes."

Geung laughed. Siri slapped his friend's forehead playfully.

"Hilarious," said Siri. "Sadly, we don't have time for comedy. The security people will be here soon to throw us out. Tell me what you see."

Mr. Geung ran his eyes over the body like a scanner passing over a document. He flipped over the corpse and scanned what Nurse Dtui referred to as the B side. He looked up at Siri and shook his head. Siri gestured for him to continue. Geung lifted the arm. It folded in places arms had no right to fold. He took hold of the hand, turned down the palm, and looked surprised. He went to the other side of the table and checked the back of the left hand.

"You see it?" said Siri.

"Yes."

"Tell me."

"Scratches. On the backs of the hands."

"But not the palms," said Siri. "But if you're repelling an attack or falling, it's instinctive to hold out your palms in front of you. It doesn't do any damned good from two hundred meters, but we aren't really programmed from birth to fall from a cliff. And, even if you land on bushes, you're probably dead already and you don't have any more chance to bleed. These scratches are caked in congealed blood. My guess is they occurred before the fall."

"But how?"

"I've been thinking about that, Geung. Here's our experienced hiker. He's been to the cliffs many times before. A happy man. He takes a pretty girl to a scenic spot. They drink some wine. No stress. Next thing you know he's free-falling to the rocks below. I have just one explanation."

Siri stood at the head of the table and ran his fingers through the victim's thickening hair.

"I thought so," he said. "Geung, come and feel this."

Geung hurried over to complete his test. He, too, ran his fingers across the scalp. At first he didn't feel anything, but then . . .

"Yes," he said.

And when Geung extracted his fingers he looked at his own hand and shared a Eureka moment with the doctor. His expression went from monochrome to full-screen Technicolor. Under the nail of his index finger was a tiny piece of evidence that explained the whole damned thing.

10/2/1943

Hello my love. How are you? I miss you and the children. I have grown a small beard since you last saw me, and I look like a goat. But do not expect milk from me. I am back at the Chinese border in Lang Son on a mission. I have confirmed that our treasure is safe. I am not surprised they didn't discover it. It was officially buried under a mountain of documents. I have found a way to transport it to you through the tunnel of love. Do not be surprised when you see it. I shall be home soon. Do not worry about me.

"How did you rescue it from the river?" Phosy asked.

"It didn't make it that far," said Daeng. "We have a guardian angel, don't forget."

"Crazy Rajhid?" said Dtui.

Daeng smiled. Rajhid, the occasionally mad Indian, lived on the riverbank, where he climbed trees, impersonated frogs, and swam naked, mostly at night.

"We can't get any privacy," said Siri. "Madam Daeng and I go down to the riverbank often . . ."

"To catch clams," said Daeng, smiling.

"But we can never be sure of any personal moments because he's always there," said Siri. "Or at least the threat of him being there is always hanging over us."

"He has saved our lives on more than one occasion," Daeng reminded him.

"Which is the only reason I don't shoot him," said Siri.

"And he did rescue your loose diary page," said Dtui. "What do you make of it?"

Nurse Dtui was walking around the restaurant with her little daughter, Malee. The tables were skyscrapers and the aisles were streets. In this game, Malee was blind for some reason and her mother was a guide dog. Dtui was certain her daughter would be a novelist when she grew up.

"We haven't read the whole thing yet," said Daeng.

"And half of it's in Japanese," said Siri. "But we're plodding through the Lao. Cross-referencing events in the diary with events during the Japanese occupation."

"The page you just read was obviously cut from the diary with a sharp blade," said Daeng. "We assume it was important for some reason. There was a short message stapled to it. It said, 'Dr. Siri, we need your help urgently.' Grammatically correct but untidy, probably not written by a native Lao."

"What are you planning to do?" asked Phosy.

"Nothing until I've read the whole diary," said Siri.

"And he's painfully slow," said Daeng.

"One sips at a fine wine, my dear," said Siri.

"And in the meantime, we won't know who sent us the diary, who needs help, or what help he or she needs," said Daeng.

"If it's from Toshi himself, he'd be about your age now, Siri," said Phosy. "He might be one of those fanatical Japanese soldiers that hang out in the jungle for thirty years after the war ends, refusing to surrender. When's the last date in the diary?"

"August fourteenth, 1945," said Daeng. "It was the day before the Japanese Emperor's notice of surrender was broadcast."

"And what did he write on that day?" Dtui asked, a little dizzy from her guide-dogging laps.

"Dtui, I'm disappointed in you, really," said Siri. "I only folded over the corner to see the date. Do I look like the type of person who would skip to the last page of a story?"

"Well, yes, you look like exactly that type, especially if it solves the mystery of why he's writing to you."

"See what I mean?" said Daeng. "A thoroughly annoying man."

"Then there's no point in having a mystery in the first place, is there?" said Siri. "Let's all just skip to the last day of our lives and see what happened. A book is like an orgasm."

"Siri, I don't—" Phosy began.

"You want to get as much mileage out of it as you can before it's all over," Siri continued.

"There goes another of our family secrets," said Daeng.

"Just words to the wise to a young couple starting off on the trail to marital bliss," said Siri.

"Do you mind if we change the subject?" Phosy asked. "I'm sending Captain Sihot off to Vang Vieng this afternoon."

"Ah, you've grasped the concept of delegation at last," said Daeng, pouring everyone another cup of tea.

"I've always known the concept but until now I've been the best man for the job."

"See how modest your daddy is?" said Dtui to her daughter.

"Can't see," said Malee.

"Right, sorry. I forgot."

"In fact, I should be there doing this myself," Phosy continued. "If we get this wrong we'll be answerable to the Vietnamese."

"But if we get it right they'll be beholden to us," said Siri.

"And you're quite sure?" Phosy asked.

"As sure as I can be until we get an eye witness," said Siri.

"Transport out of the region would have been impossible without being noticed," said Phosy, "so it had to have been a local girl."

"Do you think she'll be willing to talk?" asked Dtui.

"Sihot has to find her first," said Phosy. "He's from around there so I'm hoping the locals will talk to him. If he finds the girl and shows her what we believe happened, there's no reason why she shouldn't speak up. She's not a suspect."

"But she might be a local girl who agreed to go for a hike—if you know what I mean," said Daeng.

"Sihot's got a way with people," said Phosy. "I'm trusting he can leave there with the girl's reputation intact."

"Assuming it was intact before he gets there," said Siri.

CHAPTER THREE
Creative Writing

2/30/1941

A word about my posting. They have sent us to Thakhek in Laos. It's a small, pretty but unremarkable town on the Mekong, a hand-grenade toss across the river from Thailand. But it is strategically situated exactly halfway down the country. The Thais have signed memoranda of cooperation with half the planet as a sort of insurance they'll still have allies no matter how badly things turn out. But with the bulk of the French forces busy in Europe, this would be a good time for the fickle Thais to nuzzle up to us and claim back some real estate stolen by Laos and their French minders. Japan agreed on the condition that we could trample all over Thailand at will. To show us how much they love their northern neighbor, Thailand has declared war on England.

We are a small unit of eight Japanese with orders to tolerate but not interfere with the French administrators in Thakhek. They, in turn, have been ordered to ignore us. We are not a particularly frightening band of warriors but we represent an immense army. They tell us that eventually Thakhek will be the center of Japanese operations in the region. We are here to lay the groundwork. We are instructed to nod at the locals in a friendly manner, to not rape the women, and to pay for goods at the market at the rates the vendors charge us. It isn't what I expected to be doing when I became a pilot but I like it here.

"He's a pilot," said Daeng. "How come he's working on a ground crew and not dropping bombs?"

"I'm sure we'll get around to that," said Siri.

It was bedtime, which generally came an hour before sleep. They'd spoon on the thin mattress and look at the stars through the window and sum up their days and philosophize. It was the happiest time for both of them.

"Do you think he's one of them?" said Daeng.

"Them?"

"A *kamikaze.*"

"If he is, he's not very good at his job. This is a long diary."

"Are you really sure you don't want to . . . you know . . . flip to the last page, or the first page or whatever it is?"

"Yes."

"It might be urgent."

"If it was urgent he'd send me a telegram. No, Toshi wants me to read his diary at my own pace. Come to my own conclusions."

"It's not exactly action-packed, is it? Twenty pages into the Lao section and nobody's dead yet. We know more about the wildflowers than we do about the war. And they've sent him to Thakhek, of all places. Not much action to be had there."

"You've been there."

"A few times, after the French came back."

"It used to be a gambling mecca," said Siri. "Thais would row across the river, lose all their money, and row back, assuming they hadn't lost their boat at the card tables. Bars. Brothels. Opium. Laos was the sin capital of Asia."

"Then we won the war and spoiled everything."

"It'll all come back, you mark my words. When the old soldiers die off there'll be a reawakening. There's a lot of money to be made from debauchery."

"What a pessimistic husband you are."

"But don't you think it's intriguing?"

"Debauchery?"

"The diary. All those little teasers here and there: the treasure, studying Lao even before he knew he'd be transferred here."

"You're easily intrigued."

"And he mentions his wife and the kids just that once."

"Perhaps he wrote letters to them."

"I hope he did," said Siri. "I'd like to think he was a romantic like me."

They let the peace overwhelm them for a while. The cicadas serenaded the night birds and accompanied a distant growl of thunder.

"Siri?"

"That's me."

"Should I be concerned that you haven't vanished for a while?"

"You want me to?"

"Well, yes, considering it's your other life. You're heavily invested in the spirit dimension. You used to go over to the other side often to make sense of this world."

"I know."

"In fact, you haven't chatted with Auntie Bpoo since . . . since Civilai died."

She felt his body tense. Siri had entered a love-hate relationship with the spirit world some five years before when he discovered he hosted a thousand-year-old Hmong shaman. This was not a popular hitchhiker as he'd forced Siri to acknowledge there was a dimension his scientific mind had refused to accept. Since then he'd fought with malevolent spirits, traveled to the Otherworld, traded insults with his transvestite spirit guide, and talked with the departed. And now his closest friend was on that other side.

"I've been busy," he said.

"No, you haven't. It's as if . . . as if you don't want to go there because you'll have to talk to him. Bpoo's your guide. She'd make it all possible for you. She'd have a dramatic location set up for you both. She'd have an Otherworld log beside the Otherworld Mekong, you and him sitting there drinking fake rum and sugarcane juice and eating supernatural baguettes. It'd be fun."

"It won't. Can we not talk about it?"

"No. We talk about everything. This is a thing."

The thunder rumbled as if it was stipulated in some celestial script.

"I miss him," said Siri.

"Of course you do."

"He was my dearest comrade. But it's as if he's shed a few dimensions and exists in a new form. It's not him. When I shake his hand or kiss his cheek I feel nothing. The spirit world is a circus of illusion. I can create images and Bpoo can put them into a format that's recognizable to me. I think I see my dead friend. I believe I can hear him speak. I'm conned into accepting a full-blown production and the more I wish it to be real, the more real it becomes."

"You can't believe otherwise," said Daeng. "Your trips to the Otherworld have influenced events here, so it isn't just your imagination. You've been able to make changes in this world from your experiences."

"But I can't bring anyone back," said Siri. "And then what happens if I prefer my relationship with Civilai over there? I'd be gone for days at a time. No *maître d'* noodles. No drinks by the river. Until now I've been able to control it. It's the first time I haven't been left to the whim of a dead transvestite spirit guide. I'm earthbound. I've learned how to shut the door. I'm afraid to open it again."

Daeng smiled and kissed his cheek.

"I miss that warm empty place on the mattress and the stories when you come back, but I'd miss the real you a lot more."

6/2/1941

I should like to talk more about our vegetable patch but let me first introduce my dear colleagues here. There are eight of us, nine if you count the dog but I'll tell his story later. There's no need to memorize the names. As I proceed, I'll talk about them in more detail. Our commander is Major General Dorari Momoyotsu (怒贏罟脾四). He's a sweet man, small with a huge shiny skull. From behind, it looks like he's wearing a pink motorcycle helmet.

I am his second-in-command. Below me is Captain Jame Nomishige *(邪目耳滋)*. He is our quarter-master. He isn't fit for active duty because he lost an eye in one battle and a leg in another. I joke that it was very clumsy of him. But despite his age, he is a wonderful stores man. Next is Second Lieutenant Tetsukimo Souben *(泆膽藻麵)*. He's very tall for a Japanese and skinny as a bamboo pole. Then there is Warrant Officer Ukabane Orimimi *(迂屍淶耳)*. He's as strong as an ox and a little scary to look at. His face is all battered and misshapen. Corporal Yatsusuki Hokobei *(奴犁夸謎)*, on the other hand, has a smooth, kind face but he's built like, as they say, a concrete latrine. Private Oshiira Somai *(啞苛蔬迷)* I secretly call Quasimodo because he has a hunched back and bad skin. He sings quite beauti-fully. Last is Lance Corporal Hokofugu Hama *(餘鮭芭麼)*, who has a penchant for alcohol although he doesn't become violent when he's drunk. I've noticed that drinking brings out a hidden feminine side that perhaps only I can see.

What a colorful group we are. I confess I am dull compared to my comrades. Our mission is to prepare Thakhek for the coming-together of all the Japanese armed forces. We have been allocated forty acres of land abutting the town. With the help of local labor we will build our own little Nirvana with dormitories and roads and other facilities. Meanwhile we live in tents, which I find most invigorating.

Nineteen eighty-one Laos was wallowing in a quagmire of bad luck and naivety, a state that had set back all its dreams of the previous three years. First floods then droughts killed the crops. Bad management and apathy killed off an overly ambitious cooperatives program. Siding with Vietnam killed off any hope of aid from China. And the mass exodus and prolonged incarceration of the royalist workforce killed off a skilled middle class. So what better course of action could there be, given the total failure of the government's first three-year plan of action, than to make a new plan? The People's Democratic Republic of Laos's new five-year plan of action offered new hope and prosperity. The highlights were to revamp industry (currently amounting to small factories producing matches, plastic bags, beer, and rubber sandals), encouraging agriculture (in a country where 75 percent of the lowland was already being farmed), and to work on national highway number nine (which would need heavy equipment the country didn't possess). In the meantime, imports exceeded exports by 80 percent and experts from other communist countries searched desperately for a proletariat to stimulate. Overseas, the United Lao National Liberation Front with its snug headquarters in California was funding insurgencies and promising to rescue those trapped in Laos—as if the country didn't have enough problems.

Vientiane, the capital, had taken on the appearance of a Miss Havisham: its shuttered shop fronts laced with spiderwebs, its potted plants the color of the dirt roads, its occasional paving stones segregated by gnarled weeds. The jungle was already claiming back the outer suburbs. And yet, through all its failings, the city dug deep for something to smile about. The populace believed that a country was more than the sum of its debts and the rust of its decomposing cars. A country was the character of its inhabitants, and after thirty years of war, the Lao believed they'd earned credit just for surviving it all. And two of the happiest Lao were Dr. Siri and his wife, Madam Daeng. They had fought for independence on the battlefields and had won the right to grumble about everything. They believed also that they had earned the right to travel wherever they wished whenever they wished. The government did not agree. In order to move from one province to another, a citizen had to have a *laissez-passer*. If the citizen could not justify the trip to the satisfaction of the official in charge of such matters, it was probably easier—as Dr. Siri often put it—to pass a mature coconut through your digestive system. Even would-be travelers with dying grandmothers, soon-to-be-married nieces, or invitations from respectable village heads would have to suffer the humiliation of sitting on a wooden bench for hours while the cadre shifted the application from one side of the desk to the other.

And it was exactly this brick wall of bureaucracy that inspired Siri and Daeng to travel illegitimately as often as they could. They lied with great aplomb, they hitchhiked on aircraft, they claimed to be persons of influence but often they'd just drive through border barriers and wave. The only thing they'd draw the line at was graft. They would never pay beyond the actual price for a document or a service even if it meant watching an application slip to the bottom of a pile. That wasn't the country they'd fought for. But all around them they were beginning to hear the rustle of brown envelopes passing under tables.

"How do we get there?" Daeng asked, shoveling noodles into bowls, yelling above the happy lunchtime throng.

"Where are we going?" Siri asked.

"Thakhek, of course."

"We are?"

"Most certainly. You've been bored to tears since you resigned. You have nothing to read. Nobody to stimulate you. You hate working in the restaurant."

"I do not."

He shifted to his left a little in case there was a bolt of lightning on its way.

"And with no Civilai, you have nobody to provide you with fictional appointments elsewhere. So you're stuck. And I think it's time for a vacation for both of us."

"What about the business?" said Siri, even though he knew only too well that Mr. Geung and Tukta were every bit as competent at noodling as his wife. He looked up from the spoons he'd been polishing for what felt like a great chunk of his life. "Then why don't we go to the French Riviera?" he said.

"Because we charge twenty cents for a bowl of noodles and I'll have to work another fifty years to earn enough to get there. And you know you really want to go to Thakhek."

"It is a pleasant spot for a holiday, I admit," he said.

"And you'll be able to walk around to all the sites Toshi mentions in his diary."

"All right. You've talked me into it."

"Which brings me back to my original question. How do we get there?"

"We could always go through Thailand. We could play the deaf and dumb Thai couple again. That worked once. But I have to see Phosy tomorrow. Perhaps we can go officially as special constables."

"You'll never talk him into doing anything illegal."

"We'll see."

"But Siri."

"Yes, my love?"

"Read faster."

7/23/1941

This is such a fascinating place with three distinct groups: Lao, French, and Japanese. The Lao continue to be bemused by all the attention they're attracting. Our village headman is most kind. He provides us with workers and goes out of his way to bring us fruit and vegetables from Lao gardens. The French are like ghosts. They don't talk to us and I feel they would not even if we shared a language. None of them speaks Lao and it seems all the clerks they hire are French-speaking Vietnamese. And then there's us. We work hard and competently. We are kind to each other and to the locals.

And I promised to mention the dog. His name is Taigou, which means "big bite." I never considered myself to be an animal lover but I have become very close to two creatures since I arrived here. The first was a cat I called Hal. He was always somewhere close by watching me. He would not accept food from me but he was usually asleep at the foot of my bunk when I woke up in the morning. And then suddenly came Taigou. There's something about him that reminds me of a small person in a fur coat. One day, Private Oshiira came running to me and said there was a dog behind the latrines whose head was stuck in a teakettle. He'd obviously been dunking for water and managed to get his head wedged inside. He was galloping around like some crazed beast, running into fences and trees. I was afraid he'd hurt himself. I wrestled him to the ground and held him while my men pried off the kettle. He bit me, of course, when his head was free. It was only to be expected. But after that, the little man in the fur coat felt remorse. It was as if he understood that I was only there to help him, and from that day on, he became my protector and I became his guardian. We have adopted him as a mascot but he sleeps in front of my tent every night and nobody else's. I feel that I am getting closer to nature with every day that passes. Sadly, with Taigou's arrival, Hal no longer stays with me, although I do see him lurking in the shadows from time to time. I suppose there is some deep animosity between these two species that I do not yet understand.

Siri was on a bench in front of Phosy's office at police headquarters. He hadn't made an appointment and nobody knew where the chief inspector was. And anyone in Laos knew that making an appointment had very little effect on success in meeting the person you've come to see. But Siri had Toshi's diary so he was in no hurry. The mold from the diary cover seemed to be spreading to the doctor's skin. No amount of carbolic soap, no number of horsehair brushes would remove the stain. But he wouldn't stop reading even if he caught the bubonic plague from the thing. The Japanese had started to be more creative in his writing. He still mentioned the flowers and trees and the bloody birds ad nauseam, but he'd started to tell fables. It was as if Toshi had suddenly become aware of an audience.

12/17/1941

I was walking by the river with Taigou, taking in the scents of the wildflowers, when ahead I saw Major General Dorari sitting on a rock looking far too grey for such a colorful day. I approached him and saluted.

"Major General, why are you looking so sad?" I asked.

It wasn't my place to ask such a question to a senior officer so I expected a rebuke. But Major General Dorari had been a schoolteacher in his civilian life and I could see there was gratitude behind his scowl.

"Toshi," he said. "I am in trouble. I moved to that large colonial house on the skirt of the hill but it was too big to take care of alone so I hired a young Lao girl to clean and cook for me. She is beautiful and reminds me so much of my granddaughter whom I miss terribly. I befriended her. But the father of my maid found I had recruited the girl and he believes the worst. He has threatened to kill me for defiling his daughter."

I knew my general would never do such a terrible thing so I took it upon myself to help him. That evening, I had been invited to a wedding party for one of our road builders. I had become friendly with the Lao and was invited to celebrations often. As ever, I was the only Japanese in attendance. I knew all the village headmen would be there including the father of my general's maid. I do not drink a great deal, unlike the Lao, who drink to excess. But they have good reason to do so. I placed myself in such a position that I was certain most of the guests could hear me and I began my anecdote in my most polished Lao language.

"Major General Dorari Momoyotsu, our commanding officer, is the son of a samurai," I began. I knew I already had my audience rapt.

I continued.

"Before the samurai headed off to battle, he would have his oldest son, Momoyotsu, deliver his sword to the blacksmith for cleaning and sharpening. His father's only instruction was that he should always hold the sword in two hands and walk carefully, looking down always for stones and potholes.

"'Because the samurai sword can sense when its carrier is being disrespectful,' his father told him.

"And year after year the samurai took his sword into battle and was victorious. Momoyotsu entered his teens, and probably because he had an absentee father, he got into bad ways, listening to racy music, smoking, and chasing girls. And one day he completely forgot about collecting the sword from the blacksmith. He was with a pretty village girl as the sun was setting when he remembered. He leapt from the haystack and started to run, forgetting his belt. He sprinted to the blacksmith and banged on the door, waking the owner. He grabbed the sword from its rack in one hand and ran for all he was worth to the barracks. It was dark. The road was rocky and pocked with potholes. He'd been drinking strong rice wine so he didn't see one particularly deep divot. He tripped, his trousers fell to his ankles, the sword spun from his hand and sliced off his penis and testicles with such precision the medic at the barracks was certain Momoyotsu was a girl child."

There were tears from my audience that night, mostly from the men. Every one of them had reached instinctively to his groin when the story was told. The following morning, not only did the headman's daughter report early for work at the major general's house, not only did the headman deliver her himself, not only did he bow to the major general, but he also brought him a freshly picked jackfruit, which he handed to the general with a knowing nod.

Siri looked up from the diary to see Phosy standing over him.

"Good read?" asked the policeman.

"I'm not sure," said Siri, getting to his feet. "Have you heard of Noh?"

"The word?"

"The Japanese performance. I went to see it once in Paris. In my mind it went on for weeks. It's conducted at a pace that would make snails envious. You stay in your seat because you think something is bound to happen but it rarely does. You go to the bathroom and when you come back they still haven't completed the sentence they started before you left. It's like watching a rock erode."

"And the diary's like that?"

Phosy unlocked his office door and gestured for Siri to enter. A secretary ran in after them with a ledger full of papers to sign. The official day had begun. Phosy sat at his nice teak desk, a memento from one of his less-than-honest predecessors. Siri sat on the sofa opposite.

"He writes very nicely," he said. "He's reached a

proficiency in Lao that should make us all hang our heads in shame. But there are endless pages where he goes into great detail about clearing bushes and swimming in the river with his dog and getting the right balance of manure to mulch his infuriating vegetable garden. He's just started to tell stories, which is fun, but I'm over halfway through the diary and I'm starting to lose faith in him."

"How do you mean?"

"I don't know. I just get the feeling he's making stuff up."

"I thought you liked fiction."

"I do, in its rightful place. And I must say I'm getting fond of the introduction of make-believe in government reports. But this is supposed to be a diary. Listen to this."

Siri flipped to a page he'd marked with a sliver of paper and read.

"'I've noticed how Corporal Yatsusuki continues to gain weight. Yatsusuki is a builder and carpenter. We'd just completed a dormitory building for officers and as we were leaving, Yatsusuki got himself stuck in the doorway. It took four of us to unwedge him.'"

"See, Phosy? How many people do you know so wide they get stuck in a doorway? And there's this."

He turned to another marker.

"'I was looking for Taigou'—that's the dog—'and I found him behind the mess tent. He had another teakettle stuck on his head.' What do you make of that?"

"That dogs are stupid?" suggested Phosy.

"No. It means Toshi is so bored with his own diary that he's started to invent stories. His life is so uneventful, so perfect, that he has to make negative things up. And here I am reading it waiting for the punch line, sure that something devastating is going to happen, but when it does I won't know what's real and what's not."

"Then stop reading it."

"Of course I can't," said Siri. "Daeng wants us to go to Thakhek to walk in Toshi's footsteps but his feet aren't going anywhere I'm interested to follow."

"You could always . . ."

"I am not turning to the last page."

"Up to you."

"But we do plan to go to Thakhek regardless. Perhaps you'd be kind enough to write us up a couple of *laissez-passers*."

"Are you going on police business?" Phosy asked.

"In a way."

"What way would that be?"

"We're friends of the chief inspector of police?"

"Is that why you came here?"

"In part."

"Then I hope you have better luck with the other part."

"Right. Well, because you are the least corrupt man ever to sit at that very expensive desk, we assumed you wouldn't write us travel documents. I would have been just a little bit disappointed if you'd agreed. But we still plan to go and now you owe us a favor."

"I do?"

"Yes. You're forcing us to travel to another province without *laissez-passers*, so we need you to find us transportation that doesn't involve paperwork."

"Siri?"

"You can do it, we know you can. You of all people can circumvent the awkward bureaucracy and send us on our way legally."

Phosy laughed.

"I'll ask around," he said. "I can't promise anything."

"That's all we can hope for."

Phosy escorted Siri to the door, his arm around the old boy's shoulder.

"How did things go in Vang Vieng?" Siri asked.

"Ah, that's why I was late."

"Sihot couldn't find the girl?"

"We don't know."

"Why not?"

"We can't find Sihot."

CHAPTER FOUR
Tales of the Riverbank

2/2/1942

I was walking along the riverbank, watching the sunlight reflect silver off the backs of the low-flying terns, when up ahead I saw my friend Private Oshiira sitting beside a pool bathing his flaky feet. He looked a little sad. I approached him.

"Why do you look so sad?" I asked.

"Why, it's nothing to bother you with, Major," he said.

"Come on, old fellow," I said. "It's such a nice day, nothing could bother me."

"Well," he said, "my father always told me a man should find himself a skill and perfect it and offer it to those who don't possess that skill. After thirty years in the army it appears that my skill is cleaning latrines."

"And you are very good at it," I reminded him.

"Don't get me wrong. It's true. I am a genius when it comes to getting a shine out of old taps. You could eat your dinner off the floor when I've finished mopping. So I took my skill to the town temple, and through the Japanese interpreter, I offered to clean the temple whenever I was off duty. The abbot seemed very pleased. To me it was like a sign from heaven that my skill had been accepted. On my first evening I washed and polished all the Buddha images, especially the one they called the Great Lightness. They all shone when I'd finished. But the next evening when I returned, the abbot led me to the Great Lightness and looked at me with disappointment in his eyes; and deservedly so. The face of the Great Lightness was smudged and greasy and had no shine at all. I couldn't understand what had happened.

"That evening I dedicated an hour to the Buddhas, and before I left, the Great Lightness was shining brighter than even my most famous bathroom attachments—work that was mentioned in war dispatches to Tokyo. But the next day and the next, the abbot awoke to a grimy, greasy, smudged Lightness. And today he told me he didn't want my services anymore. That's why I'm so sad."

It was a true mystery, one that I was determined to solve. At nightfall I crept into the temple grounds. The moon was just a sliver but it afforded me enough light to see a queue of local women each bowing to the Great Lightness, saying a prayer and holding the Buddha by the ears and kissing his face with lips greasy from sticky rice and fermented fish. This behavior was quite rightly abhorred by the Buddhist council, which is why the ladies came under the cape of darkness. I learned later, you see, that the Great Lightness was believed to bestow sexual prowess on husbands and fertility on wives.

My course was clear. The next day I instructed Private Oshiira to leave his toilet brush and bucket at the foot of the Great Lightness.

"But I never use a toilet brush to clean the Buddhas," said Oshiira. "That would be sacrilegious."

"You know that, and I know that," I said. "But the ladies of the night do not. I guarantee that one small trickle of doubt in their mind will curb their overenthusiasm. The Great Lightness will welcome the dawn with a smile on his face. You watch."

And so he did.

Siri had taken to reading diary excerpts to his staff in the evenings. Mr. Geung and Tukta were addicted. It was like following a radio drama, they said, without the drama. They all knew that Crazy Rajhid was secretly listening in the shadows of the riverbank. And with every mention of Taigou, the teakettle-wearing dog, Ugly growled deeply beyond the shutters of the shop. It occurred to Siri that they were probably hosting Vientiane's first post-American book club.

"Even with the funny stories it's still dull," said Daeng.

"We're getting to know the characters," said Siri.

"Siri, there's an invasion going on all around. The Japanese are rampaging through Singapore. They've already purged Malaysia of its ethnic Chinese, and here we are hearing about a group of peculiar noncombatants living a dull life in Thakhek. And, to be honest, I'm starting to think that even if you did turn to the last page, they'd still be peeling turnips and scrubbing toilets. And we don't know why a pilot is digging ditches two thousand kilometers from the nearest action."

"It's coming, Daeng. Trust me. How about one more page before we turn in?"

"I don't know," said Daeng. "There's some rather interesting mold growing on the back garden wall I was hoping to watch this evening."

"One more page. One more page," chorused the staff.

Siri laughed, turned the page, and read:

12/16/1942

I was walking along the riverbank marveling at the thought you could swim to another country and that everything was so different on the other side.

"He certainly does a lot of riverbank walking," Daeng interrupted.

"Do you want me to read this or not?" Siri asked.

"Yes, please," said Daeng. "But I bet you a week's income he meets someone who's sad."

"Daeng?"

"Sorry."

Ahead I could see the outline of Captain Jame Nomishige with his one eye and one leg. His head was bowed. He seemed to be deep in thought so I decided to walk past him. But he looked up and called to me.

"Major Toshi," he said. "May I ask you a question?"

"See? Not sad at all," said Siri.

"Just read it," said Daeng.

"Of course," I replied.

"I am old now," he said. "As you know I am an expert in my pastime."

"Of course I know," I said. "You are a grand master of shogi. You have won many Japanese chess competitions."

"I only aspire to be a grand master, Major Toshi. But I have not been able to reach that next level; the echelon above technical skill. When I lose, and I do not lose often, I am defeated by people who overcome me at a psychological level. Every week I play against a general who passes through Thakhek with his unit. I lose to him regularly even though I'm certain my approach is technically sound."

"Then you obviously need to get inside your opponent's head," I said.

"And how would I go about that?" he asked.

"By reading his mind," I said.

The following day we went to the quartermaster's storehouse and picked up a ladder. We took a ledger from the stationery department and then selected a fine black and blue cockerel from the barracks farm. For my pièce de résistance I went to the pharmacy and ordered a special cocktail that I would pick up later. That night, Captain Jame invited the traveling general to the new mess building.

"How have you been?" the general asked.

"I knew you would say that, sir," said Jame.

"What?"

"I knew what you were going to say," said Jame. "I've been seeing a local shaman and he has taught me how to read people's minds and see the future."

"Nonsense," said the general.

"Then how could I know what you were going to say when you arrived?"

The general laughed heartily.

"Captain Jame," he said. "'How have you been?' is a fairly common greeting, don't you think? You don't have to be a mind reader to guess that."

"Then let's try something else," said Jame.

He took the ledger and a pen from his day pack. He opened the ledger, looked into the general's eyes, and started to write. But as he was writing, his lips curved into a smile. He laughed and closed the book.

"What's so funny?" asked the general.

Jame opened the ledger and held it up for the general to see. On the page was written, "What's so funny?"

The general still wasn't impressed.

"That wasn't mind reading," he said. "It was just a trick. You could be certain I was going to say something like that."

Jame turned the page, looked into the general's eyes, and started to write.

"You don't—" the general began, but he was interrupted by the sound of scratchy footsteps on the tin roof.

"What the devil?" said Jame.

The footsteps grew louder then just as suddenly, they stopped. There were a few seconds of silence before they heard an almighty "Cock-a-doodle-doo!"

"There's a damned chicken on the roof," said the general.

Jame smiled and held up the ledger and showed the words he'd written: "There's a chicken on the roof."

"Now, you know I couldn't have predicted that unless I had a gift," said Jame. "I missed the word 'damned' but you'll have to forgive me for that. I'm still a beginner don't forget."

Jame could see that the general was swaying but he needed one more example of the one-legged man's new skills to be convinced.

"Let's play a few games," said the general.

"Not tonight," said Jame. "You aren't feeling well."

"I'm feeling just fine," said the general.

"You can't fool me, General," said Jame. "You have an upset stomach. You're wondering whether you ate something bad at lunchtime. You're hoping it won't be a nasty case of diarrhea that will keep you up all night. We can play tomorrow when you're feeling better. Good evening."

That night, the general spent more time on the toilet than in his bunk. Sometimes the two overlapped. It gave him many hours to think about his encounter with Captain Jame. It hardly seemed possible the old man was able to read his mind but that "hardly" was doubt enough. He hadn't seen the many prewritten entries in the ledger that covered all the possible greetings the general was likely to make. He hadn't seen the ladder up which I carried the cockerel. He hadn't seen me creep into his tent during the afternoon and put a laxative called nigari in his green tea. And so, in his mind, there were the seeds of doubt. And the next time he met Captain Jame to play shogi, the general was so busy thinking and double-thinking for both of them that he lost every game. Jame was inside his head and would remain there forever.

"Nonsense," said Daeng. "It's all nonsense. What we need is a good murder."

CHAPTER FIVE
The Pole Jumper

Chief Inspector Phosy stepped off the military plane onto the uneven grass landing strip in Vang Vieng. A small herd of goats had panicked when the Antonov landed, then they regrouped when it took off. Phosy was accompanied by Second Lieutenant Jiep, one of the bright young generation of policemen handpicked by the chief inspector himself. There were so few men and women he could trust in his own police force. Phosy was intent on building a department he could be proud of. In total he managed two thousand officers nationwide, many of whom he had no cause to respect. Some, not threatening enough to be sent for reeducation, were left over from the old regime. Most had taken a sideways step from the military, undergone a crash course in peacetime law enforcement, and returned to their hometowns to extort money from the few people who had any. It would be an uphill task to change such a system.

Phosy was forty-nine years old in a country where the life expectancy was fifty-two. That gave him three years to fulfill his dream of a slick, efficient law enforcement network. He hoped it might grow from the twenty young people he'd selected and trained and whom he referred to as "the squad." He'd logged his absence from his office as a training day for Jiep. There were those who questioned Phosy's habit of running off and conducting investigations when he should have been signing papers and shaking hands. But he'd lost contact with an officer. Sihot was a friend. They'd worked together on numerous cases. And, as Phosy reminded everyone, no one was better qualified to find a missing person than he was.

His first call was to the police station at the intersection of the main highway; more a kiosk, as it turned out. He'd sent a message ahead to say he'd be arriving but wasn't surprised not to be met at the airstrip. So when the Antonov resumed its journey to the military camp at Kasi, they were alone all but for a herd of goats and a 1953 Renault with the word TAXI written on a cardboard sign on the dashboard. The driver had picked up Sihot four days earlier and taken him to the police box on the north-south highway. As the officers headed there, Phosy admired the beautiful setting. The dark emerald karsts stood proud above lime green rice paddies that bordered the fast-flowing river. He could understand why the Vietnamese might select this area to get away from the frantic pace of Hanoi.

Village Police Sergeant Ookum was contemplating his next case on a hammock strung between two wooden posts. Phosy prodded him awake. Sergeant Ookum focused, smiled, and said, "Hey, man. What's up?"

Phosy helped him out of his attitude and his hammock with a sound kick. The sergeant seemed more irked than censured.

"You remember me?" Phosy asked.

"Sure," said Ookum. "You're the guy who trained us in Vientiane."

"That's correct. But since then I've become the chief inspector of police."

"Wow, man. Congratulations."

Phosy shook his head, went to the only desk in the kiosk, and opened the top drawer. A small arsenal of joints was lined up in two ranks.

"Are you high?" Phosy asked.

"Only high with the honor of representing the Royal National Police Force in the execution of its duty," said Ookum, and decorated the sentiment with a jaunty salute.

"You do know there's been nothing royal since '75?" said Jiep. Phosy was pleased that the young officer had the confidence to speak up.

"Oh, yeah. Right. It slips my mind sometimes."

"I need you down off your cloud for a while to answer some questions," said Phosy.

"I'm totally off it, General. Ask away."

"Captain Sihot."

"Lovely man."

"Where is he?"

"He went back to Vientiane the day after he arrived."

"You saw him leave?"

"Not with my eyes, you know? But he said he'd be leaving then and I had no reason to doubt him. He seemed honest."

"Did you accompany him on his investigation?"

"Where?"

"Anywhere."

"I don't think so."

"Did he tell you why he was here?"

"Yeah, that I know for sure. He wanted a guide."

"Did you find him one?"

"You're damned right I did, General. Ouan down at the old resort. Public service is my creed. No job too difficult."

Vang Vieng was something of a ghost village. Close to midday there was nobody on the dirt tracks. Dogs scratched in the shade of huge water jars. The taxi passed a deserted construction site with a sign in front that read HAPPY GUEST HOUSE TO BE BUILT HERE. The owner was obviously gambling that one day there might be a rush of foreign tourists discovering this Eden. Phosy hoped, with little confidence, that his Lao brothers and sisters might keep their mouths shut, forget tourism and profits, and leave the pretty views to the locals. As Civilai used to say, tourism had a way of deleting all the wonders that attracted it in the first place.

"And what did you learn from our encounter with the local police person?" Phosy asked Jiep as they drove through the village.

"He was high, sir, on duty."

"He certainly was, boy. And why didn't he know anything about the case?"

"Because Captain Sihot wasn't confident enough to share the details with a stoner?"

"You're quite right again," Phosy said with a nod. "Which is why he asked for a guide. Someone hopefully more reliable."

"And you'll fire the sergeant?"

"Not at all. Police boxes all over the country are run by Sergeant Ookums and worse. Eventually, we'll replace them, but there are good points. The sergeant was at his post, he was in some version of his uniform, and there was a bicycle parked outside."

"Why is that a good point?"

"Because if he was corrupt he'd have a motorcycle. No, boy, he's friendly enough. I'm sure he gets along well with the locals. He'll keep."

The taxi pulled up in front of the old French resort. The cabins had long since yielded to the monsoons and many were without roofs. But, according to the sergeant, the restaurant was still functioning and provided fare for visiting cadres and those lost on the highway. There were a few wooden tables in front of a bunkerlike structure. Phosy called for service.

"Good day?"

From the rear of the building came a pudgy man with a random sort of beard that sprouted here and there like the hair of a mangy dog. He was dressed in camouflaged fatigues from a long-ago campaign.

"Gentlemen," he said, without enthusiasm. "Welcome to Ouan's restaurant. Looks like you got here just before the rush."

"We have some questions," said Phosy.

"Certainly," said Ouan, "but I don't see how you can ask questions on empty stomachs. How about a little lunch?"

The policemen hadn't eaten since early that morning but they were nervous about a restaurant that had no customers for long periods.

"How old are your ingredients?" Phosy asked.

"I have a refrigerator, Comrade," said Ouan, as if the life span of food was unlimited once chilled. "I have a generator. Take the weight off your feet. Sit here in the shade and I'll see what I can rustle you up."

He led them to the nearest table and wiped it with his forearm.

"Perhaps a drink?" he said.

"Water for us," said Phosy.

"Really?" said Ouan. "I have cold beer."

"No, we're on duty," said Phosy, although the thought of a cool beer there in the middle of dusty nowhere did appeal to him. Jiep had also perked up at the mention of it. But Phosy was the chief of police. He had to set a good example. "We're here on official business. We're looking for a colleague of ours. We believe you met him four days ago. His name is Sihot."

"Captain Sihot," said Ouan. "Of course."

"You showed him around?"

"Took him to the karst where that terrible accident happened. That poor Vietnamese gentleman."

"And where did you go after that?" asked Jiep.

"Well, he was asking about a girl," said Ouan. "He thought the Vietnamese had gone on a picnic with a local girl."

"Did you know who she was?"

"No. It's very unlikely a girl from these parts would allow herself to be entertained by a foreigner, especially a foreigner with a wife and mistress. If there really was a lass she'd have to be from somewhere else. Probably a Vientiane girl. Low morals down there. Most likely he brought a whore with him."

"We'd like to talk with some locals," said Phosy. "Someone who might know where the girl was from?"

"Certainly, Officer," said Ouan. "But first, let's get you both fed and watered. Special price for our friends in the police force. Captain Sihot loved my fried rice with river crabs. I'm an excellent chef."

They had no idea how good a chef he was because the

food was spicy enough to strip the paint off a tank. Every mouthful was like swallowing fire. They were hungry so they persevered, but it was only the introduction of two bottles of 33 Beer that allowed them to put out the flames. They completely forgot the "no drinking on duty" rule.

At first, Phosy put the dizziness down to the temperature and the food. Then he looked across the table at Jiep, whose eyelids were drooping. And when the spoon dropped from the chief inspector's numb fingers, he knew what had happened but it was too late to do anything about it. The scenery closed in on him and the last thing he remembered was Ouan standing behind Jiep with a satisfied look on his mangy face.

"You do realize he still hasn't flown anywhere?" said Daeng. "He claims to be a pilot yet he still hasn't left the ground."

"He'll take off eventually," said her husband, somewhat less confidently than on the many other occasions he'd said it. Toshi's diary had continued to meander through weird territory.

"And have you not started to wonder about the people he lives with?" Daeng pushed on. "They're freaks, every last one of them; hunchbacked, grossly fat, half blind and legless. Were the Japs really so benevolent that they'd provide work opportunities for the mentally and physically handicapped?"

"It was wartime," Siri reminded her. "They selected a team to prepare a base for the invaders away from the front line. They were probably excluded from fighting because of their physical limitations but were ideal for the work they were called on to do."

"Then what was Toshi doing there?" Daeng asked. "If

they really did select a team of misfits, what, apart from dull writing, was his disability?"

Despite the lack of excitement, Siri had persevered with his reading. Toshi's diary may have been dull but it was beautifully written and Siri was enjoying every image. He knew few of his countrymen could produce such handsome prose. His invitation to help the writer was no longer a rescue mission in his mind and more of a desire to meet the man who'd fashioned the work. It would be the getting together of a writer and a fan.

They were in the reception area at UNDP; the UN's development program, what Comrade Civilai had described as the United Nations' center of ill-advised, overfunded, pie-in-the-sky, misoperations in Laos. Siri was kinder. Even though the UN in Laos wasn't itself sure of what it was doing there, it did pump in lots of money, some of which filtered down to the communities. Perhaps that was not the way it had been intended but the most successful aid projects were invariably those which wrote corruption into the budget.

The visitors were there to meet Herbert Roper of the United Nations High Commission for Refugees. He was in charge of the repatriation program. For every thousand refugees on their way to convenience stores and Asian food markets in the West, there was a handful who'd panicked before heading overseas and decided to go back home. Some had spent years in the camps being vetted and re-vetted at a pace so slow they'd started to wonder if the West really wanted them. Many were Hmong who'd been the backbone of CIA operations during the war. The US had made a brave show of accepting its quota but pointed out that America was currently full and could take no more. But still they came to the camps. By the end of the seventies, families were leaving Laos not because they had deep ideological differences with the ruling socialist regime but because they were poor. And there were the Chinese who had suddenly found themselves victimized as a result of bad feelings toward mainland China. And there were those mountain tribes who'd fought alongside the Pathet Lao but had still been forced down from the hills by their former allies to farm the lowlands. There was any number of reasons to flee. Those who could swim took their chances crossing the Mekong. The camps didn't get any emptier and the UN started to promote the values of repatriation of refugees from the Thai camps back to Laos. Returnees were promised a place to live, forgiveness for previous affiliations, and, most importantly, a guarantee that they wouldn't be executed. It was not a tempting package unless you figured in the seventy US dollars for every man, woman, and child in the family, free farming tools, and rice for a year.

The man charged with making all this possible was Herbert Roper, an English anthropologist and linguist. He spoke a number of the languages of the Sino-Tibetan, Indo-European, Altaic, and Mon-Khmer groups and was a veritable erupting volcano of knowledge. He was the gentle type, with the build and manner of a man married to academia. But like many married men he had a secret life. His appetite for beautiful women was voracious and he unashamedly preferred the company of those who had husbands of their own. He was an unlikely but seemingly successful Lothario. Perhaps it was the thrill of the illicit that drew him to bored housewives and them to him. His list of conquests included the wives of men of wealth and power who, had they known, could have ended Roper's philandering at the end of a razor blade.

When he arrived, flustered, in the UNDP foyer he was already sweating even though he'd come from his air-conditioned office. He was dressed for a chilly spring evening in Surrey. He gave a soggy handshake to Siri but wiped his hand on his trousers before taking the hand of Madam Daeng. Siri observed that this handshake lasted a little too long for his liking. Daeng didn't seem to mind at all.

"Sorry to keep you waiting," he said unconvincingly in fluent Lao. He didn't take them to his office or invite them to sit. He'd obviously planned for this to be a brief visit. That suited Siri.

"We've been informed that you're traveling to Thakhek this weekend," said the doctor.

"By helicopter," said Daeng.

Roper only had eyes for her.

"That's true," he said.

"We would like to go with you," said Daeng.

Roper produced one of those condescending British smiles that leaves a person in no doubt they've said something utterly ridiculous.

"Of course that would be totally out of the question," he said. "Even if you were a politburo member I'd be unable to give permission for such a thing." He started walking toward the door. "I'm sorry you wasted your time here."

He noticed the old Lao couple were not following him.

"But there is a way," said Daeng.

"This is the United Nations," said the man. "It isn't a travel agency."

"Dr. Siri?" said Daeng.

Siri reached into his shoulder bag and produced a

single sheet of paper. He unfolded it and read, "Madam Wojcik. The wife of the Polish consul."

He looked up just in time to see what little color there was in the Englishman's face drain into his button-down collar.

"I . . ." he said.

"Recently returned from a trip to Bangkok where a confidential maternity test revealed that, despite her advanced years, the good lady is five months pregnant," Siri continued. "Whence a decision was made to terminate the pregnancy."

"How . . . ?" said Roper.

"You are based in a socialist state and dallying with a married woman whose husband represents a socialist country," said Daeng with a smile. "Spying is one of our fortes. How could we not know? It would appear the only ear the story has yet to reach is that of the consul."

"Who I believe is an insanely jealous man," Siri added.

"I . . ." said Roper.

"Now, for a waiter or a taxi driver that would not necessarily be a problem," said Siri.

"He could just jump on the bus and make a living elsewhere," said Daeng.

"But for a United Nations representative, particularly one with a wife and two children of his own, this situation could be a little sticky," said Siri.

"This is . . ." Roper lowered his voice even though they were alone in the room. "This is blackmail."

"Not yet," said Daeng.

"That's coming," said Siri.

"And when it does you'll be pleased to learn that we don't want money," said Daeng.

"That would be most uncivilized," said Siri. "All we want . . ."

"Is a helicopter ride to Thakhek," said Daeng.

"And back," said Siri.

"I . . ." said Roper.

CHAPTER SIX
How Does She Smell?

6/21/1943

It was a fine evening and I was watching the sun set beyond the river. I'd had a busy but fruitful day of planting tomatoes. I was about to return to the camp and resume my Lao language studies when I smelled something awful. I turned to see Warrant Officer Ukabane Orimimi standing close behind me. It was hardly surprising that he had trouble making friends. Apart from the state of his face, which was like that of an unsuccessful boxer, he had the most horrible breath. Honestly, it was as if a rat had crawled into his mouth and died there. I'd recommended mouth-washes and pineapple juice and fennel seeds but nothing seemed to make a difference.

"Major Toshi," he said. "I am so very lonely. Sometimes I think I'll never find a woman to love me."

"I believe there is someone for everyone," I said, although I doubted he'd find his ideal woman in a war zone surrounded only by male soldiers. But he needed a boost to his morale and I decided it was worth being just a tad dishonest in order to achieve that aim. At the market there was one plain Lao woman who had no nose. A feral dog had bitten it off when she was a child. What remained of the nostrils had scarred over. Consequently, she had no sense of smell. This, I decided, would be a good start for anyone getting to know Ukabane. For the next stage I trusted my instinct and the power of translation.

"This is Warrant Officer Ukabane," I said to the market woman. Her name was Moot.

Lao market women can be very direct and rude in a charming way so I anticipated her response.

"Did the bus come off as badly as him?" she asked.

"She says she's noticed you around," I translated for Ukabane.

"She has a very unpleasant face," said Ukabane, who was also cursed with the affliction of honesty.

"Warrant Officer Ukabane says you remind him of a famous actress who is very popular in Japan," I told her. "He thinks you have a very nice smile."

Her cheeks became rosy.

"He must be blind as well as ugly," she said.

"She says you look very muscular," I translated. "The type of man who would protect his woman."

Ukabane pulled in his stomach and looked away. I assumed this gesture was to afford the woman a view of his good side although neither profile would win a prize.

"She's in bad shape," he said. "Obviously never done any physical labor in her life."

"Ukabane says your figure would inflame the

desire in any red-blooded man," I told her. "He can't keep his eyes off your divine bosom."

"You tell him to take his beady eyes off my chest right this minute," she said. But her expression was more of flattery than offense.

"She says she loves listening to your voice," I lied. "So masculine and forceful. She could listen to you speak all night."

"All that in such a short sentence?" asked Uka-bane.

"Lao is a very economical language," I said.

"What are you two talking about?" asked Moot.

"He . . . No, never mind."

"Tell me."

"No," I said. "It's out of the question."

She glared at me.

"All right," I said. "He was asking what chance there might be of you accompanying him to a coffee shop one morning. Perhaps somewhere with a view of the river?"

"All that in one short sentence?"

"Japanese is an economical language," I said.

"Tell him I'd sooner get rabies and be burned alive," she said. But she said it with a smile and an eyelash flutter. I turned to Ukabane.

"What's she saying?" he asked.

"No. It's impossible."

"What?"

"She said she'd like to get to know you better."

"She didn't."

"If you say so."

"Did she?"

"She was wondering whether you might care to join her in a coffee shop one morning."

"I don't know," he said, a glimmer of a smile at the corner of his mouth. "Really? I don't know."

"I'll tell her no."

"Wait, I . . . you know? I do feel a little bit sorry for her, looking the way she does. Perhaps one small coffee wouldn't do much harm."

"He's so excited at the prospect," I told Moot. "It seems he's really fond of you. He said it's a dream come true."

"Or, in my case, a nightmare," she said. "What time?"

And that was it. I'd never seen a couple try so hard to repress their happiness. I agreed to act as a chaperone for their coffee liaison even though it really didn't matter how well things went. I wasn't about to go on dates with them into the future. The important thing was that they'd both experienced the pleasure of being desired, however briefly. There was just one more thing left for me to do. I knew Moot would never be able to smell Ukabane's nasty breath but I was sure her colleagues at the market would be only too pleased to pass on the bad news. So I felt it was my duty to investigate the source of his toxic output.

"Warrant Officer Ukabane," I said one day. "I would like to discuss your dental hygiene."

"All right, Major Toshi," he said with a slightly baffled expression.

"I would like you to go back to your tent and bring me your toothbrush. I wish to see whether you are brushing your teeth correctly."

He seemed lost.

"My what?" he said.

"Your toothbrush," I replied. "You do have one, I assume?"

"I'm not sure," he said. "What does one look like?"

The Mi-26 helicopter traced a route along the milk-tea-brown Mekong. Dark clouds still lurked on the horizon but Siri and Daeng were blessed with a fine day overhead. Word had reached Vientiane that insurgents based in the refugee camps on the Thai side had again raided Thakhek and attacked a government office. Some soldiers had been killed and valuables pilfered from private homes. But that news only made it to the Lao community, not the UN. So Roper had no cause to cancel the trip.

On board were three Bru male adults, a Lao Loum couple from a village just outside Mahaxai, and two girls whose mother had died of malaria in the camp at Ban Vinai. The girls' father had refused to travel with them to the camp. He was unable to walk long distances due to a war wound of some description. The UN had contacted him and he had requested his daughters be returned to him. They were eerily silent children, unresponsive to questions. Neither did they appear to speak to each other. They were clearly terrified.

Siri and Daeng sat on the rusty fold-down seats of the noisy chopper yelling a conversation.

"I get the feeling we're off in search of a lunatic," shouted Daeng.

"He's just a bit stir-crazy," yelled Siri. "He's using his diary as therapy. If you live in an environment where the same things happen day after day your reality cuts out and your imagination takes over."

"That wasn't a snide reference to life in our noodle restaurant with me, was it?"

"Oh, Daeng. How could you even suggest such a thing?"

"I don't want your imagination seeing me as a twenty-six-year-old beauty queen with a rum franchise."

"I have a seventy-year-old beauty queen with a rice whisky still in the back garden. Who needs a dream? I can't imagine anything better than that."

"Nicely stated."

"You're welcome."

"So, what's our plan?" asked Daeng.

"I'm about thirty pages from the end of the diary," he said. "By then, I hope we'll know who it is that needs help and why. We make contact with locals who were in Thakhek in the forties and we trace Toshi. Then we find a nice spot on the Mekong, take a cold drink, and sit watching the sun set for a few nights."

"When's our flight back?"

"Our new friend Mr. Roper has to travel to the villages with his returnees. With a helicopter that shouldn't take him so long. Three days at the most."

"Why?"

"Why what?"

"Roper's a UN official. He earns more in a week than we take in a year. Does he really need to hand-deliver refugees himself? Doesn't he have staff?"

"It's a new program, Daeng. The UN is sending refugee camp people back to their villages. People who abandoned their country. There are those who see them as traitors. The insurgent groups based overseas would like nothing better than for them to be lined up and shot by the wicked commies. Good anti-regime propaganda. Guilt by the bucketload for those who fled successfully. Massive donations to the cause. Nice homes in the Midwest for retired royalist generals. So Mr. Roper takes photos and videos of the happy reunions, teary-eyed relatives, thankful, not-assassinated returnees, and he announces that he or other UN officials will come by every three months to monitor the situation. He makes sure the local cadre hears that, takes his photo too just to confirm he gets the idea, and there's the safety package, living proof that repatriation works. Word gets around in the refugee camps and everyone decides to go home."

His voice was croaking from all that shouting so they gave up and enjoyed the scenery. There'd be plenty of time to talk when they landed. Daeng smiled at the girls, who looked away, embarrassed or afraid. Daeng could not imagine what they'd been through. While they were all together she was determined to make friends with them and learn something about them.

1/11/1944

The river has become my companion. In the rainy season, once a body of water had built up on its way from China, it was a ferocious ally, thundering past impatiently, too busy to stop and chat. But in the dry season it is a trickle that seems not to be moving at all. Now it's a lake of smoked glass with sand mounds here and there spelling out some kind of Morse code. I was at the boat port one day to receive a shipment of toys and sweets I'd ordered for children's day.

"Oh, give me a break," said Daeng.

"Shh," said Siri and continued to read.

> I was concerned about the effect of too much
> sugar on their teeth but who could resist the expres-
> sions on their little faces as they opened their parcels?

Daeng stuck a finger down her throat and made gag-
ging sounds. They were on the balcony of a rickety wooden
guesthouse with a view (if you strained your neck around
the building in front) of the river. There was one rock-
ing chair claimed by the doctor and a short wooden stool
upon which his wife perched. Siri looked down at her and
raised one bushy eyebrow. She pressed her palms together
in a short, polite *nop*. He continued.

> Along the dirt track I saw Corporal Yatsusuki
> Hokobei in extra-large sports fatigues jogging, or
> rather shuffling, at a moderate pace in my direction.
> He seemed even more enormous than usual. It took
> him forever to reach the spot where I was standing.
> He stopped, leaned forward, and seemed about to
> die. I'd only ever taken the beginner first-aid course
> so I wasn't qualified to save his life. Finally, he caught
> his breath and let loose a cough that dislodged an
> avalanche of phlegm. He reached into the pocket of
> his shorts and took out an old-fashioned fob watch.
> He looked at it with disappointment.
>
> "Damn," he said.
>
> "Too slow?" I asked.
>
> "I seem to get slower every day. It just makes me
> sad."

"Huh," said Daeng.

Siri put down the diary.

"We'll never get to the end if you keep it up with the sound effects," he said.

"You know if we do meet Toshi we're going to be deeply disappointed with him."

"What makes you think that?"

"Because he's written himself into the role of Mother Teresa. He can solve everyone's problems. Nobody's that wonderful."

"Then if we meet him we'll respect him as a great writer who was able to convince us of that," said Siri. "Whether it's fact or fiction doesn't matter. He has the power to entertain, which is a skill in itself. May I continue?"

Daeng held out her hand. Siri returned to the diary.

"Do you jog every day?" I asked.

"Rain or shine," said Yatsusuki.

"And the objective is to get fit?"

"To get thin, Major Toshi."

I looked at him. There are those who are born into thinness and, through poor judgment in the food and drink categories, acquire fat later in life. And there are those, like Yatsusuki, who are born huge, grow up huge, and remain huge all their lives no matter how hard they torture themselves with diet and exercise. Yatsusuki was an armored truck and jogging would not remove one single layer of paint. Once again, the problem was in his mind.

I wear eyeglasses. They are very fashionable and I'm proud of them. Some people attempt to make fun of me because I wear them but I do not respond to their jokes because I don't consider my eyeglasses to be shameful in any way. I was sure that I could find a way to stop Yatsusuki from jogging himself to death. My mission was aided by the arrival of Colonel Konko Asatsuba.

One evening, our team, all but Corporal Yatsusuki, was enjoying the company of Colonel Konko in the mess hut. Colonel Konko was a Tokyo man who ate only meat and could never get used to all the lizards and the abundance of rats everywhere. He was based in Vientiane and was a master of telling stories about his experiences in the army. He was a born comedian. He'd just told one hilarious anecdote about an adventure in Nanjing and we were in tears. Captain Jame confessed he was about to pee himself.

"Tell us another one," said Hokofugu.

"I'll have to start charging you," said Colonel Konko. "But you're a good audience so I'll give you one last story for free. It was something that happened in Korea. We Japanese were very popular over there for obvious reasons. I was stationed in Seoul and I was about to—"

He stopped talking and was looking toward the door through which Yatsusuki had just arrived.

"My god," said Colonel Konko.

We followed his gaze but none of us was surprised to see Yatsusuki standing there. He was on guard duty that evening and had stopped by to fill his canteen. He waved at us and made for the water jar.

"I don't believe it," said Colonel Konko.

"What?" said Major General Dorari.

"He's here," said Colonel Konko. "I've found him."

"Yatsusuki?" said the major general.

"That's what he's calling himself?" said Colonel Konko.

"That's his name," I said.

"No, it's not," said Colonel Konko. "His name is Erai Ko-oji."

He pronounced the name as if each syllable was molten gold. We looked across the table at each other then looked to the door where Yatsusuki was just about to return to his duties outside. Colonel Konko sighed.

"Ko-oji," he repeated.

"What are you talking about?" asked Jame.

"Do none of you follow sumo?" Colonel Konko asked.

There were some of us who checked the honbasho results from time to time. But we'd been overseas for so long we'd lost touch with sports back home. We all shrugged.

"When did he join your unit?" Colonel Konko asked.

"December 1940," said the major general.

"Yes," said Colonel Konko. "That would be exactly right. Ko-oji was the brightest young sumo wrestler anyone in the profession had ever seen. He had the build and the technique. Even when he was in his teens he was beating fighters with many years more experience in regional competitions. His stable held him back from the national circuit because of his age. But in July '40 the military government decided it was time to introduce new blood into the competition to build up pride in our youth and encourage the young men to fight for the homeland. Ko-oji was one of them. He was put on the program for a big basho in Tokyo. It was supposed to be a warm-up for the young men. Nothing too heroic was expected from them, just their willingness to take on the grand champions. Of course they'd lose.

"But Ko-oji won all of his preliminary bouts; won them easily. There was no luck involved. He beat the champion ozekis in seconds and inflicted a humiliating defeat on the yokozuna grand champion in the final bout. The sumo world was in shock. Never had a new fighter been so dominant. He was destined for greatness . . . immortality. But sumo is a ferociously political beast. The elders resented this upstart who'd swept through the rankings like a typhoon and shown the country the inadequacies of men considered national heroes. A true champion fought his way up the table, learning from his mistakes, honing his skill until he became the best. Crowds paid good money to watch their heroes, never completely certain of the results, never one hundred percent confident of a victory. They had, after all, followed their favorite fighters for many years through successes and failures. Who would give up their hard-earned salary to watch a tournament where there was no doubt of the victor? The whole business would collapse. But there was a role that he could fulfill that would provide a morale boost to the nation.

"It was decided that Ko-oji, after a battle with his conscience, would enlist in the great army of the empire and fight for glory, not in the dojo, but on the battlefield. And it was the same elders who pushed him into national service who decided it would be better for all concerned if Ko-oji were to fall heroically in battle: a great warrior dying for the emperor. We heard that assassins were dispatched to make sure the young wrestler never returned to Japan. But there were those in the military who had seen the young Ko-oji fight and they admired his ability. They gave him a new identity with false documents and sent him to a safe posting in the hope that he might return someday to claim the honor of which he had been deprived. And that was the last anyone ever heard of him, until now."

My unit mates sat spellbound and stunned.

"Our Yatsusuki?" said Hokofugu.

"There's no question," said Colonel Konko.

"And how do you know all this?" asked the major general.

"You know me as Konko," said the visitor, "but my pen name was Uso. Before I enlisted I was the chief sumo writer for the *Yomiuri* newspaper. I can tell you categorically that in your unit you have a brilliant practitioner of the art of sumo. But I beg you all, say nothing of this to anyone. Don't even tell him you know who he is because I am afraid you will frighten him back into seclusion. Ko-oji is safe here as long as his friends protect him."

Overnight, Yatsusuki's size and weight were no longer matters of ridicule. The jokes about his girth abated and he received more compliments about his strength. In some way, that newfound respect transcended language. Although nobody was sure how the word got out, the local people began to treat

Yatsusuki differently. The children no longer made fun of him, the girls waved, and even the French administrators looked on with admiration. Yatsusuki stopped jogging and began to carry his weight with pride. It was as if his fat had become his friend. Of course, he had no idea what had caused these changes but he loved his new status.

I met my friend Konko again a few weeks later. I knew him from the theater. He had been a brilliant Kabuki performer. But his dream was to be a character actor in the movies; a role for which he was undoubtedly qualified. I offered to pay him for his role of Corporal Konko but he insisted it was his pleasure. And so, in one sweep, I had given delight to two men.

CHAPTER SEVEN
Making Woophi

Mr. Roper had left in his helicopter that afternoon to deliver the Lao Loum couple to their village near Mahaxai. They would stay there overnight. The fussy Lao pilot had been trained by the Thais during the old regime. He was protective of his craft and objected to flying in the dark. It appeared he didn't have faith in the instruments to see him home. So Siri and Daeng had been entrusted with the task of babysitting the two girls and keeping an eye on the three Bru. The latter were easy enough to control. They were close to home and seemed so relieved to be out of the camp they spent all their time asleep. The girls were another matter. Still they didn't speak—not even to each other. Madam Daeng pulled her most popular games and tricks from the hat but there was no reaction. When they ate they stared at Daeng like street dogs afraid she'd steal their food. They would not lie together at bedtime; each kept to her own bedroll. She sang them a lullaby, one her grandmother had taught her, about ghost cats that nibble at your cheeks if you don't go to sleep, and eventually, albeit reluctantly, they dropped off.

Daeng and Siri sat in front of their room. Apart from

some silent and mysterious guest in room 4 (the manager had suggested this was a government official writing a top-secret document), Roper's team was the only clientele. The doctor had brought along a couple of bottles of Daeng's home brew and some rice snacks and Siri was reading aloud by the light of an old oil lamp. Insects dropped onto the pages and he swept them away with the side of his hand.

"See how much fun his stories are?" he said.

"Yet we still have no idea what he wants us to do," said Daeng.

"Maybe he's already told us," said Siri. "Don't forget we're only able to read half his diary."

He thumbed back through the earlier pages written in Japanese.

"Perhaps our clue is hidden amidst all this beautiful penmanship."

"Which is where it will have to stay unless you can produce a Japanese translator. I imagine they're few and far between in Thakhek."

"Fear not, good wife. Tomorrow our investigation begins in earnest and we can, at last, make sense of the mind of our grounded pilot. All will be revealed."

Nurse Dtui arrived at police headquarters at seven the next morning with Malee at the end of a rope. The child had learned how to walk but not how to walk at heel. She was a maniac for beelines that took her across roads and through hedges. Admittedly there were few vehicles on the streets but Dtui knew her daughter had to learn how to curb herself and her enthusiasm. Hence the rope. It was attached to a small pack on her back rather than around her neck but it still raised eyebrows from passersby. Dtui led her girl to the reception desk.

"Hello, Dtui. Good morning, Malee," said the old woman who sat behind it. Reception was still a novelty in socialist Laos. You'd normally walk from office to office until you found the person you were looking for, but Phosy was a leader ahead of his time. He demanded efficiency.

"Any news from Malee's daddy?" Dtui asked.

"Not yet," said the woman. "But don't forget they're in Vang Vieng. There's no post office or telephone line."

"I know," said Dtui. "But at least he could have left a message with the pilot if he wasn't going to make the flight back."

"Look, darling," said the kindly old lady, a mother and granny herself. "Here's what probably happened. Sihot went to Vang Vieng and got injured or sick. Phosy found him and arranged to take him to a military base where they have a medic. As soon as he can, he'll send word via a military wireless network and that news will eventually find its way to us."

"You're right," said Dtui. "My imagination is far too wild."

"Dtui, they're in Vang Vieng. It's a beautiful part of the country and, believe me, nothing bad ever happens there."

So, there they were; the two highest-ranking policemen in the country and a promising youngster, chained by the ankles to an iron girder that extended from one concrete wall to the other. There was a single door beyond their reach and no windows. The crack around the door provided their only natural illumination, although there was a small lamp constantly lit in the far corner that emitted a yellow glow. The lack of sunlight gave the room an eerie chill. Ouan, the resort proprietor, brought them food and water and emptied the buckets they used for their waste. But despite all their questioning and pleading, Ouan said not a single word. The policemen had exhausted all logical suggestions as to why they were there and what would become of them.

Sihot explained how he'd found his way to that room. He'd gone to meet Ouan as recommended by Ookum, the hippie police sergeant at the intersection. He, too, had been offered spicy food and a cool beer to wash it down. He, too, had fallen unconscious and had come to in this room. He'd watched Ouan drag the comatose bodies of first Phosy and then Jiep to the girder.

"Does this happen often?" asked Jiep.

Phosy and Sihot looked at each other.

"Pretty much a monthly occurrence," said Sihot. "This and getting blown up."

"God, that can be annoying," said Phosy.

"Are you making fun of me?" the young fellow asked.

"Of course we're making fun of you," said Sihot. "It was a stupid bloody question. Focus your mind on something helpful."

"Like what Ouan stands to gain from having us chained here," said Phosy.

"And where he'd find a concrete building in a village of wooden houses," said Sihot.

"That I might know," said Jiep. "I looked through the records. Apart from a busy resort, there was a concrete factory active in Vang Vieng during the old regime. It stopped operation when we took over. I imagine this is one of the factory buildings."

"See, Sihot?" said Phosy. "This is exactly why I bring in the next generation."

"You didn't think to mention that information earlier?" asked Sihot.

"I assumed you'd know."

"Do you also have a theory as to why a cement factory might need a metal girder and leg irons?" asked Sihot.

"Now that is a little worrying," said Jiep. "If I was the pessimistic type I'd guess that Comrade Ouan has a deep hatred of policemen. He lures us here by throwing an important person off a cliff, knowing we'll come to investigate. He knocks us out with some fast-acting sedative and drags us here. He's set up a torture chamber for the sole purpose of killing us slowly and painfully: pliers to the fingernails, electrodes to the genitals. That sort of thing."

The two older men exchanged another look.

"Then it's just as well you aren't the pessimistic type," said Phosy.

"It's just that he seems too . . . too gentle to be a psychopath," said Jiep.

"Some of the sweetest-looking people have been known to slit the odd artery," said Phosy.

"Or perhaps he's just the weak-minded assistant," said Sihot. "The actual maniac drives up from Vientiane on weekends with his tool kit and does the nasty."

"Enlightening as this conversation might be, what's clear is that we have to get Comrade Ouan speaking," said Phosy. "Until we know why we're here, we can't talk our way out of it. But I have a plan."

Mr. Roper and the helicopter arrived in Thakhek early the next morning. The Englishman had planned to return the three Bru to their village on the border and take back the two girls in the afternoon. But he had hit an impasse called overtime. There was a problem with the pilot's time sheet and he refused to go anywhere until he had it in writing that he'd be paid extra for taking on two trips in one day. The locals had quickly picked up on how to ride the UN's budget and Roper was not the most skilled at dealing with money matters. So he set off with the three Bru and, once again, left the silent girls in Daeng's care. They followed her like nervous ducklings.

Siri called upon his knowledge of history. He knew that the crucial year for the Japanese campaign in Indochina was '45. The six months from March to August had seen Thakhek at its busiest with the launch of *Meigo Sakusen* or Bright Moon, the Japanese *coup-de-force*. This was when the occupation became an invasion. French officials had been imprisoned or shot. Some were beheaded. Garrisons were overrun. Businessmen and their families were robbed and confined to their homes and the Japanese took over the administration of the region. After humiliating defeats in the Philippines and Okinawa, large numbers of Japanese troops retreated to Laos and Vietnam in what they referred to as a tactical withdrawal and Thakhek assumed the role of regional hub as had been planned.

Siri and Daeng went to look at the area that had served as the Japanese troop campsite on the edge of town. After thirty-six years there wasn't a lot to see. It looked like an underdeveloped suburb. There were buildings here and there the locals said had been erected by the Japanese but these were either covered in vegetation or refurbished to store hay or house cattle. Most had not survived the ravages of time.

The two little girls had accompanied Daeng and Siri on this walk around the settlement. One had allowed Daeng to hold her hand. The other flatly refused to let Siri touch her but she did remain a tail-length behind him the entire trip. Just before the old couple were about to give up and have lunch, they came across Beer.

Beer was a friendly fellow who approached them and asked what their purpose was in Thakhek. He was dressed in well-worn clothing, unimpressive but for an incongru-ous bright red scarf around his neck. He was perhaps sixty, unremarkable in build and height, but he did have a spectacular scar. It started at his hairline, gouged down between his eyes, narrowly missed his nose, and sliced through his mouth, leaving him with four lips and a truly cleft chin. Behind the gruesome scar there was something that sparked a memory in Siri's mind—one too deep to dredge to the surface.

Beer told them he was a Vietnamese from the days when Thakhek had eight times more Vietnamese inhabitants than Lao. They'd worked for the French administration and had come to take up all the jobs the lazy Lao had refused to do.

"So, what can I do for you?" he asked Siri.

"We're looking for someone who lived here during the Japanese occupation," said Siri.

"Then this is your lucky day," said Beer. "I am your man."

Siri had seen the technique before. You'd go up to a group of unemployed laborers and ask if anyone was a carpenter. They would all raise their hands. Then you'd ask if anyone could speak Russian and again, they would all raise their hands. Poverty was the real mother of invention and how hard could it be to make a bookcase or speak a foreign language? But Beer was convincing. They sat with him in a noodle and coffee shack and he spouted names and dates that sounded accurate to Siri's ear.

"Do you have family?" Daeng asked.

"Only in my mind," said Beer.

"What do you see there?"

"A big house. Servants. A loving mother."

"Everyone's dream."

"Yes, Auntie. Just a dream, I'm afraid. I was born and raised in a gutter. I've disappointed everyone since."

"I don't believe that," said Daeng. "What did you do here during the war?"

"I was a laborer," he said. "I built roads, dug ditches. I watched the Japs come and go. I learned a few phrases in Japanese so they always asked for me. I was twenty-two when they left so my memory of those days is still fresh. I have not yet reached the age of forgetfulness found in older people such as yourselves."

Siri fondly recalled the Vietnamese trait of uncalled-for honesty.

"What do you actually do for a living?" Daeng asked him. "A well-spoken man such as yourself."

"I do this," he said. "I spot strangers. I offer my services for whatever they require. I know almost everyone in Thakhek and across the river. I am the best guide." He ran a finger down the scar. "At first they take pity on me because of this," he said. "You see? I have my own souvenir of the Japanese occupation. But soon they realize I have skills. I am the most suitable person to aid you in your quest, whatever it may be."

"Was anything salvaged after the Japanese left?" Daeng asked.

"There was a sort of mass looting of everything they left behind," said Beer. "Everything that could be sold or melted down. That's where the tents went and removable parts on any planes or choppers that couldn't take off. When the Chinese came through town on the postwar cleanup it was like the Japanese had never been here."

"So no Japanese stayed on after the surrender?"

"Once they heard the Chinese would be monitoring events on the ground here, most of them decided to take their chances on the Thai side. For obvious reasons, the Japs weren't about to trust their fate to their mortal enemies. And, of course, there were no officers to make decisions for them. There were a number who stayed in the region to fight against the French but most found their ways back to Japan."

The girls were eating slowly, glaring out at nothing, mute. Noodle connoisseur Daeng had seen the state of the meal they'd ordered and given up a few spoonfuls into the bowl. Despite all his talking, Beer shoveled down his meal and gladly accepted dregs from the others. It was as if he hadn't eaten for a long while.

"What do you mean they didn't have officers?" said Daeng.

Beer shot himself in the temple with his fingers.

"They listened to the emperor's speech, marched up to the main house, shut the door, and blew themselves up. Every last one of them blown to kingdom come."

"Bad losers," said Daeng.

"It was the shame," said Beer. "They couldn't stand the humiliation of defeat. It was the first time anyone had heard the emperor's voice and there he was telling them they were to give up. They'd fought in his name. He was the sun god. They'd let him down. They didn't deserve to live anymore."

They arranged to meet Beer later that day at the town council office and walked with the girls back to the guest-house. It was a dull town that belied its notorious histories; the Las Vegas of the Mekong, the center of the French administration, the hub of the Japanese invasion. All these pasts had been erased to leave a grey and russet shadow of itself. Thakhek in 1981 was, like all provincial towns in Laos, unremarkable. The ubiquitous town square with an invariably dry fountain was there—and the market and a modest attempt at a commercial district—but it was as if the place was biding its time, awaiting the return of gam-blers and colonists and invaders to give it flavor, to bring it back to life.

The helicopter was parked on the football field out back. Mr. Roper was at the guesthouse waiting for them. He was sitting on the veranda with a glass flagon at his feet. To Siri's mind its contents looked like the type of diarrhea you got after drinking bad milk. Roper held up a tin mug to welcome the arrivals.

"Hello," he said. "Come and taste this."

"It looks like . . ." Siri began.

"I know," said Roper. "I was reluctant to sample it but I was pleasantly surprised. Fittingly, it's from Ban Woophi. The family gave it to me in thanks for returning three breadwinners to the village. Normally I would have emp-tied it over the jungle on the way back but I chanced a sip and, my goodness."

Without waiting for confirmation, he picked up the flagon and poured a few centimeters into the mugs in front of him on the balcony.

"What is it?" asked Daeng, accepting one mug.

"Goodness knows," said Roper. "They did try to explain but Bru isn't my strongest language."

"Have you considered they might be trying to kill you?" said Siri, accepting a mug himself.

"There are so many faster ways to be rid of me," said Roper. "Try it."

Siri and Daeng took a swig and grimaced as the grog bored its way through their intestines and into their stomachs. It was most certainly alcoholic and probably lethal but they enjoyed the spicy liquor.

"Good, eh?" said Roper. "If our pilot wasn't so mercenary I'd have him swing by the village again and pick up a few barrels of the stuff."

"Is he still holding you to ransom?" Daeng asked.

"Says he's reluctant to fly with the storm coming."

All three of them looked up at the single white cloud in the sky.

"So tomorrow's trip to drop off the girls will be our last," said Roper. "Where are they, by the way?"

"In their room discussing the effects of the cooperative movement on traditional Lao agriculture," said Siri.

"They're still not talking?" asked Roper.

"Not a word," said Daeng.

"I'm sure it's just nerves," said the Englishman. "Once they meet their father they'll be yakking away like nobody's business."

"I'm not so sure," said Daeng. "There's something wrong with this situation."

"Nonsense," said Roper. "All our returnees have been thoroughly vetted. I'm certain everything will be just fine."

◎ ◎ ◎

It was either breakfast or dinner. The policemen had lost all sense of time. But they were woken by the sound of the door squeaking on its hinges.

"Good morning, Comrade Ouan," said Phosy. "We were hoping to have a word with you this fine morning."

None of the men rose from the concrete to greet their captor. Ouan said nothing. The normal practice was for the three men to push their empty plates and slop buckets along the ground in front of them with the chain at its full length. Ouan would fill the plate and remove the waste. But Phosy had come up with a plan. All three of them had gathered a meter of chain behind their backs but kept the remaining chain taut all the way to the girder. In this way, from Ouan's position, it would appear that the policemen were already at the extremity of the chains with the buckets and plates as far ahead as they could reach. They would have just one opportunity to take advantage of this ruse.

Phosy kept talking to lull the man into a loss of concentration. They had to be sure he didn't notice that the chains were all a meter shorter than usual. Ouan signaled for Jiep to push his plate forward but the young man showed that he was already at his limit. Phosy had encouraged him to be patient. Unless he had a clear shot of overpowering the man he was to refrain and let Sihot have a go.

Seemingly exhausted, Ouan ladled rice onto the first policeman's plate and looked up at Phosy, who was gabbing on relentlessly, talking rubbish, tossing insults. Their captor was annoyed.

"Did you hear me, stupid!" shouted Phosy.

And that was the moment Ouan, distracted, reached for Jiep's slop bucket. Jiep pounced, taking up the slack of the chain, and grabbed the man's wrist with both hands. He shut his eyes and held on for dear life. Sihot, by far the strongest of the three, grabbed Jiep by the legs and dragged him deep into their space. Ouan was punching Jiep about the head and shoulders and wrenching at the hands around his wrist. But Jiep didn't release his grasp. Ouan was close enough now for Sihot to get a hold of his other arm and rain punches down on his chest and gut. Still they dragged Ouan forward. Sihot connected with the man's nose, which spouted blood, and the fight seemed to go out of him. Jiep and Sihot were on him like tigers on a deer, pinning him down until he lay flat and breathless beneath them. And they could feel the rise and fall of his breath as he sobbed.

CHAPTER EIGHT
The Morning After with an Orangutan

6/12/1944

Second Lieutenant Tetsukimo Souben's dream had always been to be a pilot. From the day he'd discovered I had my pilot's license and had spent time with the Imperial Army Air Force, he began to treat me as a celebrity. He had a pilot's mind. He'd studied the manuals. He knew everything there was to know about airplanes but he would never fly one.

In Japan, fliers began their training in gliders. Until you completed fifty glider hours you could not progress to the Imperial Army Air Force advanced training aircraft. It was a rule, like most rules in our country, which had been carved in stone. The space in the cockpit of the Japan-built Tachikawa training craft was 30 centimeters wide by 140 centimeters long. Tetsukimo was 220 centimeters tall, possibly the tallest man in the Japanese army. Perhaps in the whole of Japan, although there was no survey of such things. No matter how you might have bent or folded him there was no way for Tetsukimo to fit into a glider and so he'd reluctantly taken the second option, to become a mechanic. It was like a rodeo cowboy being forced to feed and water the bulls.

I liked Tetsukimo but he was bitter, especially as day after day he watched the young, inexperienced fliers take off from the airstrip at Thakhek in aircrafts they did not appreciate. I sat with him one evening and watched the Zeros flying overhead.

"How can you stand not flying?" he asked me.

"That?" I said with a laugh, pointing at the airplanes. "That, my boy, isn't flying."

He looked confused. I nodded toward the river. A hawk was cruising the air currents. It seemed to freeze in midair for some seconds, then it swooped. It barely broke the surface of the water but in its talons it held a fat catfish.

"That is flying," I said.

"But that type of flying is exclusive to the birds and the insects," he said.

"Not at all," I said. "Have you heard the story of Aki and Ako?"

"No."

"Aki and Ako grew up in a small village in Shikoku. Aki was a good scholar. He excelled in science and went on to study engineering. Ako was a boy of the mountains. He loved nothing more than to hike for days, alone, observing, learning the ways of nature. He loved to watch the birds and how they rode the air currents and played in the wind. Despite their differences the young men were good friends and they joined the air force together.

"At one stage they found themselves in a two-man

Kawasaki Ki. They completed many successful missions together. But there was an enemy spy amidst the ground crew and the man sabotaged their parachutes so that they wouldn't open. It was a week later that their aircraft was hit by enemy fire and the engine cut out. Neither man could have expected to survive the crash. Aki tumbled and fumbled with his parachute, attempting to repair it as he fell. The weight of it sent him plummeting to the ground like a rock. Ako witnessed this. He unbuckled his parachute and let it go. He unfastened the top of his leather jacket, which filled with air, and he spread himself as he'd seen the birds do so many times. He had no wings, of course, so he was still technically falling rather than flying, but he was able to catch air currents that slowed his descent a fraction. Not far below there was a lake and he attempted to steer himself in its direction. And there was a wind that day that caught him and projected him sideways so he hit the water at an angle.

"Onlookers had witnessed the whole thing. They saw Ako hit the lake at a tremendous speed and gave him no hope of surviving it. Fishermen went to look for the body and were astounded to find the boy floating thanks to the air trapped in his jacket. He was close to death, broken like a crushed sparrow, but he had endured. He was the only man ever to survive a fall from such a height."

Tetsukimo had a tear in his eye.

"Flying an airplane is one thing," I said. "You sit and stare at the instruments. You can't hear anything apart from the growl of the engine. All you smell is gasoline and you show no respect to nature. When you hit conflicting currents you call it turbulence. It's a foe rather than a friend. And the more competent you become as a pilot, the further you are from nature. In a Kawasaki Ki you find yourself in a glass bowl with no wind in your hair. You might as well be in a private cinema watching the sky on a screen."

Tetsukimo began to spend more time in the mountains after our conversation, watching the birds. He started his natural flights by hitching a small goods parachute to his back and running a line from our river cruiser. He'd build up a head of steam, and like a kite, the parachute would take off. He'd travel for miles downstream and up. From there he designed a leather suit. It had webbing beneath the arms and between the legs. He started on small hills, getting pummeled by the earth time and time again when he landed badly. But he'd revise and adapt the suit and soon was taking off from higher hills and then cliffs. I don't know how many bones he broke but I'd never seen him so happy. There may have been an Aki and an Ako but what does it matter if they didn't exist?

Thanks to half a mug of Woophi, Siri and Daeng were half an hour late for their appointment with Beer. That didn't matter too much because he wouldn't show up at all. They were in a merry state, walking hand in hand, giggling, along the dirt road. It was only when they saw the run-down stadium looming in front of them that they realized they'd been walking in the wrong direction. So they cut back past the duck pond the locals called a lake, took a shortcut through the

Chomtong temple where Private Oshiira had left his toilet brush, and, quite by accident, found themselves at the council building. They approached a young woman in the first office they came to. She was skinny enough to fall between the keys of the old typewriter she was pounding. She wore glasses with only one lens that made her eyes look like they'd come from two different donors.

"What?" she said and Siri fell into a trough of nostalgia for the days when public officials were polite and respectful. But then again he wondered whether those days only ever existed in his mind.

"Has Comrade Beer been here already?" Daeng asked her.

"Who?"

"Comrade Beer."

"Never heard of him."

Siri took over.

"Have you heard of Comrade Kayson?" he asked.

"The prime minister?" she asked.

"That's the one," said Siri. "We're here to pick up the documents he ordered a month ago. I'm Civilai Songsawat from the Central Committee."

She rested her bony fingers on the keyboard.

"I . . . I can't," she said.

"Can't what?"

"I don't know anything about documents," she said.

"Then let's talk to someone who does," said Daeng.

"I'm the only one here today."

"And where is everyone else?"

"They're over there." She nodded in the general direction of Thailand.

"Why?" Siri asked.

"To celebrate the Mekong's transition from a battlefield to a marketplace," she said.

"I beg your pardon?"

"You must have heard," she said. "It's the new Thai policy to promote peace and profit across the river. Our people were invited to Nakhon Phanom to discuss ways to mutually benefit each other culturally and financially."

In fact Beer had already told Siri and Daeng about this new fair-weather romance. A month earlier the Lao and the Thais had been firing wayward shots at each other across that waterway of peace and profit. Now the love affair was back on. No Lao official would turn down a free meal and a few cold beers with their enemy so Siri knew there would only be a skeleton staff at the council office. They'd certainly selected the most skeletal to remain behind.

"I don't care," said Siri. "We've been ordered to return with those documents before nightfall. I trust they were prepared before the junket."

"I don't . . ." said the girl. "Usually all documents come to me for a stamp. What are they about exactly?"

"The paperwork left behind at the end of the Japanese occupation," said Daeng.

"By our side?" asked the girl.

"Theirs," said Daeng.

The typist laughed and took off her glasses.

"You want all of it?" she asked.

"Of course," said Siri.

"I hope you brought a truck," said the girl.

The Japanese documents took up one side of a room the size of a royal French pantry. They were dusty like the ancient ledgers in horror films. Siri took down one file and had to blow the dust from the spine in order to make out the characters. Of course he couldn't read the contents but he could make out the date. There were at least three hundred files sorted in chronological order. When the French administrators returned to their posts they were obviously under orders not to destroy any Japanese documents. But that didn't explain why the Japanese invaders hadn't burned the lot of them. When it is staring defeat in the face, the first thing any self-respecting army does is destroy its paperwork. Siri was about to add it to his list of mysteries when the answer came to him. The Japanese officers had been too busy blowing themselves up to follow protocol. With nobody alive who cared enough to supervise a cover-up, it was not surprising the documents had survived. He opened the file in front of him hoping to find a French translation tucked inside. There were teasing general notes in French handwritten on scraps of paper saying such things as *road project to Paksane* or *advance on Vientiane*. But there were no details. They gave nothing away of either the thoroughness of the Japanese victories or the humiliation of their defeat. Siri was certain the explanation of this mission was locked somewhere inside those elegant hieroglyphics.

They couldn't take them all but Daeng requisitioned a wheelbarrow from the back of the council building and they piled in as much as they could. They took only those pertaining to the first six months of the occupation and the last three months of the failed invasion. But still the barrow was stacked high and they had to steady the top folders as they negotiated the dirt path beyond the council gate. The skinny girl watched them go and said nothing but, "That wheelbarrow will have to be returned."

The old couple wheeled their plunder back to the guest-house, where they found Roper facedown on the balcony boards. Siri checked his pulse, pronounced him "alive but soused," and decided it would be best to leave him there. For the Englishman's safety he rescued what was left in the flagon—barely half—and took it back to his room.

Daeng went to check on the girls. They looked up at her when she entered the room, not with fear or excitement but with what Daeng could only describe as resignation. It was the same look she'd seen on the faces of the animals at Dong Paina zoo. They'd been removed from every-thing they understood and had surrendered. It was then she decided to spend the night with the silent sisters and travel with them the following day. Everything about them seemed out of place somehow. She had to meet the girl's father and understand why his daughters were so afraid of the world. As interesting as the hunt for crazy Toshi may have been, it didn't trump her instincts.

Siri had reluctantly agreed to spend that night alone despite the fact that he still had half a flagon of nectar from the gods of the jungle. It was a horrible loss of romantic opportunity. He lay on his mattress that night beneath an oft-repaired mosquito net and he thought about Toshi, the pilot. His life had seemed so ideal for so long. He clearly enjoyed his time in Laos and he wrote of his coworkers with affection. He was a military man in a war but he was stationed in a place that saw no warfare. The French had a garrison nearby but they were no threat. Thousands of his countrymen were falling in battle but there was Toshi swimming in a crystal cool pond and socializing and drink-ing fresh coconut water. And Siri wondered whether that alone would be enough to turn a man's mind. Whether the guilt had got to him. Whether survival could become treasonous.

Siri turned up the gas lamp, poured a short mug of grog, and opened the diary. He was almost at the end. If there was a climax it would have to come that night. He read aloud as if Daeng were with him.

12/22/1944

I had been thinking about my friend Lance Corporal Hokofugu Hama a lot. He was the victim of an addiction and I knew he would suffer tremendously if he didn't learn to control his yearnings. But I had learned over the years that pressure from outside rarely worked. The cure always lay within. Hokofugu was a slave to alcohol and I could see he was losing the battle with his master. His favorite line was "If I ever lost control I would give it up there and then." So I decided to put that to the test.

One evening he was staggering along a dirt track (staggering was not considered losing control) when up ahead he saw a beautiful woman.

"I am lost," she said, "and I have nowhere to stay. May I come to your tent?"

He looked her up and down. She wasn't dressed like a lady of the night. She wore a sensible frock and had a long feather boa around her neck. As she was lost and had nowhere to sleep he agreed, on the condition that she would help him to walk because, he said, he was a little dizzy, perhaps from the humidity. When he awoke the next morning, he had a feather in his mouth and beside him on the pillow was a duck, staring at him lovingly. He couldn't understand what had happened. Of course he didn't tell anybody. He convinced himself it was common mistaken identity.

But a few days later, he was staggering along the same dirt track in search of booze when he saw a beautiful woman in elbow-length fur gloves. Remembering the duck incident, he tried to ignore her.

"Excuse me, sir," she said. "I am very sad because my fiancé has found another woman and I cannot sleep. Would you mind if I spent the night with you in your tent?"

Of course he felt sorry for her and she was far too beautiful to refuse so he asked her to help him walk home as he had reacted badly to some cough medicine and was a little dizzy. When he woke up in the morning he had a hangover that thumped like an orchestra of bongos and there was one hairy arm draped over him. He opened his eyes wide and saw that the arm was connected to a smelly orangutan. He couldn't believe he'd mistaken this beast for a beautiful woman. An hour in the shower was not enough to erase her stink from his skin. But still he told nobody.

A few nights later he was staggering along the same dirt track in search of more booze when up ahead he saw a stunningly beautiful woman in a full-length fur coat. It didn't occur to him for a second how inappropriate a fur coat was in a tropical country. He was determined to ignore her. Nothing she could say would force him to take her home. But as he was passing, she opened up her coat and she was wearing nothing but skimpy lace underwear beneath it. To cut a long story short, he was awoken the next morning by a deep, angry roar. He turned to see a huge black bear beside him with saliva dripping from her yellow teeth. He could feel scratch marks on his back.

Hokofugu ran so fast and so far he was listed as AWOL. But when he finally returned after a week spent in a cave, he was a changed man and he vowed never to touch another drop of alcohol in his life.

I passed on the news to Colonel Konko, who, with thick makeup and a change of wigs, had been most convincing as a woman especially under the shadow of darkness and in the eyes of a drunk. Then I went to see Nay Pom, who tamed animals to perform at temple fairs. I gave him a hamper of foodstuff in return for the loan of his duck and his orangutan and his bear.

Siri's eyelids were heavy and the lamplight was growing weak. He smiled with pleasure at the conclusion of Toshi's last story and would have lain on one side and fallen asleep were it not for one thing. The story was complete but the writing continued on the final page. The date was March 1945 and something peculiar had happened in the life of Kangen Toshimado. Siri read it silently to himself.

I suppose it's only natural that living together in a small group is likely to cause some friction. I have left the dormitory and moved back to my tent to collect my thoughts and for my safety. Corporal Yatsusuki has continued to grow. We get complaints from the French from time to time saying that . . .

There was only one more page but it did not continue Toshi's account of changes in the camp. In fact Siri had reached the stubs of pages that had been ripped from the diary. All that remained beyond the vandalism was one final sheet. It was dated 8/14/1945 and it said,

Tomorrow, I rise.

The lamp had reached the end of its wick. Siri lay flat on his mattress hugging the diary to his chest. No mysteries had been solved from his reading. No answers had been given as to the point of his mission. In fact he was more baffled than ever. Naturally he'd already read the last page. He was Siri Paiboun, the detective, after all. It was one of the first things he'd done. But he thought that by reading the rest of the diary, the meaning behind that final phrase might reveal itself. It did not. He slept for a little while but was awoken by the sound of the doorknob squeaking. He hadn't locked it. There was no light in the room but he could visualize the door opening and his wife stepping inside. He knew Daeng too well. He knew she'd never be able to sleep in another room knowing he was so close. She would crave that kiss from her Adonis, the touch of his warm hand upon her.

"I want you here naked, now, beside me," he said, patting the pillow.

There was a long pause.

"Well, if you insist," said Beer.

CHAPTER NINE
The Kyoko Protocol

The standoff showed no sign of letting up. Three policemen in leg irons were holding down a kidnapper in tears. They'd tried to get him to talk but his pathetic sobbing wouldn't let up. They'd gone through his pockets but there was no key. Time crawled by, and as if the situation couldn't get any worse, the lamplight gave out.

"You know? Even if there was a comprehensive handbook for policemen," said Sihot, "I doubt there'd be a section that got remotely close to this."

"All we need is patience," said Phosy. "Eventually we'll get words out of him. The only way matters could get worse is if we accidently killed him, so I suggest you loosen the arm lock."

Sihot let go and Ouan pulled away.

"Not so loose that we lose him," said Phosy, who still had hold of the captive's leg.

"What if he has an accomplice?" asked Jiep.

"Or a gang of them?" said Sihot.

"Let's remain positive," said Phosy. "Since our arrival we've only seen one person. He's the one who drugged us and he's the one who feeds us."

"Then how did he get us here from the resort without help?" asked Jiep.

"Second Lieutenant Jiep," said Phosy. "If you'd been observant you'd have noticed that all three of us have sores and abrasions on the back of our shoulders and dirt on the backs of our shirts. We have dried blood and bumps on the backs of our heads and our hair is dirty. But our legs appear to be fine. As none of these conditions existed before we arrived it suggests that Comrade Ouan here stood between our legs, picked them up like the handles of a wheelbarrow, and dragged us here feetfirst. Isn't that right, Comrade?"

The man groaned.

"If he did have an accomplice, they'd have taken an end each. As we aren't concussed and drenched in blood I assume this place isn't so far from the restaurant. How am I doing, Comrade Ouan?"

There was no reply.

"But the time has come for you to engage in some form of communication," Phosy continued. "I'm assuming from your obvious distress that things haven't gone the way you intended. As you can see, the situation we find ourselves in is rather bad for all of us but not without its funny side. We obviously can't let you go without finding out why we're here. So it's possible that unless we can start a conversation all of us will starve to death. I have a theory, so I'll go first. I hope you can sob and listen at the same time. It occurs to me, given the rarity of major crime in this vicinity, that the death of the Vietnamese and our abduction are in some way connected. You've generously given me time to formulate my theory so here goes.

"A local girl accompanied the Vietnamese to his favorite

picnic spot with its charming view of the valley. She may have gone innocently, fascinated by the arrival of someone exotic and far more interesting than the boys she'd grown up with. Her intentions may well have been pure enough. But the Vietnamese died. The girl was overwhelmed with emotions. She ran home to her village and came to you, her boyfriend, to expl—"

"Her father," said Ouan damply through the tears.

"I'm sorry?" said Phosy.

"I'm not her boyfriend."

"Now there's progress," said Sihot.

"To her father, right," said Phosy. "And her father knows only too well that the police are not to be trusted in this country. They would never believe the word of a poor country girl when she says she wasn't responsible for the man's death. They'd put her in handcuffs and parade her in front of the rich people's court and say, 'We have our killer!' And what do you know? A policeman arrives from the big city asking questions about local girls."

"So you panicked," said Sihot, taking up the reins. "You drugged my beer, dragged me here, and chained me up to give yourself time to make a plan."

"But what else do you know?" said Phosy. "Two more policemen turn up with the same questions. And we get the same treatment. Because frankly you don't know what else to do. You're not a killer and you're smart enough to know that more and more policemen will come looking for us. You can't kill the entire police force."

"So you're in quite a pickle," said Sihot. "And you know why that is? It's because you didn't give us a chance to tell you why we're here."

"You're here to take my girl," said Ouan.

"We're here to explain why we know she's innocent," said Phosy.

"Liar," said Ouan. "That's a policeman trick."

"I agree this would be a good moment to introduce a trick," said Phosy. "In fact we'd do or say anything to get out of here. But in this case the truth works even better than a lie for all of us. You see? In Vientiane we have a doctor friend who's very smart. He can look at dead bodies and tell how they died. And do you know what he found in the hair of the Vietnamese?"

Phosy left a gap for an answer but didn't expect one.

"He found a feather," he said. "It was the feather of an owl. And there were deep scratches on the scalp of the victim and we did some research. There are a lot of eagle owls nesting in the karsts at this time of year. And there's nothing a female owl wouldn't do to protect her young. And she'd be mighty pissed off if anyone invaded her territory. I can't imagine anything more frightening than having a five-kilogram bird dig its talons into your scalp."

"She was scared to death," said Ouan.

"I know she was," said Phosy.

"She's only seventeen," said Ouan.

"And suddenly there she is on a cliff and this guy's staggering around trying to fight his way free," said Sihot. "He tries to cover his head with his hands. He knocks over the bottles and screams for your girl to help him but what can she do? She's out of her depth."

"She ran," said Ouan.

"Anyone would have," said Phosy.

"She watched him fall," said Ouan. "The bird let go and the man screamed all the way down. It's something she'll never get out of her head. She hasn't slept since it happened."

There was a long, dark silence in the concrete room.

"So, what happens next?" said Jiep.

The helicopter left at 8 A.M. sharp. Both Roper and the pilot were sticklers for time. On board were the two quiet girls, the pilot, Roper, and Madam Daeng. If the pilot had his way, the noodle woman wouldn't have been allowed on the flight. She'd been given clearance only as far as Thakhek and back to Vientiane. But that morning she'd whispered something in the pilot's ear that obviously made him more receptive. Siri had watched from the guesthouse window and he made a mental note to ask her which particular threat to life or limb had worked on the shifty little man. She could be quite frightening.

Siri was on his way to Thailand. The small misunderstanding of the previous evening had been sorted out. Beer had gone to Siri's room with good news. He had found a Japanese. JICA, the Japanese aid agency, had begun operations in the Thai countryside and they had placed a volunteer in Nakhon Phanom, across the river from Thakhek. Beer had arranged to meet her. River guards on both sides were on the lookout for refugees fleeing Laos but the sight of an old man and a younger one with a messed-up face in a rickety rowboat didn't raise an eyebrow. Whenever Siri crossed the river, it always felt like time travel; a visit to the not-so-better future.

Kyoko was short even by Japanese standards but everything seemed to be in proportion. What she lacked in mass she more than made up for in beauty and *bon humeur*. Her smile was bracing and it came naturally and often.

Her laugh was contagious. She'd graduated the previous year in Thai language and culture from Osaka University of Foreign Studies, which had left her with a somewhat narrow career path. And, as if to prove it, there she was in the distant northeast teaching handicrafts to people with disabilities—as a volunteer.

Siri and Beer met her for lunch in a canteen with buffet-style meal choices that looked like paleontological samples. Kyoko's Thai was grammatically perfect and amusingly accented. She was a simple linguistic puzzle. Once Siri had cracked her pronunciation he was able to wade into a conversation.

"I am very excited to meet you, Doctor," she said. "Mr. Beer told me all about you."

"I'm amazed he found you so quickly," said Siri.

"I am happy to be found."

"Did he tell you what we need?" Siri asked.

"In a way," she said. "Better you tell me."

Siri hoisted a small fishing net from the floor and onto the empty seat behind him. From it he produced Toshi's diary.

"This," he said, "is the diary of a Japanese pilot."

He went on to explain how it had come into his possession and to summarize the Lao language section. Kyoko was due to teach a class in paper folding so Siri had to keep it brief.

"I'd like you to read the Japanese part at the beginning," he said. "We need to know if there are any clues as to what happened to Toshi before he came to Laos."

"Dr. Siri?" she said.

"Yes, dear?"

"Why are you doing this?" She was thumbing through the early pages.

"Because it's a mystery, Kyoko. My wife and I are easily intoxicated by them. Someone sent me a diary and asked for help. We flew to Thakhek to start to put it all together. Then we found you, another piece in the puzzle."

"You do know that the earlier dates in this volume coincide with some disturbing events in our history? And Toshi was a military man. There are likely to be some unsettling entries, I'm certain."

"If you'd sooner not . . ."

"No. No. I'm already fascinated. Many people of my father's age and older know nothing of what actually happened during the war. It's only recently that old soldiers have started speaking up. Reading this diary will be an education for me also."

"Well," said Siri. "If it's education you're looking for . . ."

He reached into the fishing net and pulled out a dozen folders. He explained how he'd come by them at the district office in Thakhek and how they were relevant to his search.

"If you get a spare moment," he said. "I have another sixty folders back in my room."

Kyoko laughed, which caused a tingle in Siri's old heart.

"I hope you don't want a written translation," she said.

"Just a brief summary would be fantastic," said Siri. "I want to know everything about his life."

"Then we should begin with his name," she said.

"His name?"

"Here on the first page dated July seventh, 1937. His name isn't Toshimado. He begins with, *My name is Uenobu Hiro and I am proud to have once served as a pilot in the Imperial Army Air Force in the service of our great emperor.*"

CHAPTER TEN
Enthusiasm Is a Hard Lie to Keep Up

When the helicopter touched down in the small village square at Vangin, the girls became animated but clearly not from excitement. Daeng could see that they were shaking with fear. She tried to comfort them but they pulled back from her. When the rotors came to a stop Roper put down the steps, but they refused to leave.

"Come on now, girls," said Roper, attempting two or three languages but there was no reaction. He and the pilot resorted to wrestling them from their seats and carrying them off the chopper. Some thirty people from the village had gathered around, smiling, waving, obviously overjoyed to see the girls, who were soon engulfed by the crowd and swept away. Roper spoke their language but Daeng did not. After five minutes of back-and-forth, Roper told Daeng that the father had not yet returned from a hunt. The villagers would take care of the children until his return. But Daeng knew the girls' names from the official file and had noticed that nobody had used those names. The pleasantries appeared to be more for the benefit of the Englishman than the children. If they were truly pleased to see the girls they kept their feelings in the soles of their feet.

"Do you see this?" Daeng asked Roper.

"See what?"

"This is not a happy homecoming. Nobody's really excited. It's a show."

"It's because we're here," he said. "You have to understand ethnic culture. The tribespeople are reluctant to show their true emotions in front of strangers. We'll get out of their hair as soon as we've attended a brief reception."

The reception was designed to be as brief as possible. In the central pavilion, on a table, there were five plates of moldy-looking sweets and five plastic beakers of something too orange to be potable. The headman, who strongly resembled a bulldog on its hind legs, ate one of the sweets and took up one of the beakers. Roper did the same. The pilot documented it all on an 8mm recorder as per Roper's instructions. Daeng took a step toward the table, then shouted, "Oh, I forgot my camera. Won't be a minute."

"The pilot's filming the whole thing," said Roper.

"I'd like some photos for my album," said Daeng.

And she ran back to the helicopter.

The headman gave a painfully slow speech. Roper nodded in agreement with some of the sentiments. They all sipped politely from the beakers, all except Daeng, who had returned without a camera and remained behind in the shadows. With the speech over, Roper said a few words in response. The villagers smiled at the tall white man who had wasted his life learning their language. And it was all over. The girls were nowhere to be seen. The visitors climbed aboard the chopper and retained their seats. Roper waved from the open doorway. Daeng did not. The pilot put on his terribly cool Ray-Bans and attempted to start the motor. Nothing happened. There wasn't so much as a cough of ignition. He tried again. Nothing. The villagers were getting restless. Some were already walking away. Enthusiasm is a hard lie to keep up.

The pilot took an aluminum ladder from stowage and climbed up to stare at the engine. Daeng shouted, "What's wrong?"

"Nothing I can see," he replied.

"Do you need any help?"

"Not from you."

"Fair enough," she said and walked away. What value was an ex–freedom fighter who couldn't disable a helicopter without leaving a trace?

"It's probably nothing serious," said Roper, whose face belied his cool optimism.

"At least it gives us more time to take in the village," said Daeng.

She set off on a tour, smiling at the householders but receiving only suspicious glares in return. The happy faces that had welcomed them were nowhere to be seen. She felt a heavy undercurrent of anger from the men as she trespassed over thresholds and allotments. Unlike any other villages she'd ever been to, there were no giggling children or curious dogs following her. In fact she saw no children over three and no dogs whatsoever. Only the wary eyes followed her. At one point at the back edge of the village she stubbed her toe on a shallow root beneath the dust. But what she kicked up was no root, it was a black electric cable. She knew she was being watched but she pulled the wire out of the earth and traced its source. Not very far into the thick undergrowth she found a bamboo hut that housed a brand-new

Cummins generator. It was a very sophisticated piece of equipment for such an isolated place. She turned back toward the village and found herself staring into the barrel of a homemade musket.

Siri and Beer were back in Thakhek by midafternoon. They banked the boat and went off in search of a woman by the name of An who had worked with the Japanese as a translator during the war. Every day, Beer surprised Siri with one more witness to the occupation. It appeared the Japanese had had an interpreter whose name was Miura. He was fluent in French. An, a Lao-Vietnamese, was also fluent in French and her own native languages. According to Beer, the Japanese were awful language learners. He cited the curse of not wanting to make mistakes. They were not prepared to go through that elementary stage of unavoidable stupidity that successful language learners endure. This, plus a belief that the rest of the world would soon be speaking Japanese, led to the remarkable statistic that 95 percent of dealings between the Japanese and the French passed through that narrow portal of Miura-*san*. To Siri that seemed like a relationship doomed from the outset. The Japanese officers coached in xenophobia from childhood would never really trust a Japanese who had been so enamored of the West as to learn its language and culture. They would view him as defective. But what concerned Siri more was why the Japanese did not utilize Toshi's language skills. He had mastered Lao. He would have stood out in a Lao town as the only Japanese who could speak directly to the locals. Was he being circumspect and keeping his ability a secret? Perhaps he had seen how foreign language skills had turned the occupiers

against Miura and he didn't want to damage his friend-
ships with his workmates.

Siri had agreed to meet An in the area of scrubland at
the foot of the hill to the east of the town. It was an unat-
tractive spot but it was significant in that it was the site
of the French colonial home that Major General Dorari
used during the occupation. According to Beer, the major
general had evicted the previous residents with threats,
although Toshi hadn't mentioned it in his diary. The
house was also the one to which the Japanese officers had
retired on the day of the surrender. As they had blown
themselves up it was no surprise that there were no walls
standing. In fact, there was nothing at all remaining of the
original building. Nothing had grown on the lot since
the explosion. Weeds had tried, and died. It was as if the
earth there was starved of nutrients.

Siri had asked to meet there on a hunch. Although he
still didn't really understand his relationship with the spirits, he'd been on whirlwind tours through the Otherworld.
He'd spoken with the dead the way a drunk in a bar might
strike up a conversation with another drunk. He'd done
everything he could to hone his skills as a shaman but still
he considered himself an amateur. And since his ornery
spirit guide, Auntie Bpoo, had gone off-line, he was finding
himself out of touch with all those gossips who could make
sense of this mission. The site of a mass suicide seemed like
a perfect spot to reconnect with the spirit world.

He took a chance and removed the lucky talisman from
around his neck and handed it to Beer. Its function was
mainly to ward off snide attacks from the *phibob*, the malevolent spirits of the forest. But he didn't know whether the
charm might block out other channels. He needed to see

if anything remained in the other dimension of the plot of land.

Beer sat on a stump and watched as Siri walked across the barren earth and sat cross-legged at its center. The doctor scooped up dirt in both hands, closed his eyes, and started to hum the tune to *"Parlez-Moi d'Amour,"* which had been one of his favorites in Paris. There was no spiritual element to it. In fact he clearly had no idea what he was doing but evocation had never been his strongest hand. After a couple of minutes it was becoming embarrassing. He opened his eyes, but all he saw was Beer on a tree stump, now joined by an elderly woman. He stood, dropped the dirt, and brushed his hands together.

And then he saw something else. It was a brief vision, electronic, as if his palms were electrodes and he was being charged somehow. Amid the buzz that shrouded him he saw creatures dancing, close, as if he were stuck in the middle of a popular discotheque dance floor. They were not human, but neither were they beasts. They were dressed in brilliant colors but their faces were white as chalk. They were drunk and raucous and clumsy but when they bumped into him he felt nothing. Within seconds it was all over.

He was a little unsteady on his feet as he walked over to the couple watching him.

"Did it work?" Beer asked.

"Not sure," said Siri, turning to the woman. "An?"

She gave him an old-fashioned *nop* greeting and he returned it. He and she were of that same generation when it was still polite to offer a prayer to a new acquaintance. The years had not been kind to her face but she had a fine head of silver hair and her spine was straight.

"Were you looking for spirits, Doctor?" she asked.

"They're like policemen," he replied. "They're never around when you need one. Were you in Thakhek when this place blew up?"

"No, Doctor," she said. "It was chaos here those last few weeks. All local communications had been cut. Nobody knew what was happening in Thakhek. Most of the Lao and Vietnamese fled. Of course the Japanese said nothing about their losses around the region, but we had the BBC from Thailand. We knew they were losing badly."

She poked a finger under her hairline and had a little scratch. Her hair slipped backward across her scalp and she righted it without embarrassment. Siri wondered why she would choose a silver wig rather than one of the coal-black beauties complete with plastic bougainvilleas on sale at the market.

An continued unabated. "You could feel it, too, in the behavior of the Japanese troops," she said. "There were deserters. There was unheard-of insubordination amongst the lower ranks. There were uniformed soldiers committing crimes. Miura protected me from drunks on a number of occasions. So we locals headed for the hills. We'd already been approached by the Free Lao insurgents. They had bases. They were recruiting. The jungle towards the Vietnamese border was so dense the Japanese army had never been able to root out rebels."

"Did you leave, too?" Siri asked Beer.

"You bet your life," said Beer.

"So neither of you witnessed the mass suicide," said Siri.

"No," said Beer.

"Then how can you be sure it happened?"

Beer looked at An.

"Miura and I had become close," she said. "Before the Chinese arrived he came to stay with me in the caves."

"He deserted?"

"Yes," she said. "But he'd never been really accepted by his countrymen. And, by then, there were already a number of Japanese deserters who had sided with what became known as the Viet Minh. Miura told us all about that last day in Thakhek as he had heard it from the superiors who came into town to investigate the incident."

"How do you suppose they'd go about something like that?" Siri asked.

"About what?" asked Beer.

"Blowing themselves up as a group effort. I mean, they wouldn't have planned it. They only heard the broadcast in the morning. You don't have a stash of dynamite in the living room just in case you feel like a dramatic end."

"Probably hand grenades," said Beer. "Something like that."

"I don't see hand grenades completely destroying a two-story building," said Siri.

"Well, Doctor, it wasn't completely destroyed," said An. "Not by the explosion. The roof and one wall to the living room were gone. And all the wood in the place was burned in the ensuing fire and there were scraps of metal lying around. But then villagers helped themselves to the bricks and the floor tiles and the surviving roofing. They even took the concrete piles. By the time they'd finished there was nothing left."

"What about the bodies?" Siri asked.

"There were none," said Beer. "The explosion didn't leave a trace of them."

CHAPTER ELEVEN
Dear Comrade Pilot

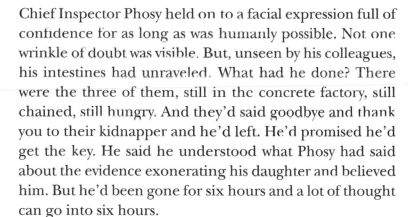

Chief Inspector Phosy held on to a facial expression full of confidence for as long as was humanly possible. Not one wrinkle of doubt was visible. But, unseen by his colleagues, his intestines had unraveled. What had he done? There were the three of them, still in the concrete factory, still chained, still hungry. And they'd said goodbye and thank you to their kidnapper and he'd left. He'd promised he'd get the key. He said he understood what Phosy had said about the evidence exonerating his daughter and believed him. But he'd been gone for six hours and a lot of thought can go into six hours.

"Do you think . . . ?" said Jiep.

"Shut up," said Phosy.

"I just . . ." said Jiep.

"Shut up," said Sihot.

Comrade Ouan had kindly put a new wick in the lamp before he left. To keep his mind off their predicament, Phosy was watching a spider construct a huge web on the wall above them. This seemed a ridiculous waste of time considering they were in a concrete room that wasn't on the flight path of any winged insects. He wondered how many more hours he'd have to study that web. He thought about Malee and whether she'd grow up to be a surgeon or just a regular doctor. He thought about Dtui and wondered whether he'd have married her if she wasn't as large as she was. Probably not. He liked big women. And he thought about whether he'd live on in history as the chief inspector who was found mummified with two good men some hundred years in the future.

He turned his head from the web to see a girl of around eight with a baby of about three months in a sling on her back.

"Are you the policemen?" asked the girl.

"We are," said Sihot.

"I'm to tell you my dad has to go away for a while," she said. "Sorry he was slow. He had to pack."

"I hope he's going somewhere nice," said Sihot.

"I don't know," she said. She looked confused. He'd disturbed her train of thought.

"What else did he tell you, love?" asked Phosy.

The baby started to cry. The three men in the room were of a mind to join it.

"I'm to tell you that Mimi is back home now and she'll be looking after us all. We don't have a mother."

"Mimi's your older sister?" said Phosy.

"Yes."

"And your dad's name is Ouan."

"I know."

Phosy's intestines returned to their rightful place.

"And did he give you something for us?" he asked.

"Only this," she said, holding up a bunch of keys. "But you have to promise."

"Promise what, love?"

"Promise that you won't keep Mimi in Vientiane for a long time. She has to look after everyone. We need her here."

"Oh, I promise," said Phosy.

"Me too," said Sihot.

"And me," said Jiep, crossing his heart and hoping not to die.

"Did you really need to break the gun barrel over his head?" Roper asked.

"I'm sorry," said Daeng. "I get jumpy when someone points a musket at me. Those things are notoriously sensitive. They go off at a sneeze."

Daeng, Roper, and the pilot were sitting on a bench in the central pavilion. They now had three gun barrels pointed at them, and these were very serious AK-47s. No danger of them going off at a sneeze. The male villagers, comfortably back in their more natural state, sat around the hut chewing and spitting and picking their noses like the thugs they probably were.

"This is the point where you tell me I don't understand ethnic culture," said Daeng.

"You've placed us in a very difficult situation," said Roper.

"Me? I'm the only one who understands what's happening here."

"Enlighten me."

"This is not a poor village," she said. "They have a Cummins generator that could only have been delivered here by helicopter. They have brand-new AK-47s. They've changed out of their flip-flops and are running around in Adidas sports shoes. In front of the huts I saw working boots but there are no farm implements to be seen.

What do they do to sustain themselves? I think you know the answer to that. The girls we brought here don't speak because they don't have a common language. They've been bought or kidnapped from remote villages. Are you keeping up with me?"

She was expecting an argument but Roper shook his head and looked down at his leather loafers.

"The refugee camp security division suspected such a thing might happen again," he said.

"Again?" said Daeng.

"Couriers bringing in children they claim to be their own," said Roper. "They register as a family to get priority for resettlement overseas. The camp communities are usually very aware of what's going on around them. A camp is essentially a large village where families mix and children play together. There were two occasions when residents reported suspected couriers, one of which turned out to be a correct call. The courier was sent home. The camp organized a program of awareness-raising, encouraging people to report suspicious behavior. I honestly believed the practice had been curtailed."

"You knew all this but you didn't see anything suspicious about these girls?"

"I'm not a child psychologist. I don't know how children are likely to respond to the death of their mother."

"Who probably wasn't their mother."

Roper's face was lined with embarrassment. "I didn't know that. I thought seeing their father would help. I assumed it was some sort of trauma."

"It is, Roper," Daeng shouted. "And you're causing it."

The guards raised their weapons. She lowered her head and her voice.

"I'm guessing this gang here specializes in kidnapping kids from different minorities. Laos has a couple hundred ethnic groups speaking eighty-five languages."

"Eighty-six," said Roper.

"Don't make me hit you."

"Sorry."

"They take kids who can't tell anyone what's happened to them because nobody understands. Our girls here can't even speak to each other. It's possible the courier could communicate with one or both of them but in situations like this the kids would be threatened. I've seen it before. They're told there are assassins in the camp listening for this or that language; killers who hate people from that community. The kids are told that speaking just one sentence in their own language will be their last. Of course, they're petrified. Mr. Roper, you've just brought two lambs back to the slaughterhouse."

Roper shook his head. "We . . . we should do something," he said.

"Good plan, Mr. Roper."

"I could talk to the headman. Reason with him."

"We should have brought the old dog some marrow bone," said Daeng. "No, there's no reasoning here. I'll give you an insight into our future. I'll play the part of the village headman. The script goes like this. 'I was expecting the UNHCR team to come and bring back our darling children but the helicopter didn't arrive. It probably crashed somewhere in the jungle. So we're mourning not only our children, but also the brave UN people who tried to bring them home.'"

"You think they'll kill us?" Roper asked.

"I'm certain that's the plan now that everything's gone wrong."

"Oh, my word."

"I think the only reason they haven't killed us already is because they're waiting for the girls' fake father to return from his hunt. And I think I know what he's been hunting. It wouldn't surprise me if he turned up here with a helicopter of his own. That landing pad's seen a lot of traffic. The village screwed up. All they had to do was welcome us, play the adoring but simple natives, give us a glass of sugar juice, and wave us off. He'd return to two girls, barely used, ready for recycling. I think Big Daddy will be pissed when he sees how badly they've handled everything."

"What do you suggest?"

"It's a small village."

"So?"

"So we take the village before Big Daddy gets home."

Siri picked up the coffee cup and could still feel the buzz in his fingers. He sat alone with An in a corner of the restaurant. Beer had gone hunting for another cast member from the occupation, a mechanic who'd worked on Japanese planes.

"Let's start at the other end," said Siri.

"You mean when the Japanese arrived?" said An.

"Yes."

"It was nutty. You always imagine an occupation to be dramatic. But these seven or eight soldiers and their officer arrive on a long boat from Thailand. What I'll never forget is that they were all standing to attention. The boat caught the occasional wake from a bigger boat or slowed down suddenly, but those Japs stayed on their feet. It was impressive. I was on the dock with the French administrator. Mr. LeHavre himself was still acting like the French were just hosting a picnic for some transient troublemakers. He wasn't about to give them an official welcome. His driver was waiting to take their leader to headquarters. We hadn't been able to find anyone who spoke Japanese. We had a French teacher who could speak English quite well. We thought if the Japs didn't have a French speaker, at the very least they'd have someone who could speak English. But we were wrong. They spoke exclusively in Japanese until Miura-*san* arrived. Not so much as a '*bonjour*.'"

"How did you communicate?"

"We didn't. They climbed up the riverbank, marched into town, and stood at attention beside the old fountain. Their leader, who I later learned was a major general, unrolled a parchment, held it up in front of him, and read from it. Orated is probably a better word for it. He had a powerful voice."

"But it was all in Japanese," said Siri.

"Every word."

"What did they look like?"

"They were soldiers. They all dressed alike apart from the commander."

"Do you remember anything odd about them? Size? Shape? Missing limbs?"

"You know, Brother Siri, in Europe they used to say all Asians looked alike. I didn't understand that sentiment until that day. It was as if they'd selected a family of octuplets to take over Thakhek. Every one of them was sunburned and robust."

"But not young."

"In their twenties. Even the major general was thirtyish. But he acted like someone much older. He treated Thakhek like it was deserted. He ignored us completely.

He took out a map and pointed in the direction of the French administration building. A couple of the men went over there to present their papers, which of course we couldn't read. A couple of others took the map to a clearing behind the old airstrip and started hammering in marker posts. It was like a cabaret and we locals were the audience. There was no interaction that day or for many days after. It was like they were operating in a different dimension and couldn't see us. We largely ignored them until the day in '45 when the occupation turned into an invasion. Well, Siri, I tell you, the wall came crashing down between our respective dimensions that day. That's when the previous years of patience were replaced by unrestricted mayhem."

"But until then?" Siri asked.

"Life went on pretty much as normal. The French and Vietnamese administered, the laborers toiled, the children studied in the temples, and the market was busy. And in the background the Japanese forces expanded. Troops came and went but we ignored them. It wasn't our war then."

"Does the name Kangen Toshimado mean anything to you?" Siri asked.

"Not from memory."

"What about a major general named Dorari Momoyotsu?"

"Dr. Siri, I tell you. We weren't on speaking terms with anyone but Miura. Once they'd all settled in he was the one running back and forth between the French and Japanese administrators passing on messages and requests from his bosses. He was the true hero of the occupation."

"And you fell in love."

"He wasn't much to look at. In fact he looked like one of those naked cats they breed in Egypt. But I was no Madonna. I was the French-to-Vietnamese-to-Lao translator. He was Japanese-to-French. We sort of filled in each other's gaps."

"I'm sure you did," said Siri with a smile.

An blushed.

"I'd like to talk to him," said Siri.

"So would I," said An. "When that particular war ended and the next threatened to drag on even longer, he went back to Japan. We exchanged a few letters but . . . you know. We had what we had."

She reset her wig at a coquettish angle over one ear and winked at Siri.

Madam Daeng had assessed the situation. The bulldog they'd been introduced to as the headman probably wasn't. If he had been, he wouldn't be waiting for Big Daddy to come back before executing the visitors. He'd faded back into the scenery following his performance at the opening ceremony. It was a younger man who ordered the captives to quit their chattering. Daeng had no idea how long they'd have before the real leader's return, so she needed to act fast. She regretted the fact she'd brained the man with the musket. It meant she couldn't play the "little old lady surprise attack." Then again, if she hadn't hit the man, the hoodlums in the village wouldn't have shown their true colors. She needed another angle.

She looked at the pilot. He seemed remarkably calm despite their dire situation. She wondered what, if anything, he was thinking. He sat by himself chewing on a blade of grass. The fact that she'd threatened to break all his fingers that morning if he didn't allow her on board probably hadn't created a lasting bond between them. Then she'd gone and scuttled his helicopter. She knew nothing about his background but she hoped it was military because she needed a soldier on her team. As they were no longer allowed to speak, she started to sing. She couldn't be certain there were no Lao speakers among her captors but, just in case, she kept her voice low.

"*Dear Comrade Pilot,*" she sang.

One or two of the men around the pavilion looked up but nobody complained about her singing. She had a good voice. She continued.

> *I'm sorry I scuttled your helicopter.*
> *You can fix it by loosening the screw*
> *At the base of the rotor shaft*
> *And flicking the switch.*
> *It's a safety component*
> *To stop the mechanics getting*
> *Accidently chopped up.*
> *Nobody ever uses it anymore.*

She added a few lines of "lalala" before,

> *If I can get you a weapon,*
> *Scratch your nose*
> *If you'd know how to use it.*

He looked at her with his head tilted to one side. And he scratched his nose. Roper had a look of horror on his face.

"*Relax, Mr. Roper,*" she sang.

In five minutes I will need you
To overpower the guard behind you.
You don't have to kill him.
Just stop him from firing.
And we can go home.
If you think you can do that
Please nod.

Roper could have wilted at such a notion but he clenched both fists and nodded. Daeng had her army, but she still needed a ruse. She got to her feet, the three guns trained on her.

"Please tell these gentlemen that I would like to excrete," she said to Roper.

He blushed but translated. There was laughter but no action. So Madam Daeng stood in front of the most sympathetic-looking of the guards and started to undo her belt. She lowered the zip in her khakis and began to squat. The men all yelled and the gathering was thrown into pandemonium until one of the armed guards was ordered to take the old woman to the latrine. She readjusted her clothing, slouched from the effort, and held on to his arm. To all of them she seemed much older now and more frail than she had been only seconds before. Roper watched her disappear behind the hut with her escort. He looked to his left, where the pilot continued to eat grass with no expression whatsoever. Roper half-turned to look at the guard behind him. He had left his AK-47 leaning against a wooden post because he needed both hands free to squeeze blackheads.

The seconds continued to drawl past and bloat into minutes. Then the soothing musical sounds of the jungle all around them seemed to become more intense in his mind, like an orchestra upping its tempo, rising to a crescendo. Roper was all adrenaline. His fingers twitched. His instincts told him it was all over, this lifestyle he'd worked so hard to earn, the career he'd forged. But if it was truly to be his last swan song, he would belt it out. Yes, damn it. He was an Englishman and his countrymen had a long tradition of dying famously. He would not go quietly.

Daeng was taking her sweet time. The guard had learned from his colleague's mistake and he sat back far enough to keep his weapon out of the reach of the old woman. She was grumbling although he had no idea what she said. He could see the top of her head above the latticed fence that served as the village latrine. The others had told him to shoot her if she tried anything. But she was staring down the barrel of an AK-47 and he knew she wouldn't be that stupid. She was old, probably older than his mother. He hated old people. He'd have no hesitation in . . .

Her head dipped below the top of the fence. First, he assumed it was all part of the natural process of doing her business but the seconds rolled by and he became anxious. What if she'd fallen down the pit? What if she'd had a heart attack? He got to his feet, hurried to the latrine, and peered over the fence.

"Shit!"

One segment of the rear fence was flat on the ground. The bitch had escaped. But how far could she get at her age? He ran into the smelly compound and through the gap. He stopped for a brief moment to guess which route she might have taken into the jungle. But that moment was his downfall. Daeng was crouching behind the next segment of fencing. He only had time to get a glimpse of her before she was on him. Not even a second to turn his gun on her. He felt her hands like metal clamps around his neck and heard the snap. And that was the last thing he'd ever hear.

While planning his attack on his captors, Roper had lost control of his bladder. Only the pilot seemed to have noticed, smiling rudely at the Englishman. But Roper had gone beyond the need for decency. He was about to launch himself at several armed guards. He'd overpower the zit-picker, take his gun, and then . . .

At that moment, two women came walking toward the pavilion. One of the guards gestured for them to go back, but they kept coming. And then there was another woman, then two more. They emerged from the huts like sleepwalkers. The guards shouted again, and again they were ignored. It was as if every woman in the village had come to the pavilion. There was dialogue too fast and too intense for Roper to pick up but the sentiment was clear. One elderly woman took the gun from one of the men, perhaps her son. Another group gathered around a second man. Roper looked behind him. The guard had gone to reason with the women and left his weapon where it was. Roper stepped backward in its direction but the pilot beat him to it.

Last to arrive at the village center was Daeng, holding the hands of the unmatching sisters, all three of them in tears.

CHAPTER TWELVE
Empirical Evidence

It was late afternoon in Vientiane. One of those fully loaded black clouds from Vietnam had just squatted over the city and dumped a thousand tons of water in five minutes. The dirt roads were mudslides rushing down to the river, diverting through shop fronts, carrying litter and flowerpots and cats too slow to get out of their way. But safe, one story up in the old Lido Hotel building, was Dtui, teaching another of her frustrating nursing classes. She'd had to take a break during the deluge while the rain hammered on the roof. Her class admired a waterfall beyond the open windows. She'd brought along an embryo in formaldehyde from the morgue, mainly to judge the reaction. Half of the country girls laughed with embarrassment. The other half said, "Eeuooh." Dtui sighed. It was like teaching chickens to fly long distances.

The only enthusiasm she saw all morning was when every girl in the room looked toward the doorway with eyes wide and tongues hanging loose. There, still dirty from the concrete factory, boots muddy from the flood, stood Chief Inspector Phosy. In her mind, Dtui ran to him, threw her arms around his neck, and kissed the living daylights out of him. In real time, she smiled and said, "Chief Inspector Phosy, can I help you?"

"Nurse Dtui," he said. "I was wondering if you could assist me. I appear to have been shot seven times."

The students gasped. She looked him up and down and saw no sign of blood.

"Only seven times?" she said.

"I was lucky," he said. "He ran out of bullets. As you are the most competent operating theater nurse in the country, I was hoping you might spare me a few minutes to remove the bullets for me."

She looked at her indestructible Soviet wristwatch.

"Class," she said. "Do you mind?"

"Go, go," they said.

In the stairwell between floors, Dtui kissed the living daylights out of her husband, then she punched him hard in the ribs.

"Where do you think you've been?" she asked.

"Vang Vieng. Nice place."

"Why do you look so messy?"

"I was drugged, kidnapped, dragged through the dust, and chained to a metal girder for thirty-six hours."

"Oh, right," said Dtui. "You go off and have a good time and leave me and Malee all alone."

"Sorry. Next time I'm abused I'll take you along."

"Is Sihot okay? And the boy?"

"Fine. I gave them the day off to get clean."

"And the girl?"

"We found her. She's willing to back up Siri's theory about the owl. She was there with the Vietnamese. She saw the whole thing. She's in the jeep downstairs."

"Why?"

"I sort of promised her father we'd take care of her."

"Which means?"

"Perhaps we could take her in for a couple of nights?"

"Phosy. We live in one small room in a dormitory."

"I could sleep in my office."

"It's like Civilai always said. My husband's the type of man who'll bring his work home with him."

"We have a big bed," he said. "If it worries you to be away from me we could always nuzzle down together and . . ."

"I'll have a blanket sent to your office," she said.

The powerful headlights of the helicopter illuminated the football field as if the World Cup was about to begin there. It was late but they'd made one or two unscheduled stops before returning to the field. Siri's bushy eyebrows were fluttering from the downdraft. Daeng leaned out and shouted something he couldn't hear. He nodded anyway and smiled. His instincts had been telling him most of the day that something had gone wrong. He was delighted to see his wife and even a little pleased that the Englishman was behind her. To be honest, he'd been alarmed that Daeng would volunteer so readily to take a scenic flight with a philanderer. Love puts a strain on trust no matter how old you are. But there she was, smiling and waving, and apparently as pleased to see him as ever. She jumped down and took his hands in hers. He could feel her stress and knew she would have a hell of a tale to tell him that night.

Roper stepped down onto the football pitch with the two girls. Their empty eyes had come alive. They both smiled at Siri and they gave off the radiance of the reborn. They were holding hands.

"They sent them back?" said Siri.

"It's a long story."

"Then we need a drink. We still have the hooch from Woophi."

"Have you been waiting for us all day?" Daeng asked.

"Most of it," said Siri. "But I would have waited on and on, taking root, growing skyward without joy, producing no fruit, not so much as a blossom until you arrived."

"It sounds like you've been reading Toshi's diary."

"To the end. But your story comes first. We can drink and talk through the night and watch the sunrise locked in each other's arms."

"Siri, the girls have been through a lot today. I really need to—"

"No," said Siri. "I need you more than they do."

"Don't panic," said Daeng. "We can tell our respective stories outside their room. They just need to know I'm there."

"Then they wouldn't miss you for half an hour or so."

"Siri?"

"All right. But I want this sacrifice to go on record."

"That's fair."

Their voices were the only sounds from either side of the river that night. Everything seemed to be cushioned in the type of humidity that invited extreme weather. Lightning was dancing silently across the horizon on three fronts but there were still stars overhead. Nature was playing her cards close to her bosom. The home brew from Woophi didn't last long but Siri had smuggled a bottle of Saeng Thip rum across from Thailand. He conceded that her story trumped his own and Daeng went into great detail in describing her day.

"Then how did you know the women would be on your side?" he asked.

"I didn't, not really. When I was walking around the village I'd noticed the odd apologetic look here and there. Something close to shame. And when I overpowered the guard who'd escorted me to the latrine, there were one or two women standing back and watching. Nobody had tried to help him. I imagined it was like in the days of the occupation with the locals watching the Japanese takeover—they saw Asians with power and it occurred to them that they weren't inferior. So it was with the women today. They see an old lady kick arse and they realize they aren't powerless. They could have a say in what's going on around them."

"I take it your original plan involved bloodshed," said Siri.

"Buckets of the stuff," said Daeng. "But I'm not averse to the Gandhi approach. Things would have been a lot different if Big Daddy had come home early. As it was, with the guns in our hands, we loaded the girls onto the helicopter, the pilot reactivated the mechanism, and we took off. Not a word was spoken."

"What do we do with the girls?"

"We get them talking. Find out what tribes they're from. Hunt out the families who had daughters kidnapped and send them home. If it turns out they were sold, the UN will find them more appropriate homes. Roper's embarrassed about the way things went. He's handling it all. He says he'll set the dogs on Big Daddy."

"So you're free to return to the Toshi mystery?"

"Honestly, Siri, I'd sooner sit on the balcony with my feet up, pigging out on red bean sweets, thumbing through Thai fashion magazines."

"You'd regret it. We've reached an exciting juncture."

"Really? You've found the mummified remains of Toshi's turnip garden?"

"Don't mock, wife. I think this will turn out to be one of our most intriguing cases."

The next day, Siri and Beer rowed past the Thai river police launch on their way to Nakhon Phanom. They glared and the police glared back. A lot of refugees made the mistake of smiling or, worse, waving: a flaming neon sign that said, HERE WE ARE, ARREST US. Those with nothing to hide had no reason to be polite. They heard shots from downriver but often the river guards on the Thai side were just shooting at birds. It was a minor disincentive to smugglers and refugees but it guaranteed roast fowl for dinner.

They met Kyoko at a comparatively upmarket roadside restaurant. She welcomed them with her smile and a polite *nop*, which on the Thai side was called a *wai*. The only difference between the two was that the Lao had yet to disguise its insincerity.

"Have you eaten?" she asked.

"No," said Beer, instantly. Siri answered with a smile.

"I'm buying you both lunch," she said.

"No, you don't have to," said Siri.

"Oh, but I do," said Kyoko. "You two have enlivened my life, expanded my horizons. I didn't sleep a minute last night."

Siri was curious to know how boring Toshi had accomplished such a feat. Many of the Lao entries—not including the fables—had put him to sleep. The waitress came and took their orders with a smile.

"Did you find it exciting?" Siri asked. "The Japanese section?"

He'd hoped for a "yes" so Kyoko's "no" floored him.

"Fascinating, yes," she said. "Disturbing, appalling, sickening? All of those. But not exciting."

"What do you mean?" Siri asked.

"Well, Doctor Siri, the diary entries begin in 1937. Hiro, who was then called Toshimado, was in Manchuria. He provides us with the dates and the times and describes in great detail the places he visited and the tasks he was ordered to perform. At that time he was a major in charge of what they called 'salvage.' They would go in behind their victorious armies and rescue goods and equipment which could be reused or sold toward the war effort. It appears the spoils of war had no bounds: valuables in empty apartments and houses, heavy equipment in factories, rings and gold fillings from deceased enemy soldiers and civilians. It's all documented with no emotion at all."

"So Toshi was a noncombatant even then?" said Siri.

"So it seems."

"Any other mention of him being a pilot?"

"None at all beyond the introduction."

"So it's possible he never flew."

"Yes," said Kyoko. "I'm only halfway through but he seems intent on demonstrating his undying devotion to the emperor and the Imperial Army. There are entries where he describes the most horrific scenes in impassive terms."

"For example," said Siri.

She turned to a page that she'd selected by inserting a pink cartoon bookmark.

"For example, this," she said. *"Today, quite to our surprise, the General made an inspirational visit to our battalion. He was so pleased with our work he penciled around one area on the map of Nanjing and gave us a suburb."*

"What does that mean?" Siri asked.

"I phoned my advisor in Bangkok," said Kyoko. "She's a historian. I read her the passage. She said that as a reward for productivity and loyalty, the senior officers would give a suburb to a unit of soldiers. There would be no holds barred. The soldiers in the unit could take anything or anybody they wished within the borders allocated. They could mete out punishment on the Chinese in that suburb for any infringement. They could destroy property, torture, kill, rape. There were no rules. It was their reward and, as the Japanese military saw the Chinese as inferior beings, there were no moral conflicts. Your friend Toshi was honored to be congratulated in such a way."

Siri sighed.

Kyoko turned to another marked page and translated, *"It was our great honor today to be able to follow the eighth battalion on their victorious march on Chuzhou. The bodies of the enemy were piled six feet high on either side of the road. There were women and children in those stacks and our glorious commander informed us that the Chinese animals were so unscrupulous that they recruited such people as spies and suicide bombers."*

The food was on the table but only Beer was eating. Siri had lost his appetite. Of course he'd learned of the Japanese atrocities in China but hearing them anew from Toshi's point of view felt like . . . like what? Like betrayal. Siri had come to like the man from his light and humorous diary entries. But to discover he was a war puppet, a man without scruples, a beast: that was more than he could take in. It was as if he'd lost a friend.

"Is it like that all the way?" he asked.

"As far as I got," said Kyoko. "There's just . . ."

"What?"

"There's something about the style of his writing that doesn't seem . . . natural."

"In what way?"

"It's a little like reading a textbook. Even the few personal entries are impersonal. Everything he sees and does makes him 'so proud to honor the emperor.' That and a few dozen other well-used wartime clichés crop up on every page. He talks about death clinically. There isn't a single euphemism. There is no difference between his choice of language describing mass rape and that talking about the lack of space in a warehouse to store rice."

"What does that say to you?" Siri asked.

"I don't know," she said, absently chasing her food around the plate. "Either your Toshi is a complete automaton . . ."

"Or?"

"Or he was expecting someone to read his diary. I got the feeling he wasn't necessarily writing for himself."

"Are you going to eat that, Uncle?" asked Beer, looking at Siri's plate. Siri slid it across the table. He noticed that Beer didn't contribute much to the thought process, but he did spare kitchen workers a lot of washing up.

"Oh," said Kyoko, "and I looked briefly through the Japanese occupation documents you gave me."

"You've been busy," said Siri.

"I'm caught up in your puzzle. I didn't have time to read it all, but I was able to pick at the troop movements in and out of Thakhek. That included the names of the first battalion to arrive there in 1941. I don't read Lao very well but there are enough similarities to Thai for me to make out the names in Toshi's unit in his diary. Even allowing for misreading and poor translation on my part, I think I can say with some certainty that there were no military personnel based in Thakhek with the names listed by Hiro."

"Not one?" said Siri.

"Not even Hiro himself."

"You're telling me he was never there?"

"According to the official lists."

"Damn."

CHAPTER THIRTEEN
An Adorable Alcoholic

"So it would appear I'm right again," said Daeng.

"You're always right, my love," said Siri. "But . . . he describes everything in such detail, even the mundane stuff. I mean, why would he bother to write about trivial things? If he was a carrot peeler, as you said, surely he'd write a diary full of excitement and intrigue to counteract his dull life. But we have a hundred and sixty pages of philosophical insights and fables and descriptions of all the beauties of Mother Nature. There isn't one death. There are no villains. Even the alcoholic was adorable."

Siri, Daeng, and the girls were fishing. Or, rather, they were sitting on a wooden dock dangling their lines in the water for the amusement of the fish.

"Except for the last untorn pages," said Daeng. "It seems Toshi's colleagues are starting to get on his nerves."

"But that's where it all ends," said Siri. "We don't have those missing pages so we'll never know what happened before his promise to 'rise.'"

"Talking about rising, shouldn't we be taking off soon?"

"We can't leave, Daeng. There are so many unanswered

questions. What about that loose sheet and the treasure? We still don't know who sent us the diary."

"I was afraid you'd say that. What's your plan?"

"Kyoko is—"

"You mention her a lot."

"She's been very helpful. She said she—"

"Attractive, is she?"

"She's gorgeous."

"Hence the risky rowing trips to Thailand."

Siri loved it. Daeng never failed to be jealous when other women made appearances in his life. If he was feeling braver he'd say something like, "In Japan, young women are attracted to older men, sexually." But he invariably came off worse as a result of making such comments so instead he said, "She told me she'd discuss matters with her *sensei* in Bangkok and see if I can get access to any other documents. Problem is, all the war records are in the hands of the Americans now and they've barely made a dent in translating everything."

"Young, is she?"

"What?"

"Keiko."

"Kyoko? I don't know, mid-twenties? But she was asking if we had any US contacts who could get us access to the data bank of records in Washington. She thinks it's the best way to find out what actually happened to Toshi after China and, for that matter, whether he really existed. If he could make up the Lao half there's no reason why he couldn't make up the Japanese half, too, including his name. So I was wondering whether we could get in touch with Cindy."

"Cindy?"

"Yes, remember? She was at the embassy in Vientiane, then moved to Phnom Penh."

"Cindy the beautiful blond second secretary?"

"That's the one."

"It appears you have a stable, Siri Paiboun."

"She was able to get us access to documents in a hurry and she was really helpful in the dog tail case last year. And she did tell us she'd be delighted to work with us again."

"I do recall."

Against all the odds one of the girls caught a fish. It appeared to be elderly. She pulled it from the water with the help of her un-sister and they chuckled together as it squirmed on the dock. By the time Siri had removed the hook and returned the fish to its retirement community in the water, Daeng had regained her composure.

"What do you hope to find?" she asked.

"If Hiro Uenobu exists or existed we might be able to find out whether he really was a pilot. He doesn't get anywhere near an airplane in the Lao or the Japanese segments of the diary. Something must have happened. And perhaps we can confirm that he was in Manchuria on the dates he gives. Then apparently he arrives in Indochina but not in Thakhek. I suppose it's possible he gives a false place name for security reasons. He seems quite knowledgeable about salvage so perhaps that part was true. Then there's a gap. His last Japanese entry was in 1940. He'd just left China and arrived in Vietnam. When the Lao entries begin he's already on his way here, or so he says. If we take it at face value, that's a gap of three months when he writes nothing. By late '41 he's in Thakhek or wherever writing fluent Lao, second in command, and having a good time with a unit of men who apparently don't exist. Doesn't this all tickle your funny bone just a little?"

Daeng had caught a knot of river weed that refused to release her hook.

"Have you ever considered that the diary might have been written by two different people?" she said, tugging on her line.

"What?"

"That soldier Hiro keeps a diary about his placement in Manchuria and he drops it."

"He drops the diary?"

"Yes, or just loses it. He's off pillaging and raping his generously donated virgins, has a little too much stolen whisky and drops it on his way back to the barracks. And somebody else picks it up, sees it's a finely crafted tome with half the pages untouched, and he keeps it for himself. When he comes to Laos he learns the language and writes his nonsense in it just to practice. Either that or he gives it to a Lao as a present."

Siri pondered silently.

"Damn," he said.

"Different language, different style, different person."

"Damn," said Siri again.

"Your friend Kimiko didn't uncover anything about his younger days?"

"No. The diary started in Shiga Prefecture, Japan, with Hiro saying goodbye to his family. He's about to be transferred to Manchuria. He's thirty-four already but we don't know anything about his early years. It really is intriguing."

"Siri, you really need a hobby that's more suitable for your age."

"The only thing suitable for my age is decomposition," he reminded her.

They heard an enthusiastic "yoohoo!" from the lane behind them, and Roper, sodden with sweat, came bounding up to them on the dock. The structure swayed. The girls shied away from him.

"Good news," he said.

"We can go home?" said Daeng.

"Not yet. I hope you can bear with me for one or two more days. I have been able to secure a cassette tape upon which we have samples of every one of the tribal languages of the region. I shall play the tape to our poor victims here and once we have established their ethnicity I can begin the process of locating their home villages."

"And what if they don't respond to their own languages?" Daeng asked.

"Why would they not?"

"They've done a good job of keeping mum so far," she said. "It's still possible they've been threatened not to use their native languages."

"Fear not, Madam Daeng. We have a linguistics expert flying up from Bangkok as I speak."

"Then the world is safe," said Siri.

"Do you suppose I could borrow the girls?" said Roper.

"I might have to go with you," said Daeng. "I think they're finding men less than trustworthy."

She threw in a sideways glance at her husband as an exclamation mark.

CHAPTER FOURTEEN
Feet Never Lie

Alone again, Siri was in his room reading—for want of an alternative—a thrilling account in the *Passasson Lao* newsletter of the minister of agriculture's state visit to East Germany. There was a hint of alliteration in the third paragraph that gave Siri a modicum of hope for his country's literary future. He was not upset to be interrupted by a shout from outside.

"Dr. Siri!"

He ran to the door and opened it to find Beer and a man in his sixties with a neat beard the color of smoke. Siri had always wanted one just like it but for some reason he'd been unable to grow facial hair. Apart from the beard, Siri might have been looking at an image of himself. He expected Beer to introduce the guest as a Lao or a Vietnamese, but in a low voice he said, "Dr. Siri. This is Yuki-*san*."

Siri nodded and Yuki-*san* ran a thumb and forefinger over his beard.

"I couldn't find the mechanic," said Beer. "But this is even better. Yuki-*san* was in Thakhek at the same time as Toshi."

"I was starting to believe Toshi didn't exist," said Siri.

"Apparently he did," said Beer. "But everyone knew him as Hiro."

Siri was recharged. A lost cause had been found.

"Then please come in," he said, standing back.

There was only tepid tea from a thermos to drink but Beer threw back three mugfuls while the two old gentlemen sipped politely and stared at each other.

"Do you speak Lao?" Siri asked.

"Only few words," said Yuki-*san* in Vietnamese. It was heavily accented but competent. Siri's Vietnamese was fluent.

"I cannot be in your room for long," said the Japanese.

"Yuki-*san* stayed in Vietnam after the Japanese defeat," said Beer, also in Vietnamese. "He fought with the Viet Minh against the French. He ingratiated himself with Uncle Ho and was given a plot of land and a wife. He now has three children."

"How do you know all this?" Siri asked.

"I tell him," said Yuki-*san*. "Walking here."

"So you aren't old friends?"

"We just met at the market," said Beer. "But I get the feeling it wasn't a coincidence. Your purpose in Thakhek hasn't gone unnoticed, Doctor."

"So, Yuki-*san*, according to the official Japanese documents, Kangen Toshimado, alias Hiro Uenobu, was not involved in the establishment of a Japanese base in Thakhek. How do you explain that?"

"Hiro come before the other," said Yuki-*san*. "Him and his unit. They come before records start. Japanese army specially want major general to come first to show important of Thakhek. Hiro come with him plus six or seven other men."

"I can't tell you what good news that is," said Siri. "I wish my wife was here to enjoy this happy moment with me. Can you confirm any other names in Hiro's unit? Captain Jame, Second Lieutenant Tetsukimo, Corporal Yatsusuki?"

"I don't know," said Yuki-*san*. "Only know Major Hiro and Major General Dorari. I deal direct with this two."

"What were you doing here?" Siri asked.

"I come many time from Cochin. I was engineer. I plan the road from Hòa Bình in Vietnam to Paksane in central Laos."

"What was he like, Major Hiro?"

"He was kind and lovely man. Everybody like him. I like him. We are like brother."

"And he was a pilot before coming south?" asked Siri.

"He don't like to talk about past life."

Siri was keen to sit down for the afternoon and hear what Yuki-*san* knew about Hiro. But first, as Beer had said, this visit could not have been a coincidence.

"Why did you come to town?" Siri asked.

"To see you," said Yuki-*san*. "Friends in Thakhek send a message to me. They say a doctor is looking for my old friend Hiro. I live in mountain with my family. I have no . . . what do you say? No resources to seek for Hiro. For many year I wonder where is Hiro? Where is Hiro? I want to see him. Drink with him. Talk about his life, my life."

"Did he also join the Viet Minh?" Siri asked.

"He leave the Japanese army and he join the Free Lao. Same enemy. Different country."

"There's a diary," said Siri. "Hiro's diary but in it he calls himself Toshi. Have you seen it?"

"No."

"He keeps his diary until August 1945. Some pages

before that are missing. These are the weeks before the Japanese surrender. Do you have any idea what he might have written there?"

"I don't know this diary."

"But do you know whether he joined the Free Lao before the Japanese surrender? Was he cooperating with the anti-French underground when still a major in the army? That might explain why he'd want to rip out the pages."

"This are questions I too want to ask," said Yuki-*san*.

"Then, at least, I should buy you a few drinks so I can hear about your visits here during the war. I have a lot to learn about your time with Hiro."

"This I want very much," said Yuki-*san*. "But cannot be today. I come back soon. We talk."

"My time's limited here," said Siri. "Are you free tomorrow?"

"Yes. I come back tomorrow."

Siri walked him to the door.

"Yuki-*san*," he said. "At least leave me something to help me find your friend. I'm running out of ideas. I need a clue to follow up on."

Yuki-*san* stopped in the doorway and did his goatee grab. Siri found himself mirroring the gesture.

"Might be something," said Yuki-*san*. "Hiro had a place. Secret place. He talk often. He call it 'tunnel of love.' He like to go there in his leave time."

"Where is it?" Siri asked.

"I don't know," said Yuki-*san*.

Siri looked at Beer, who shrugged.

"Did he describe it?" Siri asked.

"One time," said Yuki-*san*. "One time he say this place is

like enlightenment. He say sometime you are in dark for long time, then one moment everything is clear. You come out the end. You see light."

"He said the place is like that?"

"That's all he tell me."

Siri hadn't really learned anything new about Toshi other than that he'd stepped out of fantasy and become real. It should have made research easier. Now Siri was certain the name at the beginning of the diary was genuine. It was likely he used his actual name as a Japanese officer and called himself Toshi only in the diary entries: his Lao secret identity. If the records Siri had retrieved from the council office were compiled by Toshi and his team, that explained why they didn't mention themselves. It meant he could be more certain that Toshi had indeed come from the rail-head in Lang Son as Kyoko said, and had been involved in salvage operations. It even reignited the likelihood that he was responsible in some way for transporting the treasure mentioned in the loose page. Everything and anything had become possible as a result of Yuki-*san*'s visit. Perhaps Major Hiro had handpicked his team for Thakhek, choosing only those with disabilities and problems because . . . because he was kind. But why would a kind man find such pleasure in the bloodbaths of Manchuria? Siri was getting there, but there were still too many questions.

He had sufficient confidence now to send what he knew to Cindy at the US embassy. Her Lao was good enough that he'd have no need to put together a translation. He sent Beer back across the river that afternoon with the message. The Thais had state-of-the-art communications systems and ran daily pouches between embassies in the

region. Siri considered accompanying Beer, perhaps dropping in to see if Kyoko had learned anything new from the
diary and the files. But an item in a Thai radio broadcast
that morning had described a Thai wife who had sliced off
her husband's penis because she smelled another woman
on his collar. She'd attached the organ to a helium balloon
and set it free, knowing it would never be found in time to
reattach it. Siri's eyes had watered at the thought of it. It
was too soon for another visit to Kyoko.

Daeng returned to her room at about 5 P.M. She woke her
husband.

"It's happy hour," she said.

"I never understood why happiness should be restricted
to just an hour," said Siri, pulling himself from sleep.

She gave him a kiss. He gave it back.

"It's because normal people in normal jobs work hard
all day and then worry all night," she said. "They can only
squeeze an hour of happiness between the two."

"Thank heavens we aren't normal," said Siri, getting
creakily into a sitting position. "What news of the linguist?"

"Astounding," said Daeng. "He's young."

"Attractive?"

She knocked him onto his back with a pillow and held
it to his face.

"Roper speaks a mere seven languages," said Daeng.
"Young Malcolm is fluent . . ."

"Does he have firm biceps?" Siri asked, but his words
were muffled in kapok.

". . . fluent in twenty regional languages and dialects."

She removed the pillow before it was too late.

"Twenty," she said. "Can you believe it? He didn't even

need the cassette. He started speaking to one of the girls in her own language just from the way she looked. The shape of her face. She answered straightaway. Seemed so pleased. It turns out her name is Mim and she's Khua. Not a lot of Khua in the world. Some two thousand in Laos, he estimates."

"And the other one?" he asked.

"Her name's Uwa and she's Jeh. Far more common. Roper could speak it but she'd been warned not to trust anyone who knew her language. There were probably a lot of Jeh speakers at the camp. But the minder had told her if she spoke to anyone she'd be shot."

"Do you know where they're from?"

"They're so very rural, Siri. Isolated villages. The only world they knew was bordered by mountains. If their homes had names they'd never been told. And Siri . . . ?"

"I'm listening."

"They weren't kidnapped."

"I was afraid of that."

"They were sold. The girls remember Big Daddy arriving in a helicopter, shaking hands with their parents, and being herded aboard. The village I went to with Roper was the depot. All their acquisitions passed through there on their way to the border and the camps. It's like when Phosy shut down the traffickers on the Thai border, except this was legitimized at the camps with UN paperwork. They hire someone to be the mother, she and the kids are registered at the camp, the NGOs push for single mothers to be fast-tracked, and whoosh, there they are in Wisconsin. They're met by American agents who sell them to the highest bidders. The women who acted as the mothers are probably sold into some sort of bonded labor."

"You're angry."

"I am not. I am thoroughly pissed."

"And when you're angry you have a habit of making unilateral decisions."

"Nonsense," said Daeng, searching the wardrobe for something to drink.

"So you haven't done anything outrageous?" he asked.

"Of course not."

She went to the bathroom and ladled cool water from the tank onto her feet. This confirmed it for him. Her feet never lied.

"I'm going to be a father, aren't I?" he said.

She came back and sat beside him on the bed. She put a hand on his thigh.

"Just for a little while," she said.

Siri hadn't needed a lot of persuading. He'd been taking in strays for some time. And his conscience would never have allowed those two scared girls to be returned to the families that had sold them. After a day that seemed to rid the two of their devils, they slept now without fear of what the future might bring. Siri and Daeng sat on the balcony in front of their room.

"So now you can tell me about Toshi's revival," said Daeng.

It was an annoying night. The heavens were tossing rain here and there. The balcony was covered but the occasional splash on the wind would water down their drinks then slap their faces. But they weren't about to give in to it. Siri told her about Yuki-*san* and his relationship with Major Hiro. He said that if she was free from mothering responsibilities the next day, Daeng should join him at the only functioning restaurant in town. She could meet the Japanese and see what she thought of him.

"Where did he go?" she asked.

"When?"

"When he left you," said Daeng. "He said he had to go and he'd see you for lunch tomorrow. So where did he go?"

"I don't know," said Siri. "He probably has influential friends here from the old days. A lot of ex–freedom fighters are somebodies now."

"Like us?"

"Exactly. Why are you always so suspicious?"

"Because it keeps us alive," said Daeng. "Because your mind needs quality control sometimes. You're a book reader. You're easily fooled by a clever phrase or a deep thought. It diverts your instincts. You should always be expecting an attack."

"Can I expect an attack tonight?"

She laughed.

"It might wake the children," she said.

"I doubt it," said Siri. "I put two teaspoonfuls of rum in their rice porridge."

"If I thought that was true I'd leave you for Malcolm. He has an aquarium."

"Why doesn't that surprise me?"

CHAPTER FIFTEEN
The Tunnel of Love

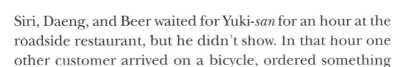

Siri, Daeng, and Beer waited for Yuki-*san* for an hour at the roadside restaurant, but he didn't show. In that hour one other customer arrived on a bicycle, ordered something to go, and went.

So there were only three of them for lunch. Roper was with the governor putting in an official complaint about Big Daddy's clan. The girls were with Malcolm. Siri and his party were the only seated customers. Having learned from their previous noodle experience, they did not order noodles. They ate sticky rice with a few assorted dips, most of which were so spicy they couldn't tell a carrot from a chicken liver. But the owner had a few bottles of beer from across the river and the current Singha Beer ad campaign was "We put out your fire." Which was appropriate.

Their own Beer was busy mopping up the dips with the leftover rice.

"Do you think anything will happen to Big Daddy and his gang?" Siri asked him.

"No," said Beer. "You'll all go home and that official report will be lining the bottom of a parrot cage in the governor's garden. If they've got access to a helicopter there have to be at least some military bigwigs in on the racket. And there'd be sufficient volume to make it worth everyone's while. There are still family groups headed on foot toward the border. They'll be easy pickings for someone like Daddy and his team."

"No worries," said Siri. "We'll get the chief inspector of police on it when we get back."

"Right," said Beer with a distinct lack of belief.

"And getting back might come sooner than we expected," said Daeng. "Roper's talking about heading off tomorrow morning."

"And leaving the Toshi case dangling?" said Siri.

"It's not a case, Siri," said Daeng. "Right now it's still a story. And without your Japanese witness there's nothing else you can do."

"We still have clues," said Siri.

"Like what?" said Daeng.

"Like the Tunnel of Love, for one. Where do you think that might be, Comrade Beer?"

"Difficult to say, Doctor," said Beer. "Khammouane Province has more tunnels and caves than people."

"But are any of them notably loveable?" asked Siri.

"I'm not a fan of confined spaces myself," said Beer.

"But if it's a tunnel it must lead somewhere," said Siri. "To enlightenment, if we're to believe Toshi's description. So we'd be looking for a tunnel that leads to Nirvana. If he went there on his days off it's unlikely to be too far away. Easy access."

"Well, it doesn't exactly go to Nirvana," said Beer, "but there's one very long tunnel that leads to a quaint little village that doesn't get visited that often. And the name's right. It's called Thum Huk."

"The cave of love," said Daeng. "How appropriate."

"There are other more famous caves and tunnels," said Beer. "But they're far. Thum Huk you can get to in half a day."

"How do we go?" Siri asked.

"By river."

"How about it, wife?" said Siri. "Are you in the mood for an adventure?"

"Ah, you know me, Siri," said Daeng. "Always up for a wasted day on the trail of someone unimportant."

"Let's go, then," said Siri.

The longboat arrived at the entrance to Thum Huk, which gaped not with wonder but with foreboding. The tunnel mouth seemed to say, "Enter if you dare."

"How long a walk is it?" Daeng asked the skeletal boatman, who must have been well into a second century.

"Eight kilometers," he said. "But no need to walk. The river goes right through to the other end. That's where you'll find the village of Sawan."

He reached in front of him and produced an old helmet with a flashlight attachment. He put it on his head and switched it on. It was much too big for him. Only his chin was visible beneath the brim, but that didn't seem to stop him from navigating. The engine howl became a growl once they were inside. The headlamp was the only illumination and it gave out a dreary halo of light just far enough ahead to know what it was you were about to hit. Yet the boatman did not reduce his speed. In fact he was so self-assured he'd turn his headlamp from time to time to give the glimpse of a stalactite or a tower of crystal. The passengers screamed, "Look ahead!" but Siri was confident the boatman had done the trip so many times he could forfeit his eyesight and still negotiate the caves safely. Some caverns were palatial, the flutter of bats far overhead. Some were mere passageways with sharp turns.

In Paris, Siri had gone to the fair with his first love, Boua. They'd queued for the actual Tunnel of Love where you traveled in a teacup along claustrophobic passages and around sharp U-turns at four kilometers an hour. And if his lips had not been clamped to hers and his eyes not closed, he would have noticed the occasional illuminated display of stuffed mice dressed as people acting out the natural stages of love; the high school crush, the meeting with the parents, the country walk, the wedding, and, in true French style, the crime of passion with the cuckold mouse lying in a pool of blood, his unfaithful wife leaning over him with a bread knife. This was not that type of tunnel of love, but Siri remembered that Toshi had also made mention of it. In the loose sheet from the diary he'd said, *"I have found a way to transport it to you through the Tunnel of Love."* Siri was sure this was the place.

They all squinted when they once again hit sunlight. The jungle beyond the tunnel was lush and there were fruit trees growing naturally on the banks of the river. Very soon they reached a landing. The boatman moored his vessel and his passengers walked into a happy-looking village. The wood, bamboo, and rattan houses were standard but solidly built. Each one was surrounded with multicolored flowering shrubs and fresh vegetables. Fat chickens pecked at the dirt and dogs and cats lazed beneath the bushes, too content to care about the new arrivals.

Siri had no idea where they were going or what they'd do when they got there. But when they passed the first house, they saw a large woman seated at a loom in the shade. She was smoking a cheroot. She showed no surprise.

"Welcome," she said. "The school's that way. You'll see it on the hill at the end of the dirt track."

They thanked her even though nobody had made mention of a school. On the way they passed some twenty or thirty houses, all of them displaying the same attention to detail, all brightly flowered and clean. If somebody was home, they'd smile and wave and ask after the visitors' health.

"Have you noticed?" said Daeng to her husband.

"The houses?" said Siri. "They're all new. There isn't one old structure in the village."

Even the village pavilion in the square was pristine. The grass roof was neat and not yet grey with age. The beams were white and had seen no intrusion from insects. The grass around it was freshly mown and the trees were pruned. The tall concrete village pillar, six hands around, stood facing the pavilion. It had been carved with amateurish elephant motifs. It reached a little under four meters. There was a jumble of offerings at its base that suggested spirit worship was alive and well in Sawan.

"If it wasn't so difficult to get here I'd say this was a government show village to impress foreign visitors," said Siri.

They marched on past the square and found the school exactly where the woman had said it would be. It was a large single room with a neat straw roof. They could hear the musical chant of times tables. The walls didn't go all the way to the roof so they could see the head and shoulders of the teacher, a handsome man of about sixty, tall and lean. Clean white shirt. Crew cut. No glasses. He

looked over the screen wall and saw the visitors. He waved
and Daeng waved back. The teacher said something to his
class, they stood, chorused the words "Thank you, teacher,
for your lessons. See you tomorrow."

And some twenty children of different ages and sizes
left the building in an orderly fashion and nodded and
said "*Sabai dee*" as they passed the visitors. The teacher
called for them to join him in the schoolroom.

"How are you?" he asked and shook their hands.

"We didn't mean to disrupt your school day," said
Daeng.

"It was almost time to stop," said the teacher. "I am Satsai. Can I have your names?"

They handed them over gladly.

"And how can I be of service to you?" said Satsai.

Siri knew that rural villages near the towns received
their fair share of public officials from the various
departments responsible for education, health, and infrastructure as well as the odd request for donations for
nothing in particular. Then there'd be village seminars
explaining the intricacies of Marxist-Leninist philosophy.
Given the absence of telephones, the village wouldn't be
unused to surprise visits. As he still wasn't sure why he was
there, Siri didn't know what approach to make.

"We're not with the government," said Siri. "I'm a doctor, or at least I used to be. I'm now retired and working
harder than ever in my wife's noodle shop. They are, incidentally, the best noodles in Vientiane. And Comrade Beer
here is our guide and cultural attaché."

There was no nod between the two and Siri wondered
whether they may have met before. They all sat at the little
desks that were planks of wood on tree stumps. The seats

were a smaller version of the desks. The visitors felt like giants.

"So, how can I help?" asked Satsai, sitting on his own, real-size desk.

"Well," Siri began. "I'm in search of a Japanese major by the name of Hiro Uenobu, although some may have called him Toshi."

He studied the teacher's face, hoping for a sign of recognition, but there was none. So he summarized the whole story, the diary, the research, the trip to Thakhek, and finally the reason for their traveling through the Tunnel of Love that day. Teacher Satsai looked on in fascination.

"It's a marvelous story," he said. "Wouldn't it have been a spectacular ending if you'd arrived here to find your soldier in front of the blackboard teaching social studies?"

"It would have been nice, yes," said Siri.

"But I'm sure your guide here has told you how many caves and tunnels there are in our province. You'd need a year to visit them all."

"This one just happened to be convenient," said Daeng. "This was the closest to Thakhek and it's appropriately called *Thum Huk*. But as we're here, could I ask you something personal?"

"Of course."

"Apart from being devilishly handsome"—she and Siri exchanged glances of varying intensity—"you seem to me like a highly educated and eloquent educator. Your blackboard writing is gorgeous. Our country is desperate for qualified professionals. If you were in Vientiane I'm sure you'd be teaching at college level."

"And your question is why am I teaching in a one-room school in rural Khammouane?"

"Exactly."

"I was born here in Sawan," said Satsai. "My father was the headman. Before this school was built, he taught his children at home from old textbooks. When he was young, he'd left the village to get an education in the temple. He returned, married, and passed on what he'd learned to us. He believed that only through education can we develop ourselves and our country."

"That doesn't explain why you're still here," said Siri.

"I left for a while," said Satsai. "As I was a rare Lao who could read and write and add up, the French administrators recruited me as a low-level official. Actually I didn't have any choice, but my father encouraged me to go. 'Every experience is an education,' he said. I learned French quite quickly. They liked me because I picked things up easily. They said I was the only Lao they'd met who wasn't stupid and lazy. That was part of my education too, bigotry and racism. It was only by leaving this village that I could learn to appreciate its simplicity and honesty. We aren't on the road to anywhere here. We're isolated, so we're untouched by all the antisocial diseases that infect the planet. That's why I came back, to immunize our children and prepare them to survive."

"Wow!" said Daeng.

It was a word she used rarely. Siri took her hand to bring her back down to earth.

"When did your people settle here in this valley?" he asked.

"Three generations back," said Satsai.

"Really?" said Siri. "I couldn't help noticing all the buildings here are new."

"That's very observant of you," said Satsai. "It's true.

Our original village was burned to the ground in '75. This whole valley was charcoal. The only thing that survived was our village pillar. Its survival inspired us to begin again. We rebuilt, replanted, and remained."

"Was it a natural fire?" Daeng asked.

"No, Comrade. We were attacked."

"In '75?" said Siri.

"It was a few months before the Pathet Lao took over the country," said Satsai. "We'd been safe here all through the wars. If anyone comes by river, we hear them and we have time to know how to react. The only other way is to get here by air. And for that we had no defense."

"Who attacked you?"

"Americans," said Satsai.

"That's ridiculous," said Siri. "No offense."

"It is ridiculous, Doctor. Yet it happened. Three US helicopters circled once. The only thing that saved us was that there was only one place they could land and that was on the village square. Most of us were at a meeting here at the school. They started shooting even before they hit the ground. We lost four villagers immediately. The rest of us climbed the hills and took refuge in the caves. There are hundreds up there towards the ridge. We all know the tunnels really well. It was an escape plan we'd formulated with the royalists against the communists but there we were fleeing our old allies. We still don't know what bad intelligence directed them to our little hamlet but they had a hornet in their helmets about something. We weren't even politically active here.

"The Americans were on the ground for an hour. We didn't know what they were doing. When we heard the choppers take off, we sighed with relief, but we could already smell the smoke. We returned to an inferno. It was still the dry season, so the bamboo burned fast and the vegetation caught immediately. We did our best to put out the fires, but they'd used gasoline. It hung in the air. Every photo, every keepsake, every stitch of clothing was gone. And there was nobody to report it to. The royalists had fled with their tails between their legs and the Pathet Lao hadn't yet arrived. By the time there was a new administration in place, we were old news. All we could do was start again. But even today we ask, why? What had we done? There were no American servicemen based in Laos. So this team had to have flown over the mountains from Vietnam—a last-gasp effort before they were called back home. But we had no idea what they wanted."

The anorexic boatman was there at the dock waiting for them. He complained it would be dark before they arrived back in Thakhek and insisted on another fifty Thai *baht* to cover the cost of extra fuel. Evidently darkness used up more gas. The ride back through the tunnel network was even more thrilling because the old man's helmet lamp had become temperamental. It went off at will and returned at just the right moments. Twice they sideswiped embankments. At one point the light did not return and the boatman turned off his engine and listened.

"Why have we stopped?" asked Beer.

"I'm taking advice from the spirits of the cave to guide me out," said the old man. "But they need an offering."

"Money?" asked Daeng.

"That or cigarettes," said the boatman.

Beer handed him three old cigarettes from his top pocket and miraculously the light returned.

"They say they are placated," said the old man. He restarted his engine and carried on. But with the return of the lamplight, Siri noticed something he'd missed on the outward journey. It was a formidable discovery, one that would turn the whole investigation on its head. When they finally reached the dock in Thakhek, the boatman thanked them for their custom as they climbed out of the boat, but Siri remained aboard.

"Nice ride," he said.

"Thank you, brother," said the boatman, anxious to be off.

"I was admiring your helmet."

"Isn't it a beauty?"

"I couldn't help noticing the insignia."

"The what?"

"The characters written on the side."

"Oh, right."

"Japanese, isn't it?"

"What? Might be. I don't know."

"Where did you get it?"

"I didn't steal it."

"I didn't say you did."

"It was a present from a friend."

"Where did you meet this friend?"

The boatman was getting more and more flustered with the inquisition.

"On my boat," he said.

"And you'd take him to Sawan from time to time."

"It was a while ago. I'm getting old. I can't remember details."

"Do you know what the letters on his helmet spell out?"

"No."

"They spell out the name Uenobu Hiro."

These were the characters at the back of the diary. Siri saw them every time he opened it. He knew them by heart.

"Never heard of him," said the boatman.

"No," said Siri. "I bet you haven't. But I wouldn't be surprised if you knew him by his other name: Toshi."

CHAPTER SIXTEEN
Well, Blow Me Down

Daeng and Siri were walking back to the guesthouse along a dirt track lit only by fireflies and a grubby moon on the horizon. They'd arranged to meet the boatman the next morning for a return trip to Sawan. They'd assured him he wouldn't get into any trouble for what he'd told them. Whether he believed them or not they'd know the next day.

"All right," said Daeng. "I can think of one or two reasons why he'd lie."

"Satsai didn't exactly lie," said Siri. "I think if we played back a recording of the conversation, we'd hear he cleverly avoided saying that he didn't know Toshi."

"We're calling him Toshi again now?"

"Just to avoid confusion. We can't keep switching back and forth."

"All right," said Daeng. "The obvious reason is that he had no idea whether we were who we said we were. So he was being cautious."

"Yuki-*san* said Toshi would go to the tunnel during his leave," said Siri. "What if he met a girl and took her to Sawan for discreet liaisons?"

"More importantly, now that we've established he was a regular at Sawan we should also ask ourselves whether the American attack was connected in any way. If Hiro was—"

"Toshi."

"If Toshi had deserted and was fighting with the Free Lao or the Viet Minh, it's possible he had a rebel cell based in the mountains. The caves are perfect hiding places."

"But it looks like the Americans weren't there looking for people," said Siri. "They didn't make an effort to search the caves. Shooting those four villagers would only have frightened the others into hiding. No, it seems to me they were there looking for something. And, if they found it, they burned down the village to cover their tracks."

"But what were they looking for?" said Daeng. "Intelligence information? Records? Maps? They were there for an hour, so they did a thorough search. Satsai said there were even metal detectors left behind."

"Let's think about it logically," said Siri. "It was a coordinated covert operation by a group of American soldiers acting outside—"

"But were they?"

"Were they what?"

"Were they Americans?"

"The teacher said . . ."

"The teacher said there were three American helicopters," said Daeng. "It was wartime. A lot of US hardware was shot down and repaired. How do we know who was flying the choppers?"

"You're right."

"I'm always right."

The conversation had lasted all the way to the guesthouse. They checked on the girls, who were sleeping soundly in their room on the ground floor, and they walked up the staircase to the balcony. The talisman around Siri's neck buzzed deep like a wasp with a bad cold but, to his detriment, he ignored it—put it down to a glitch in the Otherworld. He took their room key from his top pocket, unlocked the door, and pushed it open.

Boom!

There was a muddle of sounds and smells. A scream of "Siri! No!" The smell of hot flesh. Heat. Smoke. Shock. He noticed he was leaving the ground but not landing.

And next thing he knew, there he was on a bench in an airport. It was a cramped and busy place. The planes parked on the taxiway were all pink and purple. The sun had holes in it. He looked at the man sitting to his left.

"Oh, shit!" he said.

"Hello, little brother," said Civilai.

"Really?" said Siri. "I don't hear from you for months and the day I finally get to talk to you is the day I die?"

Auntie Bpoo, the spirit guide, who was dressed as a highly decorated pilot, stepped up to the microphone to announce a departure and read a list of the passengers.

"But first," she said, "a poem."

"No," Siri shouted.

All the passengers looked at him. Most of them were in a sorry state, missing this or that limb. There were one or two conditions that Siri recognized: a poisoning, a garroting, a drowning. Being a coroner would be of no value at all in limbo. Knowing how you died is of no use whatsoever once you've gone.

"Not a poem on my last day," Siri yelled at the top of his voice.

Auntie Bpoo ignored him.

Who are they? she began.
> *To display themselves*
> *These media elves?*
Celebrities
Without a skill
No role to fill.
> *Famous dull nonentities.*

"Rubbish," said Siri.

"What makes you think it's your last day, little brother?" said Civilai.

"Are you serious?" said Siri. "Look around. All these obviously dead people are about to step on a flight. The satire is intense. Auntie Bpoo's symbolic but hairy hand has never been less subtle. I'm on my way. You're here to see me off."

Civilai laughed.

"Actually, you're here to see me off," he said.

"You're already departed," said Siri.

"No, I was just sitting here on standby watching the flights leave. Every day I'd give my ticket to this or that granny in a hurry to join Granddad."

"So you aren't dead?"

"Of course I'm dead. Absolutely. Death by alcohol. No more certain way to kill yourself. But I've very kindly hung around here in the transit lounge so we could get together from time to time when you crossed over. Tell a few jokes. Reminisce a bit. Solve the problems of the world over glasses of something tasteless that looks like rum. We sit on a one-dimensional log and look over what I remember the Mekong to look like."

"What's wrong with that?"

"To tell the truth, Siri, I'm not having that many new

experiences over here. I'm not padding out my resumé at all. I've been living my death vicariously through you. The spirits you can talk to are the ones that refuse, point-blank, to admit we're not around anymore. Bpoo will never move on. Some of these old farts have been here in the transit lounge forever. Look at that poor bastard."

Siri followed Civilai's gaze to a dusty old man in a thread-bare navy blue uniform with arrows sticking out of it.

"All ages and types ready to hit the road," said Civilai.

Two young boys of about twelve sat in the front row. They were identical down to the shoes and the pigtails. One had his arm over the other's shoulder. Auntie Bpoo called the flight number and the boys stood and turned to face each other. One boy's nose was bleeding. The other smiled and wiped away the blood with his scarf, then handed it to the brother as a keepsake.

"Sorry to have kept you waiting," said Bpoo over the loudspeaker. "You can board now."

Only one boy was leaving. The other watched his brother exit the lounge and walk to the pink and purple airplane and when he was out of sight the other twin sat. Without warning, his head split in half like a fresh water-melon and Bpoo called for a cleaning crew to mop up the debris.

"That was messy," said Siri.

"I'm ready to board, too," said Civilai. "There's peace at the end of this. I thought I'd stay to make you happy but you aren't. Like you, I'm just clutching at straws. My being on call won't make you any more content. Best to be off."

They stood. Hugging would have been a waste of time but they didn't need nerves or body mass to smile at each other one last time. When Civilai was the last passenger in the line to pass through the departure gate, he showed Bpoo his ID. Siri shouted from across the room, "Are you sure I'm not dead?"

"Of course you're not dead, you fool," Daeng whispered in his ear.

Siri was on a mattress. He was surrounded by people with concerned looks on their faces. The guesthouse owner and his wife were there. There was Roper and the two girls. There were one or two new guesthouse patrons he recognized, not including the guest in room 4, who remained mysterious. There was a man in the top half of a policeman's uniform with basketball shorts below, and Daeng. And seated back-to-back on the floor, handcuffed together, were two very shady characters who looked like they'd been run over by a herd of buffalo.

"Are they part of this story?" Siri asked sheepishly.

"The gentleman on the left, the one with the long greasy hair, that's Big Daddy," said Daeng.

"You don't say?"

"He didn't take the girl-power rebellion in his village very well. He came to town to get his children back and get even."

"What happened?"

"Hand grenade," said Roper. "Booby trap. Blew the door to your room right off. No idea how you survived it."

Siri looked up into the knowing eyes of Daeng and pushed himself into a sitting position.

"I'll tell you later," she whispered.

"I'm not sure you should be moving," said Roper. "We tried to find a doctor to look at you but there was nobody at the clinic."

"It's all right, Mr. Roper," said Siri. "I'm a doctor. And I think what I most need right now is a glass of rum and bed rest. Lots of both."

"Of course," said Roper.

The visitors filed out of the room and the owner returned with a bottle of rum. But Siri was already asleep. It was late when he woke up. Daeng, still dressed, was holding on to him and she was awake. He could see the small ember of a mosquito coil reflected in her eyes. A storm raged outside the room.

"I fell asleep," he said.

"Almost as soon as everyone left."

"I suddenly felt exhausted."

"You got blown up."

"Right. The details are a bit fuzzy. Would you like to talk me through it?"

She manipulated him into a spoon position. He didn't groan so she was sure there were no serious injuries.

"We came back to the guesthouse," she said. "You were unlocking the door but I noticed scratch marks around the handle. I heard a pin drop. I threw myself at you."

"As you always have."

"I need to give you a quick seminar on booby traps at this juncture," she said. "There are indoor booby traps and outdoor booby traps. If our door had opened outward, the attacker would only need to fasten a grenade to something in the room that didn't move and tie the string from the grenade pin to the inside door handle. The victim opens the door, pulls out the pin, steps inside, and *bam*! You wouldn't be here listening to this."

"I feel I need to thank the gods for indoor booby traps," said Siri.

"The indoor booby trap is more complicated," said Daeng. "You duct-tape the grenade to the floor facing away from the door. You find a length of cane or a chopstick. You tape one end to the door and the other to the grenade pin. Thus, when you open the door, you push the stick, which pushes the pin out of the grenade. This is much better for us."

"Why?"

"Because the doorframe takes the bulk of the force of the explosion. You feel the blast. It knocks you off your feet but you're not hit by twenty kilograms of teak."

"Just by a flying wife."

"Exactly."

"I assume you've learned this from experience."

"Terrorist school."

"Where do the two thugs fit in?" Siri asked.

"Ah, right. This might be a little violent for your taste."

"I'll chance it."

"There we were on the ground, you because you'd been hit by the blast, me because I'd thrown myself at you. You were unconscious. I was winded and I needed to take a couple of minutes to pull myself together. It was dark out there. In fact, the only light was from the room curtain, which was smoldering. But it was enough to see this dark shape climbing over the balcony railing, followed by another. I've found that curious onlookers usually take the stairs so I knew these two ninjas were up to no good. One of them was holding a machete. He walked over to you and put two fingers on your neck to see if you were alive. He raised his weapon. He was there to finish you off, then me, no doubt. As you know, Siri, I still have a few moves."

"Oh, I know."

"And I recall someone famous once saying 'the best form of attack is to run screaming in the opposite direction.'"

"It was in Sun Tzu's *The Art of War*," said Siri.

"So I got to my feet and ran screaming. As I expected, both of them gave chase. I was the one they were after, you see? No offense intended."

"I should be grateful."

"It was lucky I wasn't dressed for a night out. Wearing a *phasin* would have made everything very difficult. I'd gone with the unflattering fisherman's pants and a peasant jacket. That fashion choice gave me a few options. When I was sure the first of the thugs was close enough, I fell forward onto my left side, which left my right leg free to place a kick upward between the man's legs."

"Ouch."

"I knew he'd be busy counting his testicles for a while so I turned my attention to thug two, alias Big Daddy. He was surprised to see his accomplice on the ground. He charged at me waving his machete, shouting 'Ghrrarr' or something like that. I knew from experience that would-be assassins who make wild animal noises when they attack lack confidence and are probably low on swordsmanship skills. Plus I knew he was stupid. Why else would they come to finish us off with knives after they'd woken up half the town with a grenade? Why not bring a gun? In fact, why bother with the grenade at all? Just shoot us, why don't they?"

"Sound advice which I'm pleased they didn't have access to," said Siri.

"I could only assume they wanted it to be dramatic," said Daeng. "A lesson to anyone who messes with Big Daddy. Being blown up and hacked to pieces makes a statement."

"Loud and clear."

"Now, despite all this thought I was putting into the fight, I was still on the ground and he came at me with his machete raised, using his free hand to cover his delicate parts. This left him a little unbalanced. I feint right. That's where he aims the blade. I flip to my left. The blade skims my hip and sinks into the coconut wood of the balcony. He's totally off-balance now. I trip him with my lower legs, he lets go of the machete and falls backwards and I'm on him."

"Like a cougar," said Siri.

"More like . . . well, all right. Cougar's fine. As I don't want to damage my fingers, I beat him around the face and neck with the heels of my hands, left, right, left, right. Blood everywhere. Teeth flying. But ninja one is back on his feet. He's staggering towards me, fist raised. He hasn't learned anything in those thirty seconds. I roll to my right and land another kick on his groin."

"Ooh."

"He screams and drops like a sack of walnuts and I follow up by rearranging his face. Daddy is in the crawl position, blinded by the blood. I yank the machete from the plank and I hit him twice with the handle. He drops flat on his stomach. And that was when the guesthouse manager and his wife and some of the new guests appeared."

"You don't have a mark on you?" said Siri.

"I knew you wouldn't want me to spoil my looks."

They lay for a long time counting each other's heartbeats, listening to the ceiling lizard politics.

"Siri," she said at last.

"Yes, my warrior queen?"

"When the grenade went off you disappeared for a few seconds."

"I know. It was about twenty minutes on the other side."

"Did you see Civilai?"

"He sends his love. We won't be hanging out together anymore."

"I'm sorry."

"It's fine. I have you."

They were woken next morning by the sound of the whirring helicopter rotor. Roper had told them amid the chaos of the night before that he felt it would be best to get himself and the girls out of Thakhek as soon as possible. He'd invited Siri and Daeng to go with him but they opted to stay because things were starting to get interesting at last.

"What time is it?" Siri asked.

Daeng looked at the alarm clock.

"Seven," she said.

"I thought we'd have time to say goodbye to the girls," said Siri.

"Me too. Never mind. We'll see them when we get back, and after the drama last night I'd feel more comfortable if they were in Vientiane away from the traffickers. Are you still up for another trip along the love tunnel?"

"Of course," said Siri. "Isn't that why we're still here? Why would you ask?"

"Because you were almost blown to bits last night. I thought you might need a day to recuperate."

"You're talking to Siri the Invincible, don't forget. At our age, every day has to be seized. But I do have one small request."

"Yes?"

"I was hoping we might take a little detour before heading for the cave."

"Somewhere nice?"

"Thailand," said Siri.

Daeng raised her eyebrows. "Missing your girlfriend already?" she said.

CHAPTER SEVENTEEN
Yokai

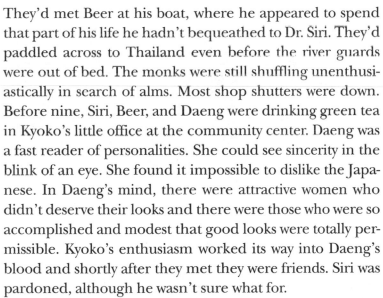

They'd met Beer at his boat, where he appeared to spend that part of his life he hadn't bequeathed to Dr. Siri. They'd paddled across to Thailand even before the river guards were out of bed. The monks were still shuffling unenthusiastically in search of alms. Most shop shutters were down. Before nine, Siri, Beer, and Daeng were drinking green tea in Kyoko's little office at the community center. Daeng was a fast reader of personalities. She could see sincerity in the blink of an eye. She found it impossible to dislike the Japanese. In Daeng's mind, there were attractive women who didn't deserve their looks and there were those who were so accomplished and modest that good looks were totally permissible. Kyoko's enthusiasm worked its way into Daeng's blood and shortly after they met they were friends. Siri was pardoned, although he wasn't sure what for.

"Look at my eyes," said Kyoko. "They are the eyes of somebody who doesn't sleep anymore. I've been through all the files you gave me. I've read and reread the diary. I've tried to forgive Hiro for the atrocities he was party to in Manchuria but I cannot. I tried to give him the benefit of the doubt that he must have written the way he did because he was afraid someone would find his diary, but I could not. I was struggling to find a reason to like him. I wondered whether he had some coded system to hide his true feelings; something hidden in the text. So I started to analyze the Japanese language."

"And?" said Daeng.

"I found nothing. Every Japanese page was clinical and unemotional. I was about to give up but then I did make a discovery, not in the Japanese pages but in the Lao segment. I'm still attempting to read everything, but what intrigued me was that there was no mention of Hiro's commanding officer or his unit in the official files, yet they feature so prominently in the Lao half."

"I may be able to explain that," said Siri. "We met a Japanese deserter in Thakhek by the name of Yuki-*san*. He knew Hiro. He believed that Hiro and his team came too early to be listed in the documents. In fact, they might have been responsible for keeping the records, which would be reason enough to write themselves out of the history."

"That's quite interesting," said Kyoko. "But I don't think so. In fact, I know for certain that his unit did not exist."

The visitors sat forward on their seats.

"Tell us," said Daeng.

"Look at this," said Kyoko.

She removed a roll of papers from her bag and opened them on the desk. The pages contained columns of Japanese characters that meant nothing to the Lao or to Beer.

"My instincts were sparked by the names of Toshi's coworkers and of Toshi himself, for that matter," she said. "He introduces them all phonetically using Lao letters, but he very kindly adds the Japanese characters—that we call *kanji*—in parentheses. I might have ignored them but for the fact that most of the names are unusual. Of course they could all be the names of Japanese men. But imagine a list of Frenchmen. You'd expect to find one or two Martins, a Thomas or two, a Petit; traditional names with one or two unusual names like Quint thrown in. But you wouldn't expect to find ten Frenchmen with bizarre names on the same list. So I wrote down here the original *kanji* spelling for each of the men in Toshi's unit. All of them were completely odd."

"How do you mean?" Siri asked.

"Well, for example, 'Kyo' in my name could be written using any one of twenty different *kanji* with twenty different meanings. You wouldn't expect your mother to choose a horrible name for her daughter, so you'd look for the meaning amongst the lovely *kanji* like 'reverent' or 'respectful.' But the mothers of the men in Toshi's unit must have hated their sons. Either that or Toshi was trying to tell us something. Of course it all comes down to interpretation, but here is a list of the meanings of the names Toshi gave to his team."

She pointed to the names one by one.

"If we are to believe the *kanji*, Major General Dorari Momoyotsu might very well have been 'a blasphemous mad donkey with four spleens,'" she said. "Lance Corporal Hokofugu Hama is 'a leftover fish with a tiny banana.' Warrant Officer Ukabane Orimimi is 'a lying corpse with blocked ears.' Oshiira's 'a mute pain in the arse who lost his vegetables,' Tetsukimo is 'a licentious being with a gall bladder like noodles,' and Konko 'a spittle of old cannabis roots.' Our friend Toshi obviously had tremendous fun selecting the most insulting names. You see? As I say, it could have just been a joke, his way of making fun of his fellow soldiers or of protecting them. But I didn't think so. The only positive impression I had of him from the earlier diary in Japanese was how methodical he was. There had to be something else.

"Look at my lists. These are the alternative ways we could write the names of the men in Toshi's unit. Some have up to thirty options. At first, I didn't know what I was looking for. I looked through the lists trying to match this or that *kanji*, and it was in the *kanji* of Jame Nomishige that I had a breakthrough. I saw something I recognized. I'm from Tokushima and our local folklore has a character called Yama Jiji. Japan has many cautionary tales to keep our children in line. If you don't eat your vegetables the carrot monster will come and bite off your feet; that type of thing. And over the years these demons took on form and became monsters in the fairy tales. Yama Jiji is a demon who knows exactly what you're thinking. You can't keep a secret from him. I used to be petrified by stories about him. So when I saw the words 'Yama' and 'Jiji' in my list of possible hidden *kanji* names for Captain Jame Nomishige, it seemed to be too much of a coincidence. At first I laughed. It was like finding Santa in one column and Claus in another: a funny coincidence.

"But I continued my search and, remarkably, in the columns of another name, Taigou the dog, I found *kanji* that spelled out Okami. This too rang a bell. I phoned my *sensei* in Bangkok—and I must tell you she has started to look forward to my calls—and she immediately identified Senbiki Okami as being another demon. Toshi's faithful dog is an evil spirit. She gave me a list of all the *yokai* she could remember."

"*Yokai?*" said Daeng.

"Yes, they're devils. They are the many demons that haunt our sleep. With her suggestions I quickly found one more, Aka Name, in the name of Oshiira, the toilet cleaner. My *sensei* asked me to fax her my lists so she could save me time in my search. In fact I knew she was as addicted to the puzzle as I was."

"So Toshi was stationed in Thakhek with a gang of devils?" said Siri.

Given his own run-ins with malevolent spirits, Siri didn't see it as at all strange that a unit of Japanese soldiers should include creatures from the dark side.

"What about Toshi himself?" asked Daeng.

"I couldn't find any hidden devils in his name," said Kyoko.

"But he's hanging out with lowlifes," said Daeng. "He must be one of them."

"Not necessarily," said Siri. "We know Hiro exists as Toshi. Perhaps he gave his unit mates nicknames to protect their real identities."

"And he gave them all devil names?" said Daeng.

"I suppose it might have been his private joke," said Kyoko. "I'll see what my *sensei* says and I'll let you know."

She poured them all tea. Beer helped himself to more cookies.

"It's funny," said Kyoko. "When I first met Dr. Siri I knew he was the type of man who'd be married to a remarkable woman. I'm always right about these things."

If there had been even an ice cube of doubt in Daeng's mind that Kyoko was extraordinary it melted right there and then.

In the boat to the caves, Siri and Daeng didn't bother to

shout above the roar of the engine because they were both lost in their own thoughts. Siri was imagining Toshi's life in Laos. He had decided to give some credence to the fact that Toshi had changed the names of his friends and himself as a sort of protection. Perhaps they had something to fear. He was based so far from the fighting it would have been easy to forget there was a war at all. He obviously enjoyed his time here. Perhaps there was a girlfriend, but there was also a wife and children back home he'd only mentioned once in the entire diary. Perhaps he had deserted from the army and moved into the jungle. Many had.

But Siri felt the key was not in what they knew already but in what they did not. It lay in those missing years before the diary began, somewhere around Toshi's arrival in Indo-china. The five pages torn from the diary. The end of the love tunnel. And, in his soul, Siri knew there was more to be learned about the tragic day at the end of the invasion when twenty Japanese officers killed themselves for honor.

To fill some of those gaps, Siri had asked Beer to stay on the Thai side and contact Cindy at the US embassy in Cambodia. He was to ask whether she'd been able to find any records pertaining to Hiro Uenobu, the pilot. He should also return to Kyoko's office later to see whether her *sensei* had been able to put more names to demons. It was just as well that Beer felt as comfortable in Thailand as he did in Laos. He had friends on both sides. But there was another reason Siri preferred Beer not accompany them to Sawan on this occasion. He was certain their Vietnamese guide and the teacher, Satsai, knew each other, and that the relationship was not warm enough for either of them to admit it. On this trip to confront the teacher, Siri didn't want any added complications.

Daeng was in a world of her own.

"What are you thinking?" Siri shouted.

"Nothing," yelled Daeng.

"Not true."

"Perhaps I'm wondering how I can replace Civilai in your life," she said. "Your jokes that only old men with a French education can understand. Your cultural references that we country Lao are baffled by. Your intellects. Your world knowledge. I could never match him for all that."

Siri took her hand and held it to his chest.

"Daeng, do you really not know how vital you are to my well-being? I can't count how many times you've saved my life, reined in my insanity, made light of my senility. Surely you know what cancels out every one of those superficial moments shared by two cranky old men."

"Noodles?"

"Love, Daeng. Love."

And to the amusement of a grinning boatman, Siri gave Daeng the type of kiss that nobody along the banks of the river would ever forget.

The fat woman at the loom still had a cheroot dangling between her lips.

"He's at the school," she shouted.

"Isn't it the weekend?" Daeng asked, not certain herself after all the goings-on.

"He likes to be there just as much when the kids aren't there as when they are," she said. "It's peaceful up on the hill."

Siri and Daeng followed the track. In Thakhek it was a muggy, hot day as the clouds gathered for another assault, but at the end of the tunnel there was a coolness. There was no breeze, just a drop in temperature of several degrees. Daeng breathed in the climate. They walked up to the schoolhouse. Satsai was at his desk mending what looked like a cordless metal cutter contraption. There was as much oil on the teacher's shirt as on the machine.

"Knock knock," said Siri.

Satsai looked up and smiled. If he was surprised to see Siri and Daeng he didn't show it.

"I don't suppose either of you have engineering degrees?" he said.

"Afraid we were born in an age before technology," said Siri.

He and Daeng sat at the miniature desk. Satsai brushed all the motor parts into a heap and wiped his hands on a rag.

"I had a feeling you'd be back," he said.

"Instinct?" said Daeng.

"Common sense," said Satsai. "You came all the way to Thakhek to solve your mystery. You aren't the types to give up. When I told you about the helicopter attack I could see a light behind your eyes. Even if that invasion wasn't connected to your Japanese pilot story, I could see I'd fueled your imaginations. You are adventurers."

"Ah, but you know it is connected to our pilot story," said Siri.

"I do?"

"Yes," said Daeng. "We know for certain that Hiro was here in your village. We assume he came here during his leave time. You weren't absolutely honest in having us believe you'd never heard of him. Your village is the connection we were looking for. We don't know if his presence caused the helicopter raid but my husband is most unforgiving towards coincidences."

"Hate 'em," said Siri.

Satsai looked up at the tight thatch of the roof. Like all the other structures, it had been assembled with care and love. He sighed.

"It's because you were sent the diary that I feel I should tell you what you want to know," he said. "The account you gave me yesterday about Hiro working in Thakhek with a group of misfits wasn't true. He wasn't there."

"You mean he wasn't there under that name?" said Siri.

"No, I mean physically he was never a part of any occupational force based in Thakhek. He'd been decommissioned a long time before."

"Damn," said Siri. "I think it's story time."

"It's a long story," said Satsai. "I think you'll want to sit somewhere more comfortable."

CHAPTER EIGHTEEN
Major Depression

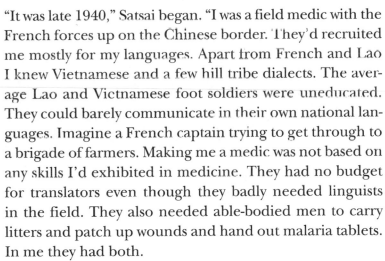

"It was late 1940," Satsai began. "I was a field medic with the French forces up on the Chinese border. They'd recruited me mostly for my languages. Apart from French and Lao I knew Vietnamese and a few hill tribe dialects. The average Lao and Vietnamese foot soldiers were uneducated. They could barely communicate in their own national languages. Imagine a French captain trying to get through to a brigade of farmers. Making me a medic was not based on any skills I'd exhibited in medicine. They had no budget for translators even though they badly needed linguists in the field. They also needed able-bodied men to carry litters and patch up wounds and hand out malaria tablets. In me they had both.

"The Japanese had arrived some two months earlier. They'd taken advantage of France's distractions in Europe and lied their way into the French-controlled region in order to stop the trains heading through to China loaded with weapons and supplies. The friction along the border was substantial and the French fortresses were on constant alert for an inevitable Japanese offensive. When I arrived, the two armies were truly strange bedfellows. There was no official conflict between the Japanese and those they called the 'white devils'—most of whom were actually Vietnamese—so the French had no choice but to allow the invaders to use their services and help themselves to supplies.

"The first I heard of Major Hiro was from the Vietnamese medics in my unit. They said a Japanese officer had gone berserk. He'd spent the day with his battalion as usual, filing reports, recording the movement of equipment. At exactly five P.M. he took off all his clothes, climbed to the top of an old unoccupied French machine gun tower, and started yelling at the top of his voice. They'd dragged him down and taken him to a medical ward in a small French hospital. It was there that I met him: a crazy man. He was sedated but still shouting in a language nobody could follow. I'm not an adherent of the spirit world but to me it sounded as if he was possessed. He spat and snarled and drooled and had to be tied to the bunk to protect the other patients. He was unnerving everyone so eventually they had to put a gag on him. His commander wanted to send him back to Japan but he was in no condition to travel.

"They assigned me to him. I was supposed to feed him. For two days he just spat everything out. He needed calming down so I started to talk to him. I didn't have much Japanese at the time so I spoke in Lao. I knew he didn't understand but it didn't seem to matter. After a few days he'd let me feed him. He seemed to relax with me. I felt good about it. It was like . . . like I was taming a wild beast. Three weeks passed and still they were haggling about when to ship him home. And then this general arrived. His name was Shosen Umiji and he'd been Hiro's commanding officer in China. He had a very simplistic approach to mental health. He came to see Hiro just that one time, looked down his nose at him and spat on the pillow. He turned to his aid and said something I vaguely understood. I was sitting at the back of the room and I memorized the comment. The French had a Japanese translator and I asked him later what had been said. The translator told me, 'Major Hiro will have to die on the battlefield.'

"The general had decided to avoid embarrassment for the family and the nation by having Hiro put down. I was astounded at how lightly he'd made the decision. I wasn't a friend of Hiro. He was a disaster; a cocktail of hateful sounds and looks. There was a devil in his eyes even when he was relaxed. But with me by his side he remained calm. In a way he had selected me. Something told me I should help him."

"So you sprang him from the hospital," said Daeng.

She and Siri were so engrossed in the story it took a while for them to notice the refreshments on the desk beside theirs. Someone had walked up from the village with three cut coconuts with straws and spoons to cut out the meat. The coconut water was surprisingly chill. Nobody had asked for or ordered anything. It was just one more nicety in a nice place: the type of village that used to exist everywhere.

"I suppose I sprang us both," said Satsai. "I hated being there. Life education can only go so far before it becomes torment. I hated the French and the Japanese and I missed my home. There was death all around me. So one day I put my ID card in the pocket of a corpse that had no head and I took his papers. I stole a horse and cart, put Hiro on the back, and headed south. Even after I'd untied him he came with me with no drama whatsoever. He'd stopped his ranting and his anger subsided. He wasn't less insane, just a different type of crazy. He dribbled and stared ahead at something only he could see. I dressed us both in peasants' clothes and we were largely ignored at roadblocks where they assumed our brains were as empty as the cart. The only possession we had was a small knapsack that was supposed to contain Hiro's personal belongings, although I never opened it. I'd blocked it inside the wooden seat along with his uniform and helmet and I forgot all about it until much later.

"We stopped for a week here and there on our way to the Lao border, living off the land. One day he turned up at the campfire with his diary in his hand. He'd taken it from under the seat. I didn't even realize he knew where his kit was. He showed it to me. I couldn't understand anything but it was beautifully written. I wasn't sure what he wanted me to do. He'd point to this or that and I realized he wanted me to tell him the Lao words. So that's when I started to teach him Lao. We began with the basics: name, where he came from, age, et cetera. I'd write it in sand or mud and he'd copy it into his diary. It was incredible how fast he picked it up. I guess all those nights in the hospital with me speaking to him in Lao language had stuck somehow. He ate it up. He was like an alien coming to earth with only a brief time to understand everything. I would give him a phrase and do my best to explain the meaning and he'd nod and write. On the journey we picked up a notebook and pencil for me and we'd communicate through Lao writing. I suppose you could say we became pen friends. But from that night we fled the hospital till he left us, I never heard him say a word."

"In all the time you were together?" said Daeng.

"Not a single utterance," said Satsai.

"And you brought him here," said Siri.

"It was the only safe place I knew. My family liked him. They understood. The war had crushed him just as it had destroyed our country. The weight of it had been too much for him. It was a month in my village before he lost his multiple nervous tics. His hands stopped shaking. He no longer drooled. He used school notebooks to express himself. The village women taught him embroidery and cooking. He read the few Lao language books we had. His diary became his private world. I didn't ask him what he was writing there. I hoped that one day he might show me.

"Since our return, we hadn't gone into Thakhek town. Before the war I would go often. As you can see, Sawan is geographically close but ideologically very far away. There was a lot of Japanese activity in the town. I thought it safer for him to stay here. If anyone came from civilization we had the caves to retreat to. But we weren't bothered that much. Someone from the village would go in for supplies and he'd tell us what was going on. There was a large troop presence by then, new buildings going up, tent suburbs, roads being blasted through the mountains. Hiro would listen to all this news like a dog with its tail wagging and he'd run off to write his diary. But I knew he wanted to go there to see for himself. I was against it but he was determined. He would dress like a bum, dirty his skin, and resummon the facial expressions from the early days of our journey. He'd take the boat through the tunnel and wander around Thakhek ignored and avoided by everyone. He'd be gone for a day or two but always came back and he'd go straight to his diary."

"He let you read it?" Daeng asked.

"Eventually he became proud to show it to me," said the teacher. "And he was such a brilliant writer. I loved his fictional stories about Toshi, his alter ego. And I wanted to believe they were a gift to me."

"Did you send the diary to us?" Siri asked.

"No. I really don't know how it got to you and I don't know who was asking for your help. I haven't seen it since '75."

"How often did Hiro leave the village?" Daeng asked.

"For his clandestine trips into Thakhek, he'd go about once a month. But his missions took longer."

"His missions?" said Daeng.

"Yes. He arrived at the school one day in his uniform with his helmet under his arm. It was the first time I'd ever seen him dressed up. He saluted and went down to the dock and he vanished. We were—or perhaps I should say I was—frantic. I didn't know where he'd gone. I wanted to put his photograph up on trees and offer a reward for his return the way the French do for lost dogs. I suppose I hadn't realized how functional he'd become, how independent. He'd learned French and Vietnamese."

"But he didn't speak," said Siri.

"I believe he could understand both and had learned to read and write. He'd also taught himself carpentry, plumbing, agriculture. He improved our fishing system. We had always been poor but Hiro did all he could to improve our lot. It was only to be expected he'd leave one day. I was afraid that was the day."

"Did anything significant happen leading up to that day?" Siri asked.

"We'd had an outbreak of diphtheria," said the teacher.

"As I'm sure you know, it's a highly contagious condition. Some of our kids died. Many were sick. We'd take them into Thakhek but the little hospital was ill-equipped. What drugs they had were priced beyond our means."

"And that was when Hiro disappeared," said Daeng. "You know, there was a page in the diary written on October second, 1943?"

"I remember," said Satsai. "I read it when he came back. He'd been gone eleven days. I don't know how he got to Lang Son or what he did or how he got back. He wouldn't tell me. But he had done something miraculous. A medical unit arrived in the village two days after his return. They treated all our children and left us medication. It was unbelievable."

"Teacher Satsai," said Daeng.

"Yes?"

"From my memory, the diary entry written in October began with the words 'Hello, my darling. I miss you and the children.' Or something like that. We thought Hiro was writing it to his wife, but he wasn't, was he?"

Satsai looked at Daeng and gave his answer some thought.

"No," said Satsai. "He wasn't married."

"The children were at your school and the darling . . ."

Again, he appeared to be weighing his reply.

"Was me," said Satsai. "I'm sorry."

"What on earth for?" said Daeng.

"I don't want to tarnish your impression of Hiro."

"Then you obviously haven't had enough time to understand my husband and me. Everything you tell us about Hiro makes us like him more."

"I suppose I'd loved him ever since our wonderful

journey in the pony cart together," said Satsai. The visitors' reaction seemed to liberate him. His face became animated and he smiled as he spoke. "He was unique, inquisitive, intelligent. I was proud to be with him and I wanted him to feel the same about me. But our trip home had been innocent. I had no intention of taking advantage of a man with such a troubled mind. When I read his diary entry calling me his darling I thought it was just a joke, but still it filled me with joy. It hadn't occurred to me he would know I was a homosexual. I thought I had disguised it so well."

"Your trips to Thakhek before the war?" said Siri.

"The French were obliging and passionate in many ways," said Satsai. "I wonder if Hiro could smell the desperation on me. I was so bent on keeping my evil identity a secret from my parents. Thakhek had been my outlet. There were cross-cultural gatherings at the old French colonial house at the foot of the hill for like-minded souls."

"That was a busy place," said Siri. "Was Beer one of your cross-cultural liaisons?"

Satsai looked at him with surprise.

"Surgeon's intuition," said Siri. "Was his wound connected to his inclination?"

A look on the teacher's face suggested he'd given up a lot already, but that the honesty was doing him good.

"Beer thought he might enlarge his experience of the world by serving the Japanese as he had the French," said Satsai. "But he ran into the wrong officer at the wrong end of a bottle of *shochu*, a last-minute attack of shame while holding a *samurai* sword. Beer was lucky his head was still attached to his shoulders the next morning."

"But meanwhile, back at Hiro's return from Lang Son," said Siri.

"I read his diary entry and we laughed and there was no pretense. It was as if we'd always been lovers. My black-and-white existence took on all the colors of the rainbow. Everyone in the village knew what we had together and nobody criticized us. In fact they were happy for us. I wish I'd shared my secret sooner. Hiro was my constant companion. We shared everything from then on. I've never known such a love."

The teacher leaned back against his chair and breathed heavily. One more burden had been off-loaded.

"And what did he bring back from Vietnam?" asked Daeng.

"The treasure?" said Satsai. "He never did say. I assumed he'd returned with money and had used it all to pay for the medicine."

Siri and Daeng exchanged a glance. They'd heard Satsai's first lie.

"Do you have any photographs from those days?" Daeng asked.

"There were a lot," said the teacher. "We didn't have a camera of our own but some of our graduates did well, traveled, and came home to visit relatives. They had cameras. They sent us copies but everything was destroyed in the raid."

"Every photograph?" said Siri.

Satsai pondered for a while, weighing up his next move.

"All but this," he said, reaching into his back pocket and pulling out a cheap plastic wallet. It was clearly not stuffed with money. He reached into one of the compartments and pulled out a photograph folded in half. He opened it carefully, like a librarian unpacking the Dead Sea Scrolls. It had obviously seen many such openings. The only thing holding the two halves together was an age-browned strip of tape on the back. The picture was almost entirely sepia from years of back-pocket sweat. He laid it down on his desk and Siri and Daeng stepped up to examine it. It had been taken in the village square. The focus was surprisingly good. Some twelve children of various sizes stood at the foot of the village pillar and two handsome men stood on either side of it. One was Satsai, as adorable in his twenties as Daeng had imagined. The other, a little shorter, cropped hair, round-rimmed glasses, was Hiro. Both men were smiling, not the grins thrust forward for photographs, but actual happy smiles. Siri was overjoyed to put a face to the writer.

"When was this taken?" he asked.

"About two weeks after he returned from that first mission," said Satsai. "The children in this photo would have been dead if it weren't for the medicine Hiro conjured up."

"Would you mind if I borrowed this picture for a day or two to show around in Thakhek?" asked Siri.

Satsai looked shocked at the thought, but then seemed to reprimand himself mentally.

"If you think it would help," he said. "But I would like it back when you're finished with it. It's the only picture of him I have."

"And what of the second mission?" Daeng asked.

Satsai stared out over the roofs of the village.

"It was the day before the Japanese surrender," he said. "Nobody was expecting it to happen so suddenly, or at least nobody in this region. The rumors were that things weren't going so well for the Japanese, but you always got

the feeling they'd fight to the death. You couldn't picture them with their hands in the air. Garu, the boatman,
was our telegraph. He'd come in with supplies or returnees and he'd sit on the dock and tell us the news from
Thakhek. Around that time the gossip was all Japanese. A
lot of senior officers had arrived under the leadership of
General Shosen. There was obviously something brewing.
There were several thousand troops stationed there and
twenty or so Zeros parked beside the landing strip. They'd
been refitted with additional fuel tanks and canisters of
high explosives to make a bigger mess when they flew into
American battleships. The generals had ordered a lot of
booze and food so there was some type of celebration that
night. Nobody in town knew what they were celebrating
but it was ironic timing. The next day, probably all bloated
and hung over, they'd go to the radio and hear the emper-
or's speech and bang goes the lot of them."

"So Hiro left on August fourteenth?" said Siri.

"That's right."

"And again with no warning?" Siri asked.

"Well, he was in his uniform again. I was having an
afternoon siesta but I was awoken by the creak of footsteps on the bamboo slats. I was drowsy. Hiro lay down
behind me and held me tight, like a mother protecting
her child. I could feel his heartbeat thumping against my
back. His uniform smelled of mothballs and the material
was unsuitable for the tropics so we were both sweating.
But the warmth surrounded me like a womb and I fell
asleep again. When I woke up, he and our only motorboat
were gone."

"And that was the last you heard of him," said Daeng.

"Yes," said Satsai.

Daeng and Siri could feel the same loss they knew still weighed heavily on the teacher's heart.

"Any idea where he went?" asked Siri.

"No."

"And he left the diary with you?" asked Daeng.

"Yes, he did. I can't tell you how many times I read through it. I even studied Japanese so I could understand the early entries. I was shocked, Doctor. I have to tell you. It was no wonder he lost his mind after all the atrocities he witnessed in China. No man with a heart and a conscience could have come through those years unscathed."

"So you don't think he endorsed the atrocities?"

"Of course he didn't. It was China that drove him insane. He hated everything about the invasion. But he understood it was necessary to document what happened there. The only way he could do that without having his records confiscated and destroyed was to describe it all favorably. He was convinced nobody would believe the events of Nanjing. He once wrote in our notebook conversations: *The best way to disguise a sin is to redecorate it as a blessing.* I didn't know what he meant until I read his diary. Everything he wrote pointed to exact locations and gave detailed statistics all presented with hurrahs and hoorays. His superiors would see nothing but a patriot in his writings. It was a work of genius. And I thought it was lost."

"Wait, when was the last time you saw it?" Daeng asked.

"I didn't check it religiously," said Satsai, "but I'm certain it hadn't been removed from the wooden chest I kept it in under the floor. I had it wrapped in tinfoil to keep the mice out of it. I'm sure it was in my house the day of the raid."

"And the village was burned down," said Daeng.

"To the ground."

"Nothing survived?"

"Not a thing."

"Then somebody on that raid must have found the diary," said Daeng.

"This is why I married her," said Siri.

"What we don't know is whether they picked it up incidentally along with other paperwork . . ." she continued.

". . . or whether it was the diary they were looking for," said Siri.

"Which means we might have to take another look at that diary with fresh eyes," said Daeng.

They were all walking together to the jetty. Daeng and Siri were drunk with information and they needed to sit down and organize their thoughts. Garu, the perennial boatman, was stretched out under a palm tree.

"How do you know it was Americans who destroyed your village?" Daeng asked.

"You mean apart from the helicopters?" said Satsai. "We all saw those."

"Yes, I'm sure you did. But you were fleeing to the caves. You didn't really have time to listen to their accents."

"There was an eyewitness who survived without hiding in the caves," said Satsai.

"Can we talk to him before we go?" said Daeng.

"Her," said Satsai and turned around and pointed to the fat lady at the loom.

"I was in a tree," said the fat woman. "Of course I didn't have these pigs back then weighing me down." She hoisted one breast in each hand to demonstrate their weight.

The visitors were sitting on her veranda eating home-made *khao lam* sticky rice in bamboo that was chewy and tasted like pure sugar.

"In fact I was what you might call lithe," she said. "But you know how it is. Find yourself an attractive husband and let yourself go. Not that time did him any favors either. Bald as a blister he turned out to be. If only I'd—"

"So you were in a tree," said Siri.

"That one there, in fact," she said, pointing to a hand-some willow that overhung the river. Not one of its limbs would have supported her weight now. "I scurried up there as soon as the shooting and the screaming started. Two of 'em came this way to secure the jetty and make sure no one got in or out through the tunnel."

"You heard them say that?" asked Daeng.

"No," said the woman. "I'm just assuming that was why they were standing on the jetty with their guns pointed at the tunnel. Truth is they didn't say a word. Just chewed gum."

"But you were close enough to see their faces?" said Siri.

"Didn't get a great look," she said. "They were all wear-ing those fancy reflecting sunglasses and had their hats pulled down over their faces. But I knew what American uniforms looked like. Saw enough of them in the comics."

"So there was nothing that made you suspicious?" asked Siri.

"You mean apart from Americans flying a hundred-odd kilometers to shoot us and burn our village down? That was pretty suspicious."

"I mean something more . . . subtle," said Siri. "Some-thing that seemed out of place to you."

"No . . . well, perhaps there was something."

"What?"

"Their uniforms were brand-spanking new. Could see the folds. But both of them had their trousers held up with rope. You'd think if a government could afford four million dollars a week to kill communists, the least they could do is spring for nice leather belts, wouldn't you?"

CHAPTER NINETEEN
The Belts Tighten

Siri and Daeng had the foresight to bring flashlights on this journey through the caves. They could enjoy the cathedral-like chambers and the twinkly crystal candelabras. They could forget that bats carry the top twenty lethal airborne diseases and that they'd probably die from inhaling bat feces so they could see the Tunnel of Love for what it was: a fairy tale. It was the ideal opening setting for Siri's movie. If his coproducer Civilai had been there they'd have already plotted out the storyboard and worked out the camera angles. But Civilai was off in Nirvana auditioning angels and Siri had to learn to put his movie career on hold. But what a setting.

Back in daylight, he sat close to Daeng on the longboat and they exchanged a smile as the light patter of river spray hit their cheeks. He was sure his wife had worked everything out, as had he.

"The diary was not only therapy," he yelled above the engine noise. "Hiro had set out to chronicle the awful things he'd seen. He was a sensitive man and he was surrounded by countrymen he couldn't relate to—couldn't understand. He had to find a way to reset his expectations. He needed to find good Japanese, but they didn't exist in his world. So he had no choice but to create them in his diary. And for five years he lived in that diary world. He saw only goodness there. And gently he came back to earth."

"But he took that first gamble," said Daeng. "He left his safety zone and went all the way back to the Chinese border, where he'd lost his mind. What was he doing there? After shielding himself from evil for so long, why would he take a chance of a relapse?"

"The treasure," said Siri. "The kids in the village were dying. They needed money for medicine. Hiro had access to something—some money source he'd squirreled away while he was in control: something that stuck there in his mind and was reactivated by the disaster in his village. The war proper still hadn't come to the region, so he went back there in peacetime. He recovered his treasure, brought it back to the village, and used it to solve their problem."

"But Satsai said he didn't know what Hiro had done to achieve it," said Daeng.

"It had to be money," said Siri. "Back then, you could only ever solve problems with money."

"What I really want to know is where Hiro went on that last day; the day of the surrender," said Daeng. "He couldn't have known it was going to happen. But something he'd heard was important enough for him to leave the village and never go back."

She looked up at the sweeping hillsides and a landscape that hadn't changed for hundreds of years.

"Do you think Hiro loved Satsai?" she said.

"It had to be something the teacher asked himself every day," said Siri.

"I'd like to believe that love finds its own level," said Daeng. "That whatever mental condition Hiro was suffering from didn't affect his natural instincts. I'd like to think that the love Hiro felt for Satsai transcended all the short-circuiting and was as natural as hunger and fear. I'd like to believe that Hiro loved Satsai without any hindrance."

Siri looked into eyes that never disappointed him.

"You know, I have an urge to take you back to my room right this minute," he said.

"If only we weren't on a gradually sinking boat," she said.

He took her hand and squeezed it gently and they both smiled.

"And you do realize we now have ourselves an antagonist," said Siri.

"Your Japanese visitor, Yuki-*san*."

"He claimed to be a friend of Hiro in Thakhek, which we now know was a lie."

"So how does he fit into this story?" asked Daeng.

"Well, that's just it. If he says he knew Hiro on active duty in Thakhek and the name of his commanding officer, what does that tell you?"

"Damn, he's read the diary."

"You see?" said Siri. "I told you this was all going to turn out to be fun."

Beer was waiting for them at the dock as if he had some innate boat-owner radar. They paid the boatman generously and asked him to make himself available in case they had any more work for him. They had questions but they could wait. They went to the bad noodle shop that had been miraculously transformed into a happening nightclub and bar through the magic of flashing Christmas lights. There was music, Thai pop on a cassette player, but Siri asked for it to be turned down. The other customers didn't object because there were none.

"Do you suppose this place would even be here without us?" Siri asked.

They ordered beer and quail eggs, which should have given them enough nutrients to serve in lieu of a meal. Beer, at Daeng's insistence, ordered dinner for himself. He'd teased them with promises of fascinating news from across the river. He opened his shoulder bag and took out Hiro's diary and a notebook of his own. Siri took the diary. He ran his fingers over the leather with renewed respect. He'd read it the first time as a journal documenting life in a small town during wartime. Now he could read it again as an act of therapy, an insight into the troubled mind of a broken man pulling himself back together with words. It added so many layers to Siri's love of reading.

"Kyoko-*san* didn't need it anymore," said Beer. "She said she'd found all the *yokai* hidden in the names of his men. There were ten of them including the dog. She gave me this list."

He put it on the table in front of him.

"There are three sheets of Japanese letters in lists with the *yokai* names circled. But to make it easier she's explained it phonetically here and written the characteristics of the demons."

	Private Oshiira Somai	Lance Corporal Hokofugu Hama	Colonel Konko Asatsuba	General Shosen Umiji	Major General Dorari Momoyotsu
Kanji	啞苛 蔬迷	餘鮭 芭麼	根古 蔴唾	腫脡　膿痔	怒羸 罾脾四
Meaning	A mute pain in the arse who lost his vegetables	A leftover fish with a tiny banana	A spitter of old canna-bis roots	A cured meat tumor with pus-filled hemor-rhoids	A blasphe-mous mad donkey with four spleens
Yokai	Aka Name	Amazake Baba	Nekomata	Shuten Doji	Nurari Hiyon
Known for	Hunch-back/skum eating	Disease spreading, alcoholism	Eating people	King of devils/drunken-ness, eating vir-gins	Sleaze/commander of monsters, petty theft
Origin	Dirty bathrooms every-where	Northeast Japan	Mountains but travel through cities	Shiga (from mixed parentage)	Okayama (brothels and expensive villas)

	Captain Jame Nomishige	Second Lieutenant Tetsukimo Souben	Warrant Officer Ukabane Orimimi	Corporal Yatsusuki Hokobei	Taigou the dog
Kanji	邪目 耳滋	洙膽 藻麵	迂屍　洣耳	奴犁　夸謎	大　嚙
Meaning	Evil eye and hairy ears	A licentious being with a gallbladder like noodles	A lying corpse with blocked ears	A boastful and puzzling slave with the shakes	Big bite
Yokai	Yama Jiji	Ittan Momen	Ushi Oni	Nurikabe	Senbiki Okami
Known for	Loudness, mind-reading	Flight with occasional violence	Cruelty, bad breath, inflicting curses	Being big and blocking others	Wolfish/ team player
Origin	Shikoku	Kagoshima	Western Japan	Grown from dark alleyways	Kochi

"She's a genius," said Daeng.

"The only one they couldn't find was Hiro himself," said Beer. "There were no demons to be found in the permutations of his name's *kanji*. She and her *sensei* have contacted a Japanese lecturer at Thammasat University in Bangkok who's a bit of an expert in those things."

"Any luck with the war records?" Siri asked.

"They found your Hiro Uenobu," said Beer, who had no problem tucking into a full meal and talking at the same time.

"Excellent," said Siri.

Beer turned a few pages in his notebook and read, "Born Shiga Prefecture 1906. His father had been a decorated soldier, so Hiro qualified for a scholarship at the military preparatory school and a direct line to the air academy in Saitama. He was in the top seventh percentile in all the courses he took and proved to be a brilliant flier. But the record states, 'Due to an injury sustained during training, the result of which his eyesight began to deteriorate, he is no longer considered suitable for the air corps.' They gave him the compassionate rank of major and attached him to the salvage battalion. He was never to fly again."

"Poor Hiro," said Daeng.

"They looked up the incidences of pilots being bumped up the ranks like that. It appears the training regime for young fliers was particularly brutal. Errors were often punished by beatings. There were common reports of cadets being struck about the head with wooden paddles. The training officers believed that suffering made for better pilots. As Hiro's eyesight was twenty-twenty when he entered the academy, it's probably fair to guess he got his disability as a result of overenthusiasm by a trainer. Hence the high compensatory rank."

"Really?" said Daeng. "They beat up their own pilots?"

"Spare the rod," said Siri to himself. Civilai wasn't around to complete the proverb.

"Miss Cindy's official records closely followed the dates and places Hiro wrote about in his diary," said Beer. "From Manchuria he was transferred to the Vietnamese-Chinese border in late 1940 and continued with his salvage operations there. That was when the Japanese diary entries stopped. But, according to the regional commander, there was an incident at Lang Son. The Japanese surrounded the garrison there and called on the French to surrender. As a rather odd gesture of defiance, the commanders ordered the troops to disconnect the breeze blocks from their 155-millimeter cannons and throw them in the Ky Cung River. This presumably to deny the Japanese the use of French weapons against their own men. Of course there were witnesses to this act and word got back to the Japanese. They dispatched their salvage team, headed by one Major Uenobu, to retrieve whatever had been dumped into the river.

"Now, it happened that some fifty years earlier, the French, at that time running away from the Chinese, had also dumped whatever they begrudged the advancing army into the same river at the same spot. Hiro and his team dived down into the murky water and retrieved the breeze blocks in a few hours. But embedded in the mud they found trunks and cases from that earlier debacle. According to the record it took the best part of a week to retrieve it all."

Beer read out the official invoice for that operation:

Description	Unit
Breeze blocks from current campaign	57
Large wooden chests	18
Small wooden cases	12
Personal suitcases and briefcases	66
Small arms/machine guns (unusable)	132

"The small wooden cases contained red wine," said Beer.

"Well, you wouldn't want Chinese Hor on your tail with cabernet sauvignon in their blood," said Siri.

"The list of contents looked quite unremarkable," said Beer. "Apart from the wine and weaponry it was mostly personal items. There was one chest of *piastre* notes that had since been devalued and were worthless. There was ammunition and sabers and one box of cutlery."

"Nothing that could be described as treasure," said Siri.

"Nor of value," said Beer. "The weapons and parts were obsolete. The banknotes were sodden and worthless, and the wine was corked. But all of it found its way to a warehouse in one of the deserted garrisons."

"Was there a signature on the invoice?" Siri asked.

"Of course," said Beer. "The head of the salvage team: Major Uenobu himself."

"So it's possible he found something of value in the chests and, as he said, buried it in paperwork where it was forgotten," said Daeng.

"Until his first mission back to Vietnam, when he retrieved the hidden treasure and used it to buy medicine for the school," said Siri. "Was there anything else?"

"Two more mentions," said Beer. "In October he was admitted to a French hospital suffering from 'shell shock.' Then in November he was pronounced dead in battle. Your researchers did some cross-referencing and concluded there was no battle anywhere on that day."

"And there he was traveling south on a pony cart while at the same time lying dead in a nonexistent battle," said Daeng. "They'd have contacted his family. They'd be mourning his death while here he was having a nice life in Laos. Of course he would have been executed for desertion if they'd found him here."

"Comrade Beer," said Siri. "I know you've had a busy day with a lot of international travel, but I'd like you to do one more trip for us tomorrow. I want you to ask around at clinics and pharmacies. See if you can find someone who remembers getting paid over the odds in 1943 to administer diphtheria vaccinations across the river. You might want to stir a Japanese officer who didn't speak into the mix to jog memories. There wouldn't have been a lot of medical facilities to choose from in wartime Nakhon Phanom."

"Why do you think the medicine would come from Thailand?" Daeng asked.

"We didn't have and still don't have the medicines or the expertise to deal with an epidemic," said Siri. "He wouldn't go to the Japanese for help and the French were already rationing food and medicines. I seem to recall Satsai saying a medical unit arrived to administer the vaccinations. We didn't have such things as medical units over here, not even in Vientiane. It had to be Thai."

Siri smiled at Beer. The Vietnamese always seemed pleased to be given an assignment even though the Lao couple hadn't yet paid him, nor had they negotiated a fee for his services. He seemed to know they wouldn't cheat him of what he'd earned. He was a poor man. His clothes had seen many washings, his sandals were made from old tires, and his trousers were held up by a length of loosely macraméd strings. It was then that it occurred to the doctor.

"They weren't American," said Siri.

"What?" said Daeng.

"The raid on the village. The helicopters were American and the men wore American uniforms but the uniforms weren't theirs. They were too big, hence the rope belts."

"How long does it take to punch a few holes in a belt?" said Daeng.

"I don't know, Daeng. But the point is—"

"They could have been small Americans."

"Unlikely, and they probably didn't care about the belts because they didn't think anyone would notice such a small detail. Perhaps only a weaver would spot a fashion anomaly so they didn't worry about it. It was all set up to make the villagers believe it was an American operation. In wartime nobody would question such a thing. Americans are historically nuts. But what if they were Japanese? There are Jap deserters peppered all through these mountains. Yuki-*san* has read the diary, or at least he knows of it. He might have found it in the village, or maybe someone on that raid passed it on to him. But that again begs the question, was the raid set up to find the diary or was finding it coincidental? Were they looking for something else but stumbled on the diary?"

"I have a question," said Beer. "I'm still not clear why Yuki-*san* would show up in Thakhek and tell you about Hiro if he was involved himself."

"He was sowing seeds," said Daeng. "Of course, he came to keep Siri searching, afraid we might leave before we had the whole picture."

"And he pointed us in the direction of the Tunnel of Love," said Siri. "He threw in the clue we needed to identify Hiro. But who is he and what does he stand to gain from our presence here?"

"There are only two possibilities I can see," said Daeng. "He wants us to find Hiro, or he wants us to find something that Hiro had."

"The treasure," said Beer.

"Exactly," said Daeng. "It always comes down to money. How disappointing."

CHAPTER TWENTY
The Case of Beer

The next morning, with the early sun at their backs, Siri and Daeng were absently tossing a mushroom net into the river and freeing anything silly enough to get caught in it. It was a futile charade because nobody on either bank cared who they were or where they were going. Beer rowed slowly, allowing the current to do all the work.

"I thought I'd be doing my homework alone this trip," he said.

"And you will be," said Siri. "But we feel like we're really close to putting all the pieces together. We had an epiphany that we're now on a treasure hunt with an evil Japanese villain watching our every move. How much more thrilling could it all be? While you're at the clinics and pharmacies, we'll go to see Kyoko and find out whether her *sensei* has any news for us. We've decided that the answer to everything lies within the ranks of the *yokai*. Hiro has led us into the world of the demons for a reason. That's where we'll find the treasure."

They docked the old boat at its usual disused pier and Beer padlocked it to a post even though they all doubted anyone would bother to steal it. He put the key under a rock. They agreed to meet back there at eleven to compare notes.

"What do we do about Yuki-*san*?" Beer asked.

"He worries you, doesn't he," said Daeng.

"If he was on the village raid, he must have accomplices who are killers," he said. "Yes, I'm excited about solving the mystery of the lost treasure, especially if there's a chance of my sharing in the spoils, but I'm not in a hurry to die for it. I'd never met Yuki before but he came straight up to me in the market and asked about you. So he knows who I am and where to find me. I'm not a fighter. I'm not you, Madam Daeng. If it comes down to it, I'm a coward."

"I understand," said Siri. "When we get back to Thakhek today we'll use our contacts to trace him. We know people at police HQ. It can't be that difficult to find a foreigner with a family, not even in the mountains. If he's on the Vietnamese side they'd have a record of him. We'll find him. Once Yuki-*san* stops being anonymous, he stops being a threat."

"I was . . . I was kind of thinking you'd already started a search for him," said Beer.

"Not so simple, Beer," said Siri. "You know what communication's like in this place. But don't panic. We won't let anything happen to you."

They shook hands and went their separate ways. Siri and Daeng took the river road, stopping to admire the pickled monkey bushes, looking across the river at the dinosaur country they lived in.

"Do you think we can find something for him in Vientiane?" Siri asked.

"Beer? Are you still collecting people, Dr. Siri?"

"More like an investment, I'd say. If his face wasn't split

in half he'd be snapped up by the UN or some NGO: hardworking, responsible, honest, fluent in half a dozen languages. He could be on a living wage somewhere."

"Have you not considered he might prefer his freedom?"

"You can only appreciate freedom if you have alternatives," said Siri. "It seems freedom is his only option."

Daeng dropped the subject. She knew her husband was already on Beer's case. There was no arguing with him. He'd probably already drawn up a list of employment opportunities.

They arrived at the JICA office long before the staff was expected to be there. But the security gate was open and there was a motorcycle parked out front. Kyoko was at her desk with *kanji* sheets in front of her. She jumped for joy—literally—when Siri and Daeng appeared in the doorway. She didn't know whether to *wai* or hug, so she did both.

"Uncle! Auntie!" she squealed. "We're almost there."

"Where?" asked Daeng.

"The conclusion," said Kyoko. "Come. Sit down. Have tea."

She poured green tea from a ceramic pot into three delicate bowls. Daeng decided that only a Japanese would travel to a third-world country with such breakable objects in their suitcase. Daeng sipped the tea politely. Siri slurped and decided it needed sugar to stop it from tasting like liquid grass. But he kept his mouth shut.

"I'm a fanatic," said Kyoko. "I've become an authority on *yokai*. I can't believe I wasted my formative years studying sociology and psychology when there was a world of demons out there I hadn't even delved into."

Siri and Daeng stared at her.

"I'm not even sure if she's serious," said Daeng.

"Oh, I am, Daeng-*sama*," she said.

"So you've found Toshi's alter ego?" said Siri.

"I have—we have," said Kyoko. "But he wasn't a *yokai*. His name was Minamoto Yorimitsu and he was a warrior dispatched by the lords of the land to rid them of Shuten Doji. Doji was the leader of the Oni devils. The legend went that Shuten Doji put on a hideous mask when he was drunk one night and was never able to take it off. He spent all his time drinking *sake* and murdering young virgins. And here, my friends, is where the fictional writing of Toshi may have come together with reality. My *sensei* tells me that a group of senior officers did go to Thakhek around the time of the Japanese surrender. One of them was the general, Shosen Umiji, who had become infamous in the region because it was he who was instrumental in implementing the atrocities in China. He had been Toshi's commanding officer for a time."

"Damn, I do believe he's the one who condemned Toshi to death at the Vietnamese hospital," said Siri.

"If Toshi had been tormented by the horrors in Manchuria, General Shosen would have had a traumatic influence on his life. If Toshi was actually using the diary as therapy, what better way to slay his demons than to confront the general in whatever form?" said Kyoko.

"I'm getting bogged down with names here," said Daeng. "So Hiro a.k.a. Toshi fancied himself as . . . ?"

"Minamoto Yorimitsu," said Kyoko. "The slayer of the head devil, Shuten Doji."

"Who walked the earth under the name of . . ."

"General Shosen Umiji," said Kyoko.

"But all through the diary Toshi's a friend of the *yokai*," said Daeng. "How could he live with them if his mission was to defeat them and overpower their leader?"

"I believe we have to look at this as Toshi living in three worlds," said Siri. "There was the peaceful world in Sawan with his friends and his lover. Then there was the fantasy world he wrote about in his diary. But there was another darker world that he was repressing all the time; the evil world of the devils into which he'd been dragged in China. His hadn't been a simple madness. He had been possessed. He managed to subdue the *yokai* for several years. But then something must have happened to reopen a portal into that world."

"There's only a hint at the end of the diary and we don't have the missing pages, but it seems that Toshi was becoming unsettled," said Kyoko. "We think there may have been an incident. Something caused the *yokai* to reveal their true identities and Minamoto Yorimitsu, the slayer, was awoken from his ignorance. We think this might have taken place during the parade of the hundred devils, which is the only time the *yokai* become visible."

"Sounds like a meeting of the Central Committee," said Siri.

"Siri, we're being serious here," said Daeng.

"Sorry, dear."

"When was that?" asked Daeng.

"It happens quite often," said Kyoko. "*Yokai* are restless. They need exercise. I have a feeling Toshi's so-called friends let slip who they really were on one of those nights. The professor in Thailand said the nearest parade date to Toshi's disappearance was August ninth, 1945."

"That would have been six nights before the Japanese surrender," said Daeng.

"And that was exactly the period the pages were ripped from the diary," said Siri.

"Exactly," said Kyoko.

"So the events of those last six days were the cause of Toshi's disappearance," said Daeng.

Siri got to his feet and walked to the window. He adjusted the louvers so he could see the garden.

"I think I understand," he said. "The diary wasn't therapy."

"What do you mean?" said Kyoko.

"What happened in that diary was real," said Siri, turning back to the women. The louver glass was spotless but he instinctively wiped dust from his fingers. There were no clean louvers in Laos.

"How could . . . ?" Kyoko began.

"It was real in another dimension, Kyoko-*san*," said Siri. "When Hiro was writing, he was in the same plane as the ghosts and the spirits. It was every bit as real as his life here with the one he loved. I know all this because I've been there."

Kyoko looked at Daeng, bewildered.

"It's true," said Daeng. "Ridiculous but true. You should try living with him."

"Toshi was troubled and confused," said Siri. "His mind had been twisted out of all proportion by what he saw in China. And somewhere along the line he had become broken and had opened a connection into the spirit world. For me it's usually a door through which I pass in order to switch dimensions. For him it was the diary. It was there in this diary world that he met the devils that had driven otherwise sane, rational men to madness. It was there he met the *yokai* who threatened to once more spill over into this world of ours. But through his diary he had been able to keep the *yokai* content by befriending them. It was his way of keeping the lid on a bubbling pot. But the arrival of the wicked overlord and his demons stacked the odds against Toshi. Everything terrible was coming together. The *yokai* were revealing themselves. There was heavy troop activity in Thakhek. Japanese soldiers were out of control the way they had been in China. There was cross-dimensional chaos. Hiro was afraid for his friends in the village. He had to go on a second mission to protect them."

"And that mission had to involve General Shosen Umiji, whom he believed to be the incarnation of Shuten Doji the demon," said Kyoko. "Or why else would Hiro have taken on the name of Minamoto? Perhaps Hiro moved away hoping the *yokai* might follow him."

"I don't see him running," said Siri. "Neither metaphorically nor literally."

"This is getting creepy," said Kyoko.

"But this doesn't take us any closer to the treasure," said Daeng, who'd had enough spirit talk for one day. "Did the professor shed any more light on the text?"

"There was a reference we almost missed," said Kyoko. "We ignored it at first because it was . . . well, it was very Western. We'd only been looking at Lao transcriptions of Japanese names. But the professor is a very thorough man and he returned to it. The name was Hal."

"That was the name of the cat that left because of the arrival of the dog," said Siri.

"Nicely remembered," said Daeng.

"In the earlier pages we learned that Hiro was very fond of the cat," said Kyoko. "But the cat left because it couldn't stand the new arrival. The new arrival was Taigou, or *Senbiki Okami*, one of the *yokai* in dog form. The professor made a list of possible versions of 'Hal,' its Japanese pronunciation being *ha* and *ru*, and with a little juggling he came up with the name: *baku*. I suppose one of the reasons we missed it is because, like 'Minamoto,' it isn't the name of a *yokai*."

"Then what is it?" said Siri.

"The *baku* is a sort of talisman," said Kyoko. "It's a guardian spirit and country people adopt it to protect themselves from the devils. *Baku* reside in the gates or the pillars of temples. They soak up bad dreams and ward off *yokai*."

"So the cat was one of the good guys?" said Siri.

"Perhaps he was protecting Hiro the whole time," said Kyoko. "We wondered whether *baku* might have been responsible for painting the idyllic scenes in Hiro's mind to subdue the *yokai* and keep him safe."

"What do *baku* look like when they aren't being cats?" Daeng asked.

"It's said the *baku* was a last-minute throw-together," said Kyoko. "The gods only had spare parts left over when all the other creatures were created. *Baku* was composed of whatever they could find. It looked a bit like a small bear with uneven dog legs and the head of an elephant."

"Well, I'll be," said Siri.

"That's your insightful face," said Daeng.

"You know? I think I have an idea," he said. "We need to get back across the river immediately."

"You're not going to share this idea with us?" said Daeng.

"Not yet. Don't want to get anyone excited. It's just a theory right now."

Siri stood but Daeng helped herself to another cup of tea.

"He does this," she said to Kyoko. "He keeps things to himself, gets himself shot to death crossing back to Laos, leaving none of us any the wiser. He takes his secret to the grave."

"Now Daeng," said Siri. "Be honest. How many times has that happened? Come on, drink your grass juice and let's go."

He kissed Kyoko on the cheek and she blushed rose.

"We'll get back to you as soon as we have news," said Daeng and she followed her husband out the door.

Twenty minutes after Siri and Daeng had left the JICA office, the phone rang. Kyoko was the only one in the office so she answered it.

"Hello, I'm phoning from the US embassy in Phnom Penh," came a voice. The caller spoke Thai with a slight American accent that Kyoko picked up on. "I was given this number in regard to inquiries from Dr. Siri Paiboun."

"You just missed him," said Kyoko. "Can I take a message?"

"If you wouldn't mind. My name is Cindy."

"Ah, yes. I've heard about you," said Kyoko. "Your help in this matter has been invaluable. Thank you for calling."

There was a very long pause.

"No, I think you must be thinking of somebody else," said Cindy.

"Why?"

"Well, actually I'm embarrassed not to have been in touch sooner," said Cindy. "Dr. Siri asked me if I could find information about a major in the Japanese Imperial Army."

"That's correct."

"I was in touch with Washington and they do have a microfiche copy of the war archive."

"Yes?"

"But they're unable to give out information over the phone, not even to embassies. I'd need to be there in person with a signed request from my ambassador."

Kyoko was silent.

"Hello?" said Cindy.

"So you haven't been able to send us information about Major Hiro?"

"No, I'm sorry."

"And you haven't spoken to anyone else about this?"

"No."

"Oh dear," said Kyoko.

CHAPTER TWENTY-ONE
Defeat Can Be Confusing

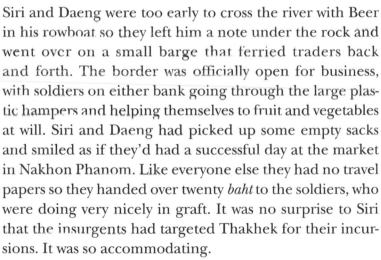

Siri and Daeng were too early to cross the river with Beer in his rowboat so they left him a note under the rock and went over on a small barge that ferried traders back and forth. The border was officially open for business, with soldiers on either bank going through the large plastic hampers and helping themselves to fruit and vegetables at will. Siri and Daeng had picked up some empty sacks and smiled as if they'd had a successful day at the market in Nakhon Phanom. Like everyone else they had no travel papers so they handed over twenty *baht* to the soldiers, who were doing very nicely in graft. It was no surprise to Siri that the insurgents had targeted Thakhek for their incursions. It was so accommodating.

They hurried back to the guesthouse. They paused in front of the door and inspected it for scratch marks. Daeng looked through the window.

"Safe," she said, but Siri turned the key gingerly. Once inside, he went straight to the bed and lifted the mattress. From beneath it he took out the diary. He thumbed through the pages until he found the folded photograph of Hiro and Satsai standing with the village children.

"Haven't you looked at that enough?" said Daeng.

"Looked, yes," said Siri. "But seen, no," he said. "Come and take a good look at this picture and tell me what you see."

Daeng perused the picture while Siri removed his sturdy Soviet magnifying glass from his shoulder bag. He always traveled with his detection equipment. He handed her the glass and she held it in front of the photo.

"Eleven, twelve children, two adults," she said.

"Anything else?"

"The village post."

"And can you see the hieroglyphics carved out of the concrete?"

"Barely."

"What can you make out?"

"Animals, mostly."

"And what's the biggest one there?"

"This one," she said. "An elephant."

"Are you sure it's an elephant?"

"Well, I'm no expert, but when I was six it's how I would have drawn one. Perhaps the artist wasn't so good at elephants. It has really short . . ."

She looked at her husband and he nodded.

"Do you think this is the *baku*?" she asked.

"Short legs. Tail of a lion. Bird feet. Doesn't that look like a desperately constructed animal to you? The *baku* inhabit temple gates and pillars to keep the *yokai* away. Village pillars are usually made of wood but this one is concrete. What if Hiro replaced the old one when he came back from Lang Son?"

"You think he might have buried his treasure under the pillar?"

"At first, yes, I considered that," said Siri. "With the type of metal detectors in common use the magnetic field is directed downwards. If the treasure had been in the ground the detectors would have found it. The reason I was so fixated on this photograph is that it didn't seem right somehow. We know Satsai is of average height. He's standing beside the pillar and I estimate there's another two Satsais' height before the top of the pillar—about five meters. When we saw it with him the other day, it would have been no taller than two Satsais, one on top of the other, if you know what I mean."

"Not really."

"The pillar is shorter now."

"How can that be?"

"When we came to see Satsai on our second visit he was mending a piece of equipment: some sort of heavy-duty cordless saw. Now, if you're cutting trees, a simple chain-saw would be sufficient, or an axe. That beast on his desk was for cutting metal and did you see any metal around there that needed cutting?"

"You think the treasure's in the pillar?"

"It's possible, and would have been simple enough to arrange. You'd just have to pour liquid cement into a wooden frame with a pipe through the center. The finished concrete structure would have a hollow channel running through it. You then melt down your treasure, be it gold or silver or whatever—and my bet is gold—and pour it into the hollow center. You erect your pillar, decorate it a bit, and all anyone sees is a tall concrete post in the middle of the square. It was the only thing to survive the raid. They burned everything else down searching for the gold. Nobody would think to look there. It's the village secret.

Whenever they need some funding for this or that project or disaster they just lop off a few centimeters from the top of the pillar. It would make sense that they used the gold to rebuild the village after the raid."

"You've got a devious mind, Dr. Siri."

"But it's possible, right?"

"Absolutely. But that means Satsai was lying to us about not knowing where the treasure was."

"Of course he was," said Siri. "Wouldn't you? His village had already been destroyed once. He knows someone suspects there's a fortune in gold in or around the village. Someone knew about Hiro and his stash and his relationship with Satsai. I bet that someone was Yuki-*san*."

"So, what do we do now?" asked Daeng.

"We try to work out why Yuki would involve us. Why did he send me the diary? We need to have ourselves a serious brainstorm and, for that, we need beer with a small *b*."

They sat on the odd chairs looking out over the water. The sun was smearing a purple bruise across the horizon. The clouds were highlighted in lilacs and mauves, the river pink. The bougainvillea bush in front of the balcony was being ravaged by a hostile gang of purple butterflies. It was the type of scene that would have graced the photo albums of all the tourists the government dreamed would one day come to appreciate the country and spend their money. But this evening only Siri and Daeng could be bothered to enjoy it. There was another ugly hotel being built on the far bank and they hoped the Lao would someday build an even uglier one in revenge.

It was a hot early evening that anticipated more rain. The couple waved paper fans in front of their faces.

Thanks to the generator the beer was cold but the ideas were not flowing.

"It has to have something to do with my reputation as an internationally renowned crime fighter," said Siri at last.

"That, or the fact that you can read at all," said Daeng.

"What do you mean?"

"Look at it like this. Yuki-*san* recovers the diary from Satsai's house in the village. He knows somehow that Hiro has gold or whatever. He can read the Japanese section but it tells him nothing. Half the diary is written in Lao language. The few academics we have here got their qualifications in French language. Most of them fled in '75. We're left with school teachers with classes up to grade six with no textbooks and college tutors with degrees in Russian. The teachers have nothing stimulating to read so they've not developed a reading habit. Hiro's diary would be beyond the comprehension of almost everyone in Laos."

"Apart from Satsai," said Siri.

"But Yuki-*san* isn't about to recruit the man from whom he'd stolen the diary to explain the hidden meanings in it," said Daeng.

"And I doubt Satsai would have seen it as anything but a literary masterpiece," said Siri. "What Yuki-*san* needed was someone with a reading background, with a track record of solving mysteries, with research resources and endless retirement hours."

"Enter Dr. Siri. Someone recommended you to Yuki-*san*, someone who admired your work. You were the perfect man for the job and, voila, here you are solving the mystery just as he planned."

"But he doesn't know that," said Siri. "All that effort would only be worthwhile if he was sitting here with us taking notes."

The screeching of the cicadas was momentarily drowned out by the grinding of cogs.

"Oh, shit," said Siri who had reached his conclusion only seconds before Daeng.

They ran into the room and started to conduct a thorough search of all the likely places. When that produced nothing, they used their imaginations. It was Daeng who found the wireless transmitter in the knot atop the mosquito net, just two meters above their nighttime conversations and intimate moments.

"It's short range," said Daeng. "He'd have to be within fifty meters."

"The mysterious guest in room four," said Siri.

They ran down the stairs to the far end of the building, where the door to room 4 was ajar. They went inside. Beside the unmade bed was a radio receiver. The headphones were on the pillow.

"Looks like he doesn't need them anymore," said Siri.

"We have to get to the village," said Daeng.

"It's almost dark."

"It's a tunnel. How much darker could it be?"

So it was that with no plan and no equipment they headed toward the river. Even before they left the guesthouse grounds they bumped into Beer coming toward them.

"Comrade Beer," said Daeng. "We need a fast boat with a light."

"Why? What's happened?" said Beer.

"We'll tell you on the way."

◙ ◙ ◙

The boat they hired was certainly faster than Garu's. They arrived at the entrance to the Thum Huk tunnel in record time. But the young driver didn't have the expertise of the old man. He had a strong beam on the front of his boat but he was bemused by all the twists and turns of the cave network. He refused to go at speed because he was afraid. There was talk of ghosts in the tunnel. So by the time they reached the village the moon was on the rise, nestled now in the low clouds, and there was nobody at the dock. A clunky old WW2 foldable launch was tied up there. There was no artificial lamplight.

"Damn, I wish I'd brought the Kalashnikov," said Siri.

"I suppose we could have planned this a little better," Daeng agreed. "But we're here now. Best make the most of it."

They'd briefed Beer on the journey. They'd told him about the revelations from Kyoko's professor and the discovery of the listening device. He'd told them how he'd spent a fruitless day at clinics and pharmacies and even made an appointment with the director of the hospital, who had nothing useful to say. Beer seemed embarrassed by his failure but they congratulated him on his thoroughness.

As they chugged painfully slowly through the caverns, Siri's detective mind had kicked in. He was impressed by the tenacity of Yuki-*san*, who'd sat in room 4 for three days listening to their deliberations, waiting for the moment to arrive when the Lao announced the location of the treasure. But for such a well-planned surveillance operation there was something lacking. Yes, they'd discussed much of the case when they were together in their room. And yes, it had proven worthwhile to transfer the listening device to their new room after the explosion. But their discoveries and insights weren't restricted to the bedroom. They'd talked on the balcony, in the boat, in the restaurant, sitting on the dock. Who was to know when and where the ultimate revelation would be revealed? To get full coverage they'd have to have another listening device attached to their clothes or in their bags, or . . . At that point, Siri had leaned into Daeng's ear and shouted a theory that only she could hear.

They walked by the light of the boat pilot's flashlight to the square where the village pillar lay on the ground, the concrete smashed. The gold or other precious metal had been removed and the sledgehammers left lying around. On one slab of concrete, the smiling face of *baku* looked up at them, his tail-end gone. He'd failed to protect the village this time, but his expression suggested all was not lost. Still there was nobody to be seen, not a soul.

"The school," said Beer.

"I know you're afraid," Daeng told him. "You don't have to come."

"I do," said Beer, his voice trembling. "I'm a part of this. I want to see my work through."

"You're a saint," said Daeng.

She went up to him and gave him a hug. Siri joined them but his main objective was not to bond with their guide. It was to remove the pistol from the back of his macramé belt. It was hidden by the tail of his shirt but the doctor had seen its outline when they docked. He held it to Beer's head and twisted the Vietnamese traitor's arm behind his back one notch short of snapping it off.

"What? What are you doing?" he asked.

"You could shout to your team at the school for help," said Daeng. "And they'd probably come to see what's wrong. But we have a gun now. We could pick them off one by one. I doubt there'd be more than six of them and this is a Makarov PM. If it's fully loaded, and it feels heavy enough, it contains eight rounds. I could even miss a couple with my first two shots and still leave you without allies."

"I don't understand," said Beer.

"Oh, I know," said Daeng. "Defeat can be confusing. We should have suspected you a lot sooner. That was a very thorough account of Hiro Uenobu's early life you gave us. In fact it contained information that one would never find in standard service documents. You could only have learned it from someone who knew Hiro and had worked with him and had access to his records. I'm assuming that someone is Yuki-*san*. I also assume he's paying you a significant amount of money for your service. Perhaps he's offered you a share of the treasure."

"And here's the way you probably imagined it all to go," said Siri. "Yuki-*san* has the villagers at the school. It's a small village so that will be about . . . a hundred people? You might actually think Yuki-*san* plans something innocent. Perhaps he'll give the villagers a warning not to tell anyone what they've seen here and let them go home. That would be only fair considering they haven't done anything wrong. Deep down, you're a good person, so you're hanging on to the hope that he isn't planning to massacre the lot of them."

"How awful that would be," said Daeng. "Bringing back memories of the war. The *yokai* let loose again."

"They aren't like that anymore," said Beer.

"You know? I was wondering whether they'd already wiped out all those innocent women and children," said Siri. "But then it occurred to me they're just waiting for you to deliver the last two loose ends. The sounds of gunfire and screaming would have echoed along that old tunnel. We might have rebelled or turned back. So, no. Your last task is to deliver us, take a step back, and watch the bullet fest."

"Of course, Comrade Beer, you're a loose end, too," said Daeng. "You've served your purpose. They don't need you anymore. I doubt they'll give you a chance to step back. You've been helpful but they have their gold now and you're not one of them. I'd say it's sayonara, Beer-*san*."

"I know you're imagining your share of the treasure," said Siri. "That thought has turned you blind."

They saw the flashlight of someone approaching along the track ahead of them.

"Your choice," said Siri, handing Beer back his pistol. The doctor nodded at him and ducked into the bushes.

The man on the path appeared around the bend. His lamp was attached to his helmet. He was in his sixties with a heavy-looking paunch but he wore full Japanese combat uniform. He raised his weapon when he saw Beer standing there with the old woman.

"It's you," said the Japanese in heavily accented Vietnamese. "What kept you? We've been waiting."

He lowered his gun and gestured for them to follow. Beer looked at Daeng, who raised her eyebrows and stepped in front of him. The silence that followed was thick as treacle.

"I . . . I . . . the boat was slow," said Beer, at last.

"Where's the other one?"

"Other one?"

"Yes, retard. There's supposed to be two of them."

"He . . . I . . . I killed him. He tried to escape."

"Shit. Major Yuki won't like that," said the Japanese. "He won't like it a bit."

He approached Daeng and for no apparent reason he slapped her in the face. It might have been for old times' sake but in those old times the prisoners didn't slap back. Daeng's left hook almost knocked him off his feet. There was a brief look of shock on the soldier's face before he pointed his gun at her chest. Siri was faster. He came up behind the Japanese and cracked him over the head with a branch. The man dropped like a coconut.

"Congratulations," said Daeng to Beer. "You've now officially switched sides."

Beer looked vacant. "I'm sorry," he said meekly, seemingly apologizing for all of the bad decisions he'd made in his life.

"How many more are there?" Daeng asked, pointing her chin at the prostrate soldier.

"I didn't plan to—" Beer began.

"I asked you how many more?" said Daeng, removing the lamp from the helmet of the Japanese.

"Five," said Beer.

"There were nine on the original raid," said Siri.

"They got old," said Beer. "They died."

"They're all Japanese?"

"Yes."

"And Yuki-*san* is the leader?"

"Yes."

"Okay. It's time for a plan," said Daeng.

CHAPTER TWENTY-TWO
Wish You Were Here

"So, you've finally come back to us," said Dtui.

Chief Inspector Phosy stood in the doorway of their room in the police dormitory wearing the same crumpled uniform he'd had on for four days. Malee was asleep in the cot, too exhausted from a day of untettered imagination to welcome her father.

"Sorry," said Phosy. "Things always seem to take twice as long as they need to."

"Is it all over?"

"Finally."

Phosy fell backward onto the bed. His wife was afraid he might fall asleep instantly so she threw herself on top of him. It was almost too much for the plywood base, which groaned and splintered beneath them.

"What happened?" she asked.

"Happy ending," said Phosy. "Mimi's on her way back to Vang Vieng on the bus with Sihot as a bodyguard."

"I'll miss her," said Dtui. "Malee was very fond of her."

"I won't miss sleeping alone in my office," said Phosy.

"Your idea," said Dtui. "What did the judge say?"

"Death by owl was the official verdict. Or at least there

was no evidence to prove otherwise. The original wife gets first grabs on the fortune but I get the feeling the minor wife won't give up that easily. That should be nasty to watch. But it's none of our business anymore."

"What about Mimi's dad?"

"Comrade Ouan? I suppose I shouldn't really say."

"Have you ever been beaten up by a girl?"

"You have to promise not to tell anyone."

"Tell them what?"

"We, ehr . . . We decided not to press charges."

She pushed him away.

"You can't be serious," she said. "The guy drugs three police officers and chains them up in a concrete room for two days and he's going to get away with it?"

"We've put it down to tough Vang Vieng hospitality."

"Phosy?"

"Look, Dtui, ours is a young administration still feeling its way. How would it look if three senior police officers allowed themselves to be overpowered and held hostage by one man? And I shouldn't have even been there."

Dtui smiled.

"Does this mean I'll be getting my refrigerator now?"

"It's not corruption. We'll just call it . . . a tactical side-step."

"I'll keep my mouth shut in return for a tactical micro-wave," she said. "They're all the rage now."

"I've brought you something much better," he said.

He was lying on his shoulder bag so he wrestled it out from underneath them.

"Close your eyes," he said.

Dtui did as she was told.

"Now open them."

She opened her eyes to see a plastic Ziploc sandwich bag between her husband's thumb and index finger.

"What is that?" she said, trying to focus on the contents.

"Guess."

"It surely . . . oh, it can't be."

"They were just about to set fire to the fellow," said Phosy. "This is a valuable piece of forensic folklore. It will be invaluable in settling arguments long into the future."

"And given that we don't have a refrigerator, where do you propose we store ten centimeters of nasal hair?"

"I suppose if it keeps growing we could eventually stuff a cushion with it."

"That's disgusting," she said, rolling onto her back. "You get more and more like Dr. Siri every day."

"Which reminds me," said Phosy, reaching once more into his bag. "This arrived today. Postman Ging special delivery. It cost me a pack of cigarettes."

"It looks like a postcard," said Dtui.

"It is. It's from Daeng and Siri."

"I haven't seen one of those since the Americans left. Is there a picture?"

He flipped it over.

"Ooh, lovely," said Dtui. "Since when did they have pyramids in Thakhek?"

"Probably not a lot of choice of postcards in Thakhek. It says, '*Greetings from Egypt.*'"

"It's the thought that counts. What did they write?"

"'*Hello and thank you for the ride to Thakhek,*'" Phosy read. "'*Not much going on. Quite restful. Wish you were here. Love, Siri and Daeng.*'"

"That's nice," said Dtui. "They could use a bit of a rest."

CHAPTER TWENTY-THREE
Silence Is Golden

The villagers were crammed into the school building with an elderly Japanese soldier stationed at each point of the compass armed with some relic from the war. Each had a sword in a scabbard hanging from his belt. The scene was lit with candles and hurricane lamps. Yuki-*san* was sitting on the teacher's desk, thumping his fist impatiently onto the wooden boards. He looked around at the old men he'd known as young warriors. They'd suffered as time passed, wasting their lives in the tropics, competing against diseases, malnutrition, wild animals, dysentery. They'd had houses and wives and had sired a battalion of ugly children, but it was not by choice. Every one of them had been waiting for this moment. There had been twelve of them to begin with, thirteen if you included Major Hiro. They were the regular core of the salvage team in Lang Son. They'd dived to retrieve the breeze blocks abandoned by the French gunners. They'd discovered all the other crates and cases. They'd called in a heavy winch to lift them out of the mud. It had taken six days to get it all out, twelve men laboring, the major in his usual trance, staring at clouds, muttering to himself.

But they were all there the day they pried open the two largest chests and saw the morning sunrise reflect off the gold. There wasn't a single thought in any man's head as to the glory of the empire or how many armored vehicles that much gold might buy. There was only greed in their hearts and a way out of the insane world they'd found themselves in. Captain Yuki it was who approached the major with his plan.

"Sir," he'd said. "We've done what we've been assigned to do. We've retrieved the breeze blocks and they've been reattached to the artillery. All the big guns are functional. Our operation under your leadership has once again been an unmitigated success. And, as you know, we were also able to salvage other objects that had been thrown into the river at an earlier time. Much of it was ruined and of no use to the military. But sir . . ."

"Yes, Captain?" said Hiro.

"You may recall that there were some items of great value raised from the river. There was gold, sir. And that gold has no claim of ownership against it. The French no doubt stole it originally and the Hor bandits before them. It is technically the spoils of war. Our beloved generals have taught us that victory deserves a reward. Recovering the breeze blocks has allowed us many great victories."

"And what is your point, Captain?" asked Major Hiro.

"We—I mean, your unit—would be honored if we could use it for humanitarian purposes. We have seen great suffering in the region and, with your permission, sir, we would like to give a little back to the people here. We would like to share the great merit that has been bestowed on our empire by helping the poor and the sick."

"That would be a very noble enterprise," said Hiro, his eyes focused on two lizards playing chase across the wall.

"But Major, we would need to be patient. We need to be able to find a place to store the gold safely for a year or two to keep it out of the hands of opportunists and thieves."

"I know exactly what you mean," said the major. "I am Major Hiro Uenobu. I am the head of the salvage unit."

"I know that, sir."

"Then leave it up to me. Have the men reseal the crates and stencil the words *Obsolete Breeze Blocks* on both. I shall bury that gold in paperwork so deep you'll need a diving bell to find it."

"Are you sure you . . . ?"

"Do you doubt my filing ability, Captain?"

"No, sir. It's just . . ."

"I know what I'm doing. Once the gold is safe, I shall share its location with you and the men. Give me thirty-six hours."

But the major didn't have thirty-six hours. He spent that day at his desk directing and redirecting the movement of containers. He stamped and signed each order. And that evening after sweeping his office and locking the door, he stripped butt naked and climbed an old observation turret. By the time they brought him down, his mind was scrambled. No matter how many documents they scoured, the men in his unit could find not a trace of the two crates. Captain Yuki and his men went to every known warehouse and storage depot. They broke open every box and case, but they could not find their gold. They visited the major every day trying to squeeze the location out of him, but by then he was already barking mad. Then, one day, he'd disappeared.

Captain Yuki took over Hiro's position and rank and continued to search for both the gold and the man who had hidden it. They hired local guides to search for him, but they had no success. They kept an eye out for him, sure that he'd return to steal their gold, and one day he did just that. They didn't see him come but one of their informants heard of a local headman who was attempting to sell a gold ingot. Yuki and his men went to the village and beat a confession out of him. His story was this: a Japanese major in uniform had arrived at the village by truck one night with an order written in Vietnamese for the headman to provide a dozen men to dive into the river and salvage some items there. The major didn't speak at all. He took the village team to the river and pointed to the spot where he wanted them to dive. The gold was exactly where the salvage team had first discovered it in its original cases. Hiro had merely returned it to the river. The paperwork story had been merely a distraction.

The headman, like most locals in the region, was over-awed by the might of the Japanese and he had no thought of taking the gold for himself. But the document had promised him one ingot in payment, for which he was most grateful. They helped the major load the gold into the truck and he went on his way with a friendly nod. The headman did have the foresight to jot down the number of the truck and he had kept the official order. Yuki noted that it was a very clever forgery, as were the travel papers deposited at every guard post between there and Thakhek. There they found the truck deserted on the bank of the Mekong River. This was another of Hiro's ruses, as he had already offloaded the gold and had not used the Mekong as a transportation route. But Thakhek became the center of operations for Yuki and his gang in their search for the treasure that would have made them all very rich men. The war ended; the salvage unit deserted and relocated to rebel bases in the central region. They had no sympathy for the cause of the men and women fighting the French, but they needed to be close to the town where Hiro was last known to have been. They went their separate ways but kept in touch, always asking if anyone had run across a mute Japanese, always hoping that Hiro would come out of hiding and lead them to their rightful booty. They aged, got out of shape, and fought halfheartedly, but the scent of the gold never left their nostrils. Then, at last, a flash of light.

They got word from a contact in Thailand who told them about a doctor who had worked at the small hospital in Nakhon Phanom. It appeared that back in 1943 he had been contacted by a Japanese officer who did not speak. The soldier had cash—a lot of it—and a prescription written in Thai for vaccines to counter the childhood condition known as diphtheria. The doctor had told him that the medicine was hard to come by as it was still undergoing tests and very expensive. But the cost didn't concern the Japanese. The doctor also told him that a qualified medical team would have to attend to the children and administer the vaccine. Again, the officer had no problem with that and even arranged transport across the river and to the site of the epidemic. The only insistence was that the Thai medical team would be blindfolded. Everyone on the team could feel that they were inside a water-filled tunnel for half of the journey. The doctor recognized the smell of bat excrement. One of them cheated and lifted the blindfold to see a beautiful quartz structure in a vast cave. Eventually they found themselves in a picturesque village in the mountains. They stayed there for two nights working with the surviving children.

Armed with this information, Yuki gathered his troops, consulted his maps, and deduced that Major Hiro had gone to ground in the cave network leading to the village of Sawan at the end of a tunnel called Thum Huk. The war with America was coming to an end. The Viet Minh had a number of captured helicopters at their disposal. The mechanic responsible for maintaining them was another Japanese deserter who had befriended the salvagers. He knew of three mercenary pilots who didn't ask questions. He suggested that nobody would miss three old helicopters for a few hours. They flew across the border, did one low pass over the village so everyone would identify the invaders, and landed in the central square certain there would be no retaliation. They searched every building and the lower caves. There wasn't much of value, so they didn't waste their time pilfering. They all knew what they were looking for and the quickest way to find it was to burn down the entire village and sweep the land around it with metal detectors. Yuki-*san* spent longer in the headman's house looking for evidence of contact between the village and Hiro. He emptied all the documents from the single metal file cabinet and trashed the place. His last gesture was to rip the mattress with his knife. And there, beneath it, was a small trapdoor leading down to two layers of bamboo flooring. And tucked between them was a box containing US dollars, some personal documents, and Hiro's diary. Yuki-*san* opened it at the last page and his heart raced. He was certain the diary would give up the location of Hiro's gold. Even after they'd burned down every house, scoured every meter of ground, and had found nothing, Yuki's heart still beat wildly. They returned to the helicopters and flew back across the mountains and Yuki began his frustrating journey through the pages of the diary.

And now he sat on the schoolteacher's desk, banging it with his fist until his knuckles bled. Arriving at this stage had been masterful on his part. By staying in the jungles for all this time he had alienated himself from his homeland, dishonored his family name. He could never return to Japan. He had no contacts and no resources. But he needed an academic to read the Lao section of the diary. It was good fortune that he'd heard of the crime-fighting doctor in Vientiane from a Vietnamese neighbor who'd spent time in Laos. Yuki had released information shred by shred to keep the doctor enthralled and he'd waited for him to fill in the gaps in his knowledge. Yuki-*san* had heard of the *yokai* when he was a child but he never would have made the connection through Hiro's stories. For that he had to thank the clever Lao—before killing him. The Japanese knew that Dr. Siri was the type who would never rest until he caught up with Yuki and his men. That's why he had to die. That's why they all had to die. A neat, clean end to the story; gory but necessary. The way the Imperial Army had rampaged through China, clinical, heartless, merciless. No witnesses. No guilt. Nobody would suspect a band of Japanese of such a massacre. It had to be insurgents. There would be clues left strategically around the village pointing to royalists in the Thai camps. With everyone gone they would cut the gold into lumps, load it onto the foldable boat, and head for the life they deserved.

There was just one small matter to take care of, but the Japanese leader was getting impatient.

"We'll give him five more minutes," said Yuki-*san*. "If they're not here then we'll assume they aren't coming. We can head back along the river and take care of the doctor and his wife and the idiot Vietnamese back in the town. Not as neat as I'd planned but we can take our time now. We'll do away with this menagerie first."

It was what Teacher Satsai had anticipated. He had enough Japanese to understand what their fate would be. So in a gentle whisper he had spread the word that upon his shout of "Go" everyone was to make a run for it, head in whatever direction they could as fast as they could. Many would be mowed down by the machine guns but at least some would get away. Satsai himself was crouched near the leader. He'd go for Yuki-*san* and subdue him the best he could.

But the plan was put on hold as Beer marched the old Lao couple into the school yard with his gun trained on their backs.

"What kept you?" shouted Yuki-*san*, jumping down from the desk.

"Sorry," said Beer.

Yuki unholstered his pistol. Siri was certain he was about to shoot the three of them in the head right there and then. There would be no discussion. Three executions: bang, bang, bang, then a signal for the massacre.

But instead there was an explosion. It was followed by another, and another. Yuki turned in time to see the third blast light up the night sky.

"What . . . ?" he said.

"That would be Chief Inspector Phosy and a few dozen

armed police officers," said Siri. "I'm sure they've already overpowered your pudgy Japanese forward guard and secured the tunnel entrance. I'm afraid that cuts off your orderly escape route. You really should have come in helicopters again."

"Your only option now is to use us as hostages and talk your way out of here," said Daeng.

There was another explosion. Yuki-*san* stood with his gun at Siri's head.

"Getting closer," said Siri.

"You could panic and get your unit of geriatrics to kill all these nice people, but you've made the classical mass-shooting mistake of placing your old boys in positions where they couldn't shoot the hostages without shooting each other," said Daeng.

Another explosion.

"Plus there's the suicide bomber element," said Siri.

"What are you talking about?" said Yuki.

Siri opened his shirt to reveal a nest of explosives with the letters *TNT* written on them strapped to his chest. A wire snaked through his sleeve down to his hand in which he held a device that looked a lot like a detonator. He rotated to give everyone a good look. There was a gasp from the captives.

"Put down your weapons," Siri shouted, "or I blow up your commander."

"No," said Yuki-*san*. "Asians of your low class do not have the courage to take your own lives."

"Usually not," said Siri. "But I have terminal horripilation. I only have two months left to live."

"Me too," said Daeng. "It's contagious."

Two of the guards had already handed over their

weapons to the villagers. Thirty years earlier they might have fought to the death, but they'd mellowed and learned to recognize fate. They'd had that one fat mango in their lives and it hadn't ever ripened.

Another explosion. Closer.

"So, let's all go together, the heroic way," said Siri. He raised the detonator and began to squeeze the button.

"No," said Yuki-*san*.

He redirected the pistol to his own head.

"Only I have the right," he said.

He squeezed the trigger, but Satsai behind him was ready. He leapt at the Japanese and wrestled him to the ground. Daeng was on them both. One of the guards had time to fire his handgun at himself and nobody attempted to stop him. He missed somehow. Lack of conviction. The last man aimed his machine gun at a group of children, but he had tears in his eyes, and he couldn't bring himself to fire. The show was over. Nobody applauded. It was extraordinary how such a large cast could be so silent. Even the cicadas held their breaths. The villagers tied up the docile Japanese and led them away. Satsai rushed to Siri.

"Don't move," he said. "Let me help you out of that."

"Don't fret, young man," said Siri, ripping off the vest. "It's only sticky rice conveniently shaped like sticks of dynamite. We raided the fat lady's house. She had a stash of it. We added the *TNT* in charcoal for effect. Best we could do on the spur of the moment. My wife's idea. The detonator was my contribution. I ripped the starter switch off your Weedwacker. Sorry about that. The best you can do right now is get on the shortwave and call the police."

"They won't come here tonight," said Daeng. "Too late. No overtime pay."

"You're right," said Siri. "Best call the army."

"But the police are already here," said Satsai.

"Well, that announcement might have been a little premature," said Daeng.

"But . . . the explosions?"

"We got our boat pilot to blow up your village diesel supply," said Siri. "One can at a time, using a cloth fuse. Added a little fertilizer to spice things up a bit. We did offer him a huge tip so I hope you can spare us a few grams of gold."

They sat around the bonfire in the village square. The Japanese prisoners were tied and corralled. A timber post had been erected temporarily to replace its concrete and gold predecessor. This was in tribute to *baku*, the poster child of vivisection, the guardian of the village and enemy of the *yokai*. The too-old and the too-young and the too-confused-by-events had taken to their beds, grateful to be alive. Only the young-at-heart sat before the flames passing around the rural Lao version of twenty-year-old scotch. What a delight that rice whisky was. It made the Woophi brew taste like methylated spirits by comparison. Its genesis was a natural pool in the depths of the caves mixed with wild rice from the lower skirts of a distant mountain. But, as Civilai always said, nothing spoils a good drink more than going into detail about how it's made. They just drank it and floated back and forth between the full moon and the ebony clouds that held it up. Daeng sat with Siri, holding hands.

"How could you be sure Beer wouldn't shoot you when you handed him back his gun?" Satsai asked.

"Faith in human nature," said Siri. "Plus the fact I'd taken out the bullets before I returned it."

"You can't leave everything to fate," said Daeng. "Now, what about the torn pages?"

"What about them?" said Satsai.

"It was you that ripped them out of the diary."

"Why would you think that?"

"Because the things Toshi saw in those last few days, the things he felt, they would have been too much for you to read over and over."

Satsai took a long suck of the straw and nodded.

"You'd been there at the beginning," said Siri. "You knew his insanity before you knew him. You'd coaxed him back, not cured but content in a way. He'd found a dimension for the demons where they couldn't get at you. Even though he shared his diary with you, the *yokai* were disguised. You weren't in any danger. But when the Japanese declared their *coup de force* in Indochina he knew he wouldn't be able to subdue the devils. They were back in the souls of the men committing atrocities. He knew that evil would reign again. And that too had to materialize through the pages of the diary."

"You tore those pages out because you didn't want to remember the man you loved haunted as he was when you first met him," said Daeng. "His demons would become yours."

"I tried to burn them," said Satsai.

"But it wasn't possible," said Siri.

"It seemed like I was being unfaithful to his . . . his process of dealing with life. I felt like I was changing the end of a story that wasn't mine to edit."

"Do you still have those pages?" Siri asked.

"Yes."

"Can I see them?"

"I'll give them to you, Doctor. Happily, I'll be rid of them. But you should decide carefully whether you want to read them. They're very disturbing."

"Where do you imagine Toshi to be now?" asked Daeng. "What do you wish for him?"

"Today?"

She nodded.

"Oh, Daeng," he said with a smile. "I imagine him to be here at this fire, drinking fine local brew and . . . and talking, telling stories about our insane days as if they were someone else's. I imagine him happy and fulfilled and cured."

"Then let us drink to Toshi's imagined life," said Daeng. "The delightful life of a grounded pilot."

Siri left the revelers around the fire and went to the compound where the enemy slept, defeated once more. The old men smiled as their dreams crumbled into dust. Only Beer sat awake, glaring up at the moon, contemplating another bad decision. The doctor sat beside him and handed him a glass of rice whisky.

"Thank you," said Beer. He sipped politely before handing the drink back to Siri.

"I had plans for you," said Siri.

"Really?"

"You were a bit too old to adopt but I could see you making a name for yourself in Vientiane."

"Why me?"

"I asked around about you, Beer. You're kind. You help people. You don't—usually—accept any work that's illegal or harmful. You're smart. In fact, as far as I could see, the only really stupid decision you've ever made was siding with Yuki-*san*."

"Well, that's the truth," said Beer, accepting another sip of whisky.

"What went wrong?" Siri asked.

Beer smiled and looked back at the moon.

"You know those angels and devils that sit on your shoulder and push you this way and that?" he said.

"I've had a few."

"Well, I had just the one. He looked exactly like me and he was always beside me with his arm over my shoulder. Every time I was just about to do something foolish he'd give me a squeeze and raise his eyebrows. He was always making those important decisions for me. Censoring me. Pushing me in the direction of righteousness."

"So where was he when Yuki-*san* came along?" Siri asked.

"That's just it, Doctor," said Beer. "Suddenly he wasn't there anymore. I was lost. The Japanese offered me a fortune to accompany you and Madam Daeng, to report back everything you said, to translate the recordings, to bring you to the village where I was afraid in my heart you'd be killed. I honestly believed the villagers weren't in any danger. He assured me they'd all be released. I knew it was wrong. I was waiting for my shoulder angel to make me see sense but the emptiness overwhelmed me. I panicked."

"Do you remember when Yuki-*san* first approached you?" Siri asked.

"It was only a few weeks ago," said Beer. "He'd heard I accepted odd jobs. He came to see me and made his offer. The other me would have said no."

"And the other you's still not around?"

"I'm more lost than ever."

Siri took the glass and looked into the milky liquid.

"I've met him," he said.

"Who?"

"The other you."

"No, I think he's just mine. I have an exclusive."

"Son, you once told Madam Daeng that in your dream you live in a big house with servants."

"It's a dream that recurs to torment me."

"But it's not a dream, is it? I believe that at one stage you did live in such a house."

Beer looked into the doctor's brilliant green eyes, which sparkled in the firelight.

"How could you . . . ?"

"It just occurred to me this evening. All the bits joined together. Your father was rich and he had great plans for you. I'd never really looked at your face. I suppose most people get no further than the scar. But now I can see the similarity. I believe that you had a brother, perhaps a twin. And the two of you were two sides of a coin, as close as could be, but opposite. Your father was a traditional Vietnamese—"

"I don't—"

"He discovered something about you that shamed him. He learned that you preferred men to women. It was unacceptable. You were expected to further the family line. He banished you. Disowned you. Sent you to work as a laborer in a foreign country. And he made you ashamed of what you were. You saw no worth in yourself. But your brother, in spirit, never left you. He was your protector. He stayed with you until his death in Laos three weeks ago."

Both Siri and Beer were crying. The drink was at their feet, forgotten.

"He's dead, isn't he?" said Beer.

"In a way, he didn't stop living. I couldn't understand why his hair and nails continued to grow but now I realize it was because you were still alive in him, just as I believe he continues to live in you."

"How . . . how do you know all this?"

"I have a curse on me that allows me to see the dead. I learn things about them," said Siri. "I usually complain about coincidences. It drives my wife mad. But I understand now that we can create them. We have the ability to draw people and events together. I was visiting a dear friend who'd passed on and you and your brother were there. I saw you as children. You were as close as any two people could be. But your brother was due to leave this world and you were there to say goodbye just as I was there to bid farewell to my friend."

"I had that same dream," said Beer. "I saw you there. It was at an airport."

"With pink airplanes."

"That's right. All my airplanes were in pastels when I was little. I was a very orthodox gay even then."

"And when the flight took off you—"

"My head split in two."

"That's right. You'd been forced to see yourself without his guidance. That scarf was the last gift he gave you. Your last physical memory of him."

"I don't suppose you met him when he was alive?"

"No, but I learned a lot about him. He was a good man, popular, like you."

"Do you think he knew he was looking out for me all those years?"

"No idea. But I am sure the belief kept you alive and safe. I'm sure he'll be really pissed off if you screw up."

"I've already let him down."

"We'll see. Perhaps you changed teams just in time. At the very worst you could be guilty of collusion in a deception. Nothing that would have you behind bars for any length of time. In fact, you saved a lot of lives today. That's worth something. And it seems to me that you have a sizable fortune coming to you."

"Me? I doubt that," said Beer. "I've been disowned by that family."

"That might not be a problem. There are tests you can take to prove you're the legal offspring. Your father can't deny you your birthright. In fact our socialist states would love nothing more than to redistribute wealth to the poor. I think you qualify as poor, don't you? Wear those sandals at the hearing. And who knows? Perhaps your father would enjoy meeting his only living son "

Almost the end of the actual story

EPILOGUE ONE
The Torn Pages

I am Dr. Siri Paiboun and I am attaching this prelude to the pages torn from Hiro Uenobu's diary as a sort of warning. The diary itself is back in the hands of Teacher Satsai, who deserves to keep it as a memento of the diarist he loved unashamedly every bit as much as I love my own Madam Daeng. I have held on to these loose pages because I am not certain whether destroying them in a traditional way would be a wise move. I'm afraid that doing so might unleash the evil contained in the words of the diary. I have attended many exorcisms, but I do not profess to be an expert. Hiro was able to subdue a mob of evil spirits for a long period of time, but not even he could keep the lid on the pot forever. His account of those last few weeks is disturbing and may offend those of you with a nervous or easily appalled disposition. Even I consider a lot of the reportage to be sickening and I strongly recommend that you skip to Epilogue Two. Reading these pages will not add any insight to the tale as it has been told. That story is complete. These last few entries would provide detail that is nothing short of gratuitous. But, as I said, I'm afraid that suppressing or destroying them would provide a back door for the *yokai* to leave that two-dimensional plane and join us in our own dimension. Those of you who are susceptible to supernatural influences might inadvertently trigger such an exodus. If you doubt the strength of your skepticism at all, I beg you not to read these pages. And if damage is done, do not say you haven't been warned.

3/10/1945

I suppose it's only natural that living together in a small group is likely to cause some friction. I have left the dormitory and moved back to my tent to collect my thoughts. Corporal Yatsusuki has continued to grow. We get complaints from the French from time to time saying that he is blocking the road and they can't budge him. Still the weirdness goes on around me. The major general has taken to crossing the river most nights. He returns disheveled with the scent of cheap women on his uniform. And he always carries a sack. It's empty when he leaves but full to bursting on the way back. One morning he'd had a little too much to drink and forgot his sack on the boat. I took a peek. It was full of objects old and new, some valuable, some still wrapped in plastic. I have a feeling he steals those things, but I cannot prove it.

Captain Jame is almost always naked now, day and night, and he's not a pretty sight. How am I to concentrate on our shogi games with him sitting opposite me like that? Taigou the dog came to the tent last night and he had a deep wound on his side. And, oddly, he had another broken tea kettle on his head. He bit my hand when I freed him and he ran away.

One day I saw Second Lieutenant Tetsukimo Souben jump out of a tall tree. I thought perhaps he was trying to kill himself but his descent was so slow it was like watching a kite come to ground. Warrant Officer Ukabane Orimimi's breath is worse than ever. You can still smell it an hour after he's left the room. Sometimes I can smell his stink in my tent, although I don't see that anything's missing. I went into the latrine one day and found Private Oshiira licking the officers' toilet bowl. I was disgusted. He sleeps there now and never comes to the mess tent. His skin is grey, and he has infections all over him. Lance Corporal Hokofugu Hama is back on the alcohol with a vengeance. He drinks beyond the bounds of his salary. With a week still to go before payday he's in the town knocking on doors, begging for booze. But nobody ever seems to get angry at him. And I may be mistaken but he appears to be turning into a woman. Nothing makes any sense to me.

8/14/45

The Arrival of General Shosen Umiji

It was the night when hell unlocked all its doors. The black rain has been falling for a week. The mountain mud flows down into the rivers and kills the fish. The overflow is destroying the crops. Everywhere there are puddles like old engine oil that smell of mildew and rotting flesh. There was a full moon somewhere behind the granite clouds last night and it seemed to send out a signal for every hidden demon to attend the march and show itself. It was all brought about by the arrival of General Shosen Umiji. He had been the commander of the forces in Nanjing and it was he who instigated the campaign of cruelty and hatred and was so successful in our victories over the Chinese. He had risen to that lofty position following his victory in a duel. Shosen Umiji—then a colonel— had been challenged by a cavalry commander to see who could behead twenty Chinese the fastest. Shosen Umiji was from my hometown. He had been a kendo champion in school. I'm sure everyone at home cheered when the result was announced in the local newspaper. He won by a good five seconds. It is a record that still stands. Since then, Shosen Umiji has remained a darling of the Imperial overlords and has risen to the rank of general.

There he was standing on a makeshift stage in front of the old French colonial house. Thousands of men had come to greet him. He wore no hat but the rain didn't seem to stick to him as it did to the rest of us. Six months ago Japan declared that the occupation of Indochina was now officially a *coup de force*. We could stop pretending to be polite to our insufferable French hosts. We had taken the whole of the region in a day and had resorted to the same barbarism we'd enjoyed in Manchuria. Thakhek was now the center of operations, a chance to regroup, refresh, retrain. We had to find some answer to the unimaginable threat that we were losing our grip over the countries we'd occupied. The troops who stood there in front of the general were a defeated lot. Their uniforms were tattered and they all sported souvenir wounds of the campaign. And as I stood in front of the stage with the other regional commanders and our own Major General Dorari, I could see the faces of every one of the men and it appeared to me they were deformed in some way. It was as if they'd been made of clay and were melting: eyes into cheeks, noses into chins. My colleagues stood in the front row at attention, perfectly still, perfectly silent, looking up at the general with something close to love in their eyes. There had been no meeting of officers to announce this assembly. Every man had arrived there spontaneously. The general had insisted that I stand in front with my back to him alongside our major general and some four lieutenant colonels I'd never seen before.

The general was giving a speech that used the words "victory" and "massacre" and "pride" a great deal. But it was then I noticed something else. All the men in my unit were looking at me and smiling. And behind them, every eye on every man, wherever that eye had settled in those shifting faces, was also looking at me. To my left, Major General Dorari was looking at me. And when I turned, the general, his mouth now as big as his entire head, was looking at me. The speech came to an end and Colonel Konko took me by the hand and invited me to enter the house with him. He showed me to a spare room and suggested I sleep. I was fatigued and greasy from the heavy rain and tired, so I lay down.

I was awoken by a chorus of screams. My room was dark. The door was open. I passed a bathroom on my left and a cockroach the size of a crocodile ran in front of me, leaving a trail of slime. It stopped and looked up at me and I could clearly see the face of Private Oshiira, the toilet licker. He vomited over my boots. I was terrified. What was happening to me? My legs refused to run. The screams were louder now. Awful smells wafted around me. The cockroach stopped at another door and like a greasy trained seal, it beckoned me forward. I stepped over it and entered the next room. The house inside had changed shape. The rooms were larger now and there were doors everywhere. An earthquake below me seemed to be rearranging the parquet flooring. This next room contained a large king-size Jacuzzi. All around the four walls were some hundred women in sheer negligee chained by the necks. They were lined up numerically with the numbers pinned to their breasts. Many were dead. Many were wishing they were. Major General Dorari in leather was leaning over one, about to climb on top of her. His body had shrunk since I'd last seen him and his head had stretched upward and backward like a giant gourd. He looked at me and smiled before burying his bayonet in the woman. Her scream ceased but those of others around them grew louder. I couldn't stand to watch so I made for one of the doors. But as I passed the bubbling Jacuzzi I could tell from the smell that it was not full of water but of stale sake. Lying on the bottom of the Jacuzzi beneath the surface of the liquid was Lance Corporal Hokofugu Hama. He was no longer a man. His face was unchanged but his body was that of a wizened old lady and her skin was covered in hard blisters and lumps like a smallpox victim. She was inhaling the sake, sucking it in through her mouth and her nose and her anus, getting larger and larger with every suck until her skin burst and the Jacuzzi was filled with her organs.

(I did warn you. It doesn't get any better. SP)

I ran to the nearest door, tripping over cockroach Oshiira as I went, so I stumbled into the next room. But this was no ordinary room. It was constructed entirely of the enormous scrotum of Corporal Yatsusuki, which formed a perfect cube, small festering hairs poking out here and there. And through the translucent skin I could see him sitting in the ceiling rafters masturbating. In his other hand he held the severed head of a Chinese woman.

As there was only one door, I returned the way I'd come, but that room had also changed. It was now a slop kitchen and on the central gas range were several enormous pots full of unskinned rats being stirred by Warrant Officer Ukabane Orimimi. He had taken the shape of an ox with six legs. His breath was now so toxic that when he breathed into the pots the rat stew turned red as chili and sizzled. It was too much for the rats, who tried desperately to escape the pots, screeching. Ukabane breathed in my direction and I could feel my uniform stick to my skin as if I were in the path of a nuclear explosion. I had to get out. The Oshiira cockroach—his legs dropping off one by one—was indicating another door through which I ran, but on the far side I dropped into a pit and sprained both ankles. It was as silent as a tomb down there and I could see nothing. Then, slowly, I heard the flap of a bat above me. Its excrement dropped onto my head. But it was no usual bat. I could sense its wingspan was some ten meters. It came closer and at one point it opened its eyes and emitted a bloody red glow. It was the face not of a bat but of Second Lieutenant Tetsukimo Souben. His body was one long white strip of cloth and he began to wrap himself around my neck. I felt the noose tighten. Because of my injury I could not run. I fell to the ground and a pack of rabid wolves surrounded me, prowling closer. Its leader was Taigou, my once faithful dog. He pounced on me and buried his teeth into my arm. He was eating me alive. I kicked and punched my way free and dragged myself through the next door. I was in a concrete room and sitting in a far corner was Captain Jame, naked. He had removed his wooden leg and the eye patch. He now had only the one eye in the middle of his forehead. His withered leg was tiny and gangrenous and it dangled from his hip.

"What is happening, Jame?" I asked.

He opened his mouth to reply but from his throat came the loudest sound I'd ever heard. I put my hands to my ears but my head vibrated from the noise. It was like the roar of a dozen jet engines. My eardrums burst and pus shot from my ears. The walls began to crack and one huge slab of concrete fell onto Jame and crushed him. His one eyeball rolled out from under the rubble and across the floor to me. Before my eyes it started to grow a new Captain Jame around it. I could stand it no more. I crawled to the next door and let myself in. Great General Shosen

Umiji was asleep in a king-size bed. All around the bed, half asleep but with one of their many eyes on me, was a barrier of oni devils faithful to the demon overlord. He wore nothing and his huge bloated stomach seemed bigger than was humanly possible. His skin was wrinkled, and his toenails and fingernails were bloody. Beside the bed was a drip tube running from a cask of whisky to an artery in his arm. From a distance it appeared he was wearing makeup, but further inspection told me he was sleeping in a white mask with horns and huge fangs. Across the room was a cage and inside were some ten blond European children crammed together, petrified. My every instinct told me I had to kill this general, but I didn't know how. I had no weapon. I knew the oni were lazy beasts and that they would soon fall asleep if I was patient. Within an hour my suspicions were confirmed. I took a scabbard from one sleeping oni and I leaned over the bed. I needed to be sure this was the general. I tried to remove the mask but it was stuck. I pulled harder and still it would not give. The mask opened its eyes and its mouth drooled blood and it smiled. I happened to look at the bedside table and there I saw my mistake. There was the actual mask, that of a wrinkled old man with a red nose, the impassive face of a military tactician—General Shosen Umiji. That was the mask behind which Shuten Doji dwelled.

"You have no way to destroy me," said the general. And all the oni came to attention at the sound of his voice. They gathered around me and pulled and pushed and grabbed at my flesh and drew their daggers and I chanced to look up. There was a mirror above the bed like that in the most respectable brothels and I could see myself clearly. I was no longer Hiro Uenobu or Kangen Toshimado. I recognized this new me immediately. I was Minamoto Yorimitsu the warrior and I knew my mission. I looked back at the general and I said,

"I know exactly how to destroy you."

EPILOGUE TWO
Tomorrow I Rise

It wasn't the first time Hiro had stolen the village longboat and traveled back through the tunnel, but it would be the last. Without a lamp he negotiated the caverns instinctively, as if he had always been an eel or a bat. He emerged even before the sun had risen and he took in the scents of the early morning blooms and enjoyed the laughter of the shrews even louder than the growl of the boat engine as he worked his way to Thakhek. He had two visits to make. The first was to the old white colonial house where the senior officers had met the evening before. There were sentries at the bottom of the driveway, but they had no discipline. They played cards under a bamboo shelter and barely looked up when he passed. The empire had fallen to ruin. It was decaying before his eyes. But Hiro was at his most senior, his most decorated. He had spent many hours embroidering his new rank and his esteemed ribbons of valor. He was a full general now and deserved to be.

The front door to the house was ajar. He walked through the large, high-ceilinged rooms, stepping over drunks and debaucherers. Whores from Thailand gathered in the kitchen, cackling and comparing their bruises and their take-home pay. There were puddles of vomit and urine and empty bottles and broken glass. Somebody had been mortally injured judging by the amount of blood everywhere. Hiro went to the master bedroom. The door wasn't locked but when he pushed against it there was resistance. He had to lean into it with some force in order to give himself a view inside the room. There was a body behind the door, a boy, fourteen or so, covered in blood. But it didn't concern Hiro whether he was dead or not. In the scheme of things, it was irrelevant. All he needed was to identify the figure on the bed: sleeping deeply, naked, snoring. He entered the air-conditioned room, which stank of sweat, and leaned over the man. There is often little in an old man's face to distinguish him from any other old man. With hair cut close to his scalp and skin browned by a tropical sun, he could have been a cyclo rider or a street barber. There was nothing of character in the face Hiro saw before him. There was no smile of contentment. There was no outward sign of a dream under way: no evidence that this old man was living in two dimensions simultaneously. The only thing clear was that this was General Shosen Umiji, who had wreaked brutality upon innocents in China, who had destroyed lives and handed out party favors as a reward; this was the same bastard demon Shuten Doji who led the dark forces of the underworld. There was no mistaking him.

Hiro was about to leave when he discovered a third identity. Beside the bed was a passport and air ticket. Both were in the name of Lee Kwan Hong, a Singaporean. The ticket was from Bangkok to New York. The passport contained an unlimited visa for the United States. The photograph was that of the devil who lay there on the sprung mattress.

General Hiro walked in sprightly fashion—somewhere between a march and a fox-trot—to the airfield. He handed his flight papers to the second lieutenant in charge of aircraft. The man, his neck button unfastened, looked Hiro up and down and saluted halfheartedly. He stamped the orders and led the general to one of the newest Zeros. It was fitted with canisters of high explosives and three additional gas tanks, two of which were not connected to the engine. Every day, the second lieutenant escorted young fliers to the craft that would become their coffins. The youths were always silent, resolved, sad that they'd lived so little, dreamed so wastefully. They were all trapped in the purgatory of imperialism, unable to confess they felt no allegiance to that old man locked away in his palace in Tokyo. He rode a white horse and spoke only to his nearest advisors. None of the young pilots wished to die for him. The honor they carried to their violent cremation was one not of nationhood but of personal pride. They would not be remembered as cowards by their peers, or the ground crew that waved them off. They kept their spines straight and their lips clenched. If one man refused to take to the sky, if he dared question the sanity of sending an entire generation off to a fiery death, if he wondered aloud how his country had sunk to allowing a gang of old generals to pervert its customs and hold its culture to ransom for glory, every other suicide pilot would echo those thoughts silently. But they'd band together to hammer down the nail that stood up and they'd climb into the cockpit and shed tears all the way to hell, but not back.

The second lieutenant looked again at the decorated general who stood bolt upright before him. He, too, was silent but there was no doubt, no fear in his eyes. This general climbed the ladder, inserted himself into the cockpit like a foot into a tight shoe, engaged the engine, checked the instruments, and taxied to the end of the runway. The ground crew might have admired him, a high-ranking officer who was opting to give his life for the emperor sooner than surrender to an inferior enemy. Or they might have felt pity for him, a lonely general with nothing to live for. But they had to admit he sure as hell could fly. He turned into his takeoff and was airborne in seconds. He was soon in the clouds and on his way to Halong Bay, where kamikazes were reportedly picking off cruisers and landing craft at will and bidding their farewells to the world. The second lieutenant sighed and returned to his logbook, but another sound made him look up. The Zero was back. It performed a perfect loop-de-loop followed by a figure eight. The Zero was never known for its maneuverability. Inexperienced pilots had trouble just keeping it on an even keel. But the general was putting on a show like no one had ever seen before. He barrel-rolled and rose skyward and again he was gone. The second lieutenant smiled and raised a thumb to the mechanics and when they all believed he'd finally gone on his way, there he was again, flying low and straight now. He barely missed the top spire of the temple.

"He's too low," shouted one of the mechanics.

"I think he knows exactly what he's doing," said the second lieutenant. He laughed. He knew that what was about to happen would never find its way into the war records. Some historian would turn it into another myth of valor and honor. The guilty victims would become the heroes as they always had and those who knew the truth would be snuffed out. A row of tents shimmered as the

Zero skimmed over them. Infantry men looked out from the flaps. The horses panicked in the corral. The engine roared. The Zero tipped a wing over the market, leveled, and slammed in a ball of fire and a thunderous *boom* into the side of the old colonial house.